STORIES OF DOWRY ...

Seema Sirohi was born in New Delhi. She completed her bachelor's degree in English literature from St Stephen's College and joined Jawaharlal Nehru University for a master's in Sociology. She went on to study journalism at the University of Kansas, Lawrence, and returned to India to pursue a career. She joined the New Delhi bureau of the Associated Press, covering major stories of the day, including Indira Gandhi's assassination, the Bhopal gas leak, the militancy in Punjab and Kashmir and India's intervention in Sri Lanka. She moved to Washington in 1988 and joined Inter Press Service for a year where she wrote about US policy towards Asia and Africa. She became the Washington correspondent for *The Telegraph* in 1989, writing political stories, analytical pieces and tracking the difficult relationship between India and the United States for eight years. She also lived in Eastern Europe for three years while the region was undergoing historic changes after the fall of the Berlin Wall. She wrote articles from Prague, Bratislava, Vienna and Budapest. She returned to India for three years and researched this book.

SITA'S CURSE

STORIES OF DOWRY VICTIMS

Seema Sirohi

HarperCollins *Publishers* India
a joint venture with
THE INDIA TODAY GROUP
New Delhi

First published in India in 2003 by
HarperCollins *Publishers* India
a joint venture with
The India Today Group

HarperCollins *Publishers*
1A, Hamilton House, Connaught Place, New Delhi 110 001, India
77-85 Fulham Palace Road, London W6 8JB, United Kingdom
Hazelton Lanes, 55 Avenue Road, Suite 2900, Toronto, Ontario M5R 3L2
and 1995 Markham Road, Scarborough, Ontario M1B 5M8, Canada
25 Ryde Road, Pymble, Sydney, NSW 2073, Australia
31 View Road, Glenfield, Auckland 10, New Zealand
10 East 53rd Street, New York NY 10022, USA

Typeset in 11/14 Aldine

Printed and bound at
Thomson Press (India) Ltd.

In memory of
my father
who would have been proud
and for Chris, Mandira and Kabir

Contents

Preface

The past decade was an exciting time of dramatic change for India on both political and economic fronts. Old ways of thinking were discarded by a nation eager to occupy its place on the international scene. Bold strides were made towards modernization, and the razzle-dazzle of the market economy made urban India a glittering arcade of dreams and enterprises. There was a sudden rush, a buzz about how fast and how deeply the country was transforming.

But improving the status of women didn't seem to be a priority in this scramble. Women were left largely on their own to face the pressures brought about by the changes. Their problems remained and in some cases even got aggravated as an unintended consequence of the rapid leaps. Attention had shifted completely from the myriad social ills affecting them, rarely generating national debates or cries for action. One such issue that suffered from a desperate lack of attention was dowry deaths – a crime so gruesome and calculated that it ought to outrage any modern society. Women were being killed every year by greedy husbands and in-laws but those in power rarely seemed bothered. Their stories lay buried in the inside pages of newspapers, alongside reports of car accidents and thefts. It was a change from the 1980s when the politicians as well as the people seemed seized of the matter.

My aim was simply to refocus attention on dowry deaths and hopefully convey the enormity of this problem. After initial research into many cases, I chose six real-life stories of women who were harassed, tortured, killed or forced to commit suicide over dowry. They belonged to different classes and castes and represented the regional spread of the problem. They were all remarkable women and while learning about their lives, I discovered their quiet bravery, their steely determination to make things work despite enormous odds. Carrying the burden of tradition and custom, they tried to create a little space for themselves in a hostile environment. But they were shut out.

In writing this book, I had only my journalistic skills to bank on and I used curiosity as the basic tool. It is not an academic book and makes no pretence in that direction. Most of the research is from primary sources, including police officials, lawyers and women activists who gave me their valuable time.

No endeavour of this kind is entirely one's own, nor was this book. I would like to thank writer Amitav Ghosh who encouraged me to pursue goals beyond journalism. I am indebted to him for the generosity of spirit and friendship and the consistent interest he and his wife Deborah Baker showed in this project.

Once I started on my research, I was sustained by many friends – some old and some new – who helped at every juncture with information, logistics and, most importantly, in revival of spirit. They provided a safety net into which I could fall when needed and carry on, and I am deeply grateful. In Kolkata, I would like to thank Aveek Sarkar who gave me the opportunity to pursue the idea and helped me at every stage. I am grateful to Shaktidas Roy, the legendary librarian of the Ananda Bazar Patrika Group who made the right files appear magically from shelves. The American Center library was a great resource and I would like to acknowledge everyone there for their help in locating articles and tracking down data. I would also like to thank Jasodhara Bagchi for giving me her valuable time and Rajashri Dasgupta for providing insights and perspective as I struggled to draw conclusions. Ranjit Pachnanda was a well of information and always cheerful. I would also like to acknowledge Anuradha Kapoor of Swayam who works with dowry victims in the city. My friends Gouri Chatterjee and Sajeda Momin gave me encouragement during our many late-night sessions, as we wondered about life and its many turns.

In Delhi, Sujata Mehra, old collegemate, was my family, friend and guide. She opened her home on my many visits and explained the intricacies of law. I would like to thank my former professor and family friend Yogendra Singh and his daughter Neerja Singh for providing the initial contacts into the world of social research and guiding me to the right people. Kuldip Nayar, veteran journalist and columnist who has been a friend and guide ever since I joined the world of newspapers, kept tabs on my progress, prodding and always enquiring. I would also like to acknowledge the help provided by S.R. Meena, the chief statistical officer at the National Crime Records Bureau, who was always prompt in responding to requests.

There are many friends in Delhi who helped in ways they are probably not aware of but they were my back-bone. Manini Chatterjee listened and encouraged. Ritu Sarin was always ready with suggestions and information. Jyoti Malhotra was charmingly wonderstruck and impressed that her friend was trying something different. I was always welcomed warmly by Jyoti, Nandan Unnikrishnan, C. Raja Mohan, Nirmala George, Javed Ansari, M.K. Venu and Chitra Padmanabhan to lively get-togethers where we reminisced and debated and argued. I would also like to remember our dearest friend Jassi, a journalist par excellence, who is no longer with us. He would have been a cheerleader.

I am grateful to Amit Agarwal at HarperCollins whose sharp editing skills and keen eye helped in giving the book a clearer focus. He always gave me good feedback.

In Chandigarh, I was fortunate that Nishi Malhotra introduced me to many interesting people. She and her friends were gracious and generous with their hospitality. I would also like to thank Ayesha Banerjee and Geetika Bhandari for their keen insights on life in Punjab. My old friend and former colleague Harbaksh Singh Nanda stood by me when times got tough. In Bangalore, I was lucky to have the office infrastructure of Alan Rosling alongwith his trusted driver Swamy to travel in the area. Without Swamy, I wonder if I would have been able to accomplish as much. I would also like to thank Sherree in Bangalore who showed me the city in a way only a resident can.

Finally, I am indebted to my husband Chris Sandrolini and my children Mandira Rosa and Kabir Mandela for keeping the faith and always cheering from the sidelines. They were my daily inspiration, my constant companions. Without their unflagging confidence in me, this book would not have been possible.

Introduction

More than nine thousand women are killed in India every year in dowry-related crimes. But that is only the 'official' figure. In reality, the number may be twice as high, for many of the dowry deaths are unrecognized as such – they are simply recorded, and dismissed, as 'unnatural deaths' by the police.

The scourge has been growing steadily despite stringent laws, greater awareness and the spread of education. The phenomenon has become so commonplace, so numbing that it rarely excites comment these days. The victims become mere jottings in police blotters, dying a second death. There is no outrage and the anger seems to have dissipated. Even women activists today seem to be a resigned and dismayed lot.

Statistics are sobering, especially so at the end of the 'Decade of the Girl Child (1990-2000)' observed by the South Asian countries. During the decade, the National Crime Records Bureau[1] (NCRB) in New Delhi recorded a 38 per cent increase in dowry deaths and a 225 per cent rise in cases of torture and harassment for dowry in India. In 1990, at least 4836 women were killed in dowry-related crimes but by the end of the decade, in 1999, the number had grown to 6699. The figures vastly underestimate the real picture because suicides and 'accidental deaths' are not included. Similarly, 13,450 cases of dowry harassment were registered at the start of the decade but by its end, they had ballooned to 43,823, with Maharashtra, Rajasthan and Uttar Pradesh recording the highest numbers. A report based on data from 1987 to 1990 and compiled by the Department of Women and Child

Welfare of the government of India found that a dowry death occurs every one hour forty-two minutes.

The book is an attempt to refocus attention on this blood-chilling crime against women by bringing their stories to light. It is an exercise in 'extended journalism', where I have tried to recount the stories of six women from different communities and classes to show the spread of the problem. It is the women and their families who speak here, without the abstraction of theory. They are not mere statistics on a chart but real voices. Voices that need to be heard for anyone to understand the magnitude of the dowry scourge today.

Sure, much has happened since the 1970s when the wound of awareness was first inflicted on the national consciousness and the country learnt about 'bride burning' and suspicious 'kitchen accidents' involving young women. Activists took to the streets in protest, special police cells were created to combat dowry deaths, and an entire National Commission for Women was instituted to assess the situation by a government looking for a way out. Awareness grew among both women and men but so did the crime through the 1980s. Parliament made stronger laws, taking the unusual step of shifting the burden of proof on the accused under certain circumstances, but dowry deaths rose adamantly, even defiantly.

Came the 1990s, a seminal decade in Indian history. The country tried to shake off its old socialist policies, desperately playing catch up with the rest of the world. Economic liberalization changed the way an average urban Indian ate, dressed and worked. It allowed him giddy dreams of globalization. The privileged and the educated began discussing India's place in a unipolar world. They measured it by the number of multinational entries and asserted it with the power of a nuclear bomb. They didn't want to be held back by persistent social problems. A whole generation of journalists grew up covering cocktail parties and fashion shows. In the breathlessness of the nineties, they seemed to forget about the women.

A new millennium dawned. But the women – most of them, anyway – continued to inhabit the land of Manu[2]. The same Manu, the ancient chronicler of life and law, who first gave the concept of 'devaluation' to the world. It was the devaluation of women. Manu had listed 'killing a woman' as a minor crime alongside stealing of grain and livestock, killing a servant or commoner and professing atheism. He declared that women should always be under the control of men – first the fathers, then their husbands and finally their own sons. 'A woman is not fit for independence,' he announced, laying down pivotal rules of Hindu society. 'When her father or her brother with her father's permission gives her to someone, she should obey that man while he is alive and not violate her vow to him when he is dead.' It was a treatise so influential that thousands of years down the line, he continues to play godfather to Indian men, informing their attitudes and actions. His pronouncements have been internalized, secured in the national psyche and accepted without much questioning. His modern spokesmen are the theorists of the Hindutva brigade who say there is nothing shocking in Manu's decrees, as K.R. Malkani claimed in his latest book, *India First*[3].

The winds and waves of globalization and the infotech revolution may be sweeping India but men still speak the language of domination vis-à-vis women, the outward appearances of 'modernity' notwithstanding. As sociologist Dipankar Gupta[4] observes, 'Our modernity is very, very superficial. If modernity has to do with gadgets and gizmos and consumer items, we are modern. But in terms of how we relate to other people, to those of the opposite sex, to those who are superior to us, to those who are inferior to us, to those who are outside our society, we are quite traditional. We do not have a healthy respect for the individual. We look at others through a perspective that is still very traditional though our clothes, our cars and our stereo sets may give a contrary impression.'

Besides, education and exposure may not always lead to enlightened thinking. Education can also be used to justify unbalanced social arrangements. Men have used education to better argue their case for continued supremacy. 'While women may use their education to challenge the power structure, men may use it to perpetuate it,' says Samita Sen[5], a reader in Calcutta University's history department.

Apart from the 'old', tried and accepted reasons of patriarchy for the degradation of women, pressures of modern-day society have added many 'new' reasons for violence against them. Sen says the process of modernization in India has occurred at different rates for different sections of the people, creating its own social tensions. 'Something is happening to the social positioning of middle-class men and their sense of masculinity and they are feeling trapped.' While women still see marriage as an end which 'settles' them in life and accept family decisions, men are tied to the family because of economic subsidies from parents, inheritance and housing shortages in cities. They may be more oriented to exercising sexual choices today thanks to the influence of the media, increasing consumerism and familiarity with Western social mores but the family often prevents them from making individual choices in marriage. When the pressure mounts they succumb to arranged marriages.

'They do it because it gives them access to capital which is very important for middle-class men to build assets. It can either come through inheritance or through dowry. All this has made marital relationships more volatile. They take out their bitterness on women,' says Sen, who also works with the women's organization, Sachetna.

The kinds of employment open to men earlier are no longer feasible in a shrinking job market. Self-employment, as seen in the sprouting of thousands of STD booths, cybercafes and small goods stores in urban areas, is today a key to social mobility. So we have the bizarre spectacle in Delhi's narrow lanes of neon-lit cybercafes, their modems humming beside wretched cries for help from women being slowly tortured to death. The swanky skyscrapers, bowling alleys and accoutrements of India's 'modernity' hide an ugly scene behind, of women dying at the altar of greed. They continue to burn in the badlands of Bihar, they continue to die in India's Silicon Valley in Bangalore, and they continue to be murdered in Uttar Pradesh. For dowry.

Dowry generally constitutes the gifts given by the bride's family to the groom and his parents either in cash or kind. It also includes what is given to the bride but may not exclusively be regarded as her property. The concept can be traced back to the scriptures, which, while describing the ritual of marriage, talk of gifts accompanying a daughter as she leaves for her husband's house. It was a purely voluntary act and it earned spiritual merit for the father. Today, it is an extortionist custom.

Eminent Indian sociologist M.N. Srinivas[6] calls dowry deaths the 'sati' of the twentieth century and for good reason. Over the past three decades, dowry deaths and 'bride burning' have spread to communities where the concept of dowry was once unknown. Communities that once gave 'bride price' to the girl's family because they were taking away a 'productive' member of the family now demand dowry. The Mizos in the northeast and the Kallars in Tamil Nadu[7] are prime examples. A need to emulate upper castes and claim compatibility with their social norms is at the root of the change. Dowry deaths have also risen in Kerala, inspite of its higher literacy rates and better social indicators. And in Bangalore, the police report an average of hundred 'unnatural deaths' of women a month.

Patricia Uberoi[8], a Delhi-based social anthropologist with the Institute of Economic Growth, says dowry is on the rise because of market forces and the failure of community restraints. 'The quantity of dowry is definitely connected with the market. Earlier it was home produced bedding, embroidery which the girls and women of the family themselves created but today dowry is part of the cash economy. Earlier the various communities had their own rules and magic numbers about how many saris or spoons they considered appropriate for a dowry. There were community constraints and negotiations were conducted within limits. And if the dowry exceeded limits, the panchayat would meet and exercise control. Today those restraints have broken down while the market forces have strengthened. Historically, dowry has gone through growth and contraction depending on boom times and recession. It is not clear where this time it is on a single trajectory of expansion.'

Dowry has become a bribe paid to a husband to keep the bride's body and soul together. A woman is a mere conduit to a 'good' dowry – the definition of good being flexible and expandable. The boys are on sale and there are few discounts in the marriage market. There is no 'buy one, get one free' here. It is a transaction weighted against the woman. In fact, it is a sale where even after the price is paid, satisfaction is not guaranteed. And ironically, the sale is never complete with marriage – the buyer is expected to keep paying in cash and in kind during festivals, to celebrate childbirth and to mark ritualistic occasions. Any excuse is good enough to keep the one-way street laden and moving with gifts. The latest, most expensive status symbol will do – a Honda car, a flat in an upscale area or a ticket to go abroad. Prospective grooms hunt around like loan sharks for the best deal, making blatant and threatening demands. It has been honed into a business with no attempt to hide the commercial nature of the transaction. It has become the quickest way to climb the social ladder, acquire the latest symbol of wealth and mark your presence in society.

A large percentage of the dowry victims are from the middle, lower middle and lower classes living in cramped conditions although crime statistics do not classify cases according to the families' economic background. Ranjana Kumari[9], director of the Centre for Social Research in New Delhi, observed in a 1985 study of 150 dowry victims in Delhi that 'while desertion and harassment cases are more among higher income groups, middle income groups show higher dowry death rates'. The same is true today even though more middle-class families are using the law and going to the courts, especially in urban areas, where awareness is heightened. Lower classes are largely being helped by non-governmental organizations (NGOs) working in slum areas. But in the upper classes a deafening silence prevails about dowry-related violence and all domestic violence in general, giving rise to the myth that wife-battering is a pastime of drunken labourers.

The Numbers Graph

Statistics in India hide as much as they reveal, especially when it comes to women. For all the cases reported, there are thousands of others that are not, in a society where the fear of stigma, shame and a shocking lack of awareness of legal rights tend to silence the victims. Many domestic crimes are not registered while others may be wrongly classified. But proportionally more cases are being reported today than they were two decades ago.

Even though women activists question police statistics, with prominent feminist Madhu Kishwar openly heaping scorn at them, the NCRB has made a considerable effort to compile all-India crime figures. It brings out an annual report and over the years its collection of data has improved and its statistical base has expanded. The figures give a fair idea of the national picture. The earliest national figures available for dowry deaths are from 1983 when 427 women were killed with the number climbing to 990 in 1985. Four years later, in 1989, there were 4215 women dead. As mentioned earlier, the steady climb has raised the number to 6699 dead for 1999. (It must be kept in mind, however, that in the nineties, the statistical base expanded to include figures from more districts as compared to the eighties and seventies.)

The dowry death numbers increase dramatically if one includes women who committed suicide or died 'unnatural deaths' because of dowry disputes. If they are counted, the official figure would be over 9400 for 1999, with Uttar Pradesh and Bihar logging the most deaths. So, by the government's own admission, more than 9400 women are killed or die annually over dowry. The astonishing rise of 225 per cent in cases of torture and harassment for dowry registered under section 498(A) of the Indian Penal Code (IPC) in the past decade is most likely because of the many special Crimes Against Women cells operating in major cities. Hundreds of families come daily to these offices to register complaints about dowry.

Other heinous crimes against women have registered a similar increase. According to the National Crime Records Bureau, rape cases rose by 62 per cent and kidnapping and abduction by 36 per cent in the past decade. Molestation cases recorded a 37.5 per cent increase, from 20,194 cases in 1990 to 32,311 cases in 1999. The number of sexual harassment cases registered remained more or less in the same range – 8620 in 1990 and 8858 at the end of the decade.

Statistics or not, the trend is chillingly clear – young brides are dying horrific deaths and husbands are blithely passing them off as accidents. If a 'stove burst' designed to look like a kitchen accident was once the favourite mode of elimination, today other methods have evolved. They hang women from ceiling fans, they give them poison, even electrocute them. Then they make up a story and spread it.

It was an accident, it was a gas leak, it was a suicide, she was depressed, she couldn't adjust, she was mentally unsound. Whatever.

And few ask the question why she committed 'suicide' or how the gas actually leaked or what she was doing cooking late at night. If she burnt herself, why was her body removed before the police came? If she consumed poison, what about the scratch marks on her body, the cigarette burns on her legs? Don't her husband and his family have to answer? Why didn't they do something to save her from the omnipotent, all-consuming gas flames? If it were an accident, she surely would have cried for help? Didn't they smell anything as they watched their favourite serial on Star Plus? Why was the door bolted from the outside?

There were and still are no clear answers. Because the politicians who have the power and can make a difference do not seem to care. Because we have lived with many shameful social arrangements for thousands of years.

Because as a civilization we do not value women no matter how many temples we build in the service of various goddesses. Because we do not want to risk real change. Because real change demands concerted action and a strong political will.

Even as the system has failed the women, it has bred a new kind of contempt towards them. Men accused of dowry murders remarry even while the case is in progress, have children and move on. They successfully paint themselves as 'victims' while grabbing another dowry. Parents of daughters care little about their future so long as they are able to marry them off. The sooner the 'responsibility' is discharged, the better. Ranjana Kumari's 1985[10] study of dowry victims in Delhi referred to earlier revealed that in 69.13 per cent of the 150 cases, parents sent their daughters back to the husbands despite full knowledge of the torment they were undergoing. Of these, 77.9 per cent of the victims returned only to be deserted while 11.5 per cent were killed.

Not Just a Hindu Problem

Dowry deaths are not restricted to the majority community. They are also being recorded among Muslims and Christians although police statistics along community lines are not available. Although minority communities in India, having adopted some Hindu practices, have had a tradition of giving dowry, Muslim boys today are also demanding and getting dowry, thanks to their success in Gulf jobs. The feeling that if a family spends money on the son's education, they should be able to 'recover' it, has grown. Muslim social workers and NGOs say that as a phenomenon dowry deaths were first noticed in the community in the 1980s but it took until the mid-1990s for the women to openly raise their voices because of the hostility they faced.

Hasina Khan[11], a Bombay-based social activist and member of the women's organization Aawaz-e-Niswan, told me, 'Some of the men were connected to political parties and they would threaten our families. If we organized a dharna, they threatened to throw acid on our faces. But as more and more Muslim women came out, there was greater acceptance.' If the woman sought divorce or khula because of constant harassment, the man often kept the dowry and the mehr as compensation. The mehr is a sum of money or property promised by the husband to be paid or given to the wife in consideration of the marriage. It is a token of respect, and obligatory under the Muslim Personal Law. Ironically, however, as dowry demands increased during the 1980s and '90s, the amount of mehr began decreasing. If a family asked for a high mehr, the boy's side accused them of 'selling' the daughter. Among middle class and lower middle class Muslim families, mehr has become a mere token and can be as low as one thousand rupees – not a sum that will help a woman survive. Upper-class Muslims feel they don't 'need' the mehr while the poor have little knowledge of it being a right under law.

Hindus and Muslims imbibed traditions and practices from each other ever since India came under Muslim rule, social osmosis being a factor of the interdependence in a pan-Indian set up. Religious conversions either by the sword or because of the oppressive caste system established the two-way street of exchange.

Dowry as a transaction between Muslim families was found in Balban's[12] time when arrangements were made to help poor families cope with dowry. Firoz Shah Tughlak did something similar and established the *Diwan-e-Khairat* whose officers investigated cases and gave grants so indigent girls could marry. Abul Fazl in *Ain-e-Akbari* mentions that

Akbar was forced to appoint *Tui-begs* or masters of marriage who acted as modern-day counsellors and kept a check on large dowries. As for the elite, dowry was an instrument of building alliances through marriages and gaining social acceptability. Akbar accepted a large dowry from Raja Bhagwan Das whose daughter married Jahangir. Aurangzeb demanded the fortress of Ramgiri when his son Prince Sultan Muhammad married a princess from Golconda.

When the National Commission for Women held public hearings for Muslim women a few years ago, stories of dowry deaths, harassment and torture came pouring out. The hearings were held in twelve cities across India between 1997 and 1999. Oral testimonies showed that dowry was a 'growing menace' among Muslims and cases were reported from every state without exception. In a subsequent report, commission member Syeda Saiyidain Hameed[13] described how some Hindu practices had penetrated the community. Greed, infused with Islamic beliefs, had led to a truly grotesque form of violence against women. Muslim men were using the sanction for polygamy to grab a new dowry while divorcing the first wife with the easy method of 'triple talaq', where a man can get rid of his wife by simply pronouncing the dreaded word three times. Some were even using 'postal talaq' – using a postcard to announce the divorce – to secure another dowry. Another sad fallout of this unique cultural 'symbiosis' was the 'growing incidence of teenage girls being married to old men from the Gulf in exchange for a lump sum payment to their destitute families'. An equally deplorable variant of this 'bride sale' was when Muslim men from the north (Kashmir, Delhi, Rajasthan) travelled to southern cities (mainly Hyderabad and Bangalore) to marry local girls without demanding 'dowry', only to take them back and force them into prostitution.

Dowry also afflicts Indian Christians, especially in the south. Having originally come from the Hindu community and lived among them for centuries, old traditions survived in the new faith. The Syrian Christians of Kerala and the Roman Catholics of Mangalore are known to deal in lakhs of rupees when conducting dowry negotiations. Christian families take out matrimonial advertisements in popular magazines and newspapers, openly offering cash with the bride. Cases are mounting in southern states daily as NGOs gear up to check the virus.

Dowry disputes and suspicious suicides are being reported from beyond India's borders – from the United States, United Kingdom and Canada, where members of an upwardly mobile Indian diaspora indulge in their own version of greed. The local police are faced with a social evil they don't even understand, let alone confront and curb. A study in Britain found that the suicide rate among South Asian women was four times higher than the national average and that 30 per cent of them died of burns. Members of the successful Indian community abroad are making huge dowry demands because they consider themselves a far more lucrative 'catch' compared to their brethren in India. They earn in 'dollars' and live abroad – a dream that many Indians want to share.

Rampant Consumerism

The process of economic liberalization has given a boost to the practice by providing new attractions and raising aspirations. If a two-wheeler scooter was once a coveted dowry item for the middle class, today it does not enter reckoning. Their rising aspirations are now pegged on four wheels. What was considered an adequate dowry in the 1980s – a sofa set, beds, a sewing machine and kitchen utensils –

is today demanded and provided in the slums. The middle class has moved to a more expensive list – refrigerators, cars, air conditioners and even a flat. If the boy is an IAS officer, the price skyrockets because of the power and prestige built into the job, to say nothing of the possibilities for corruption. An IAS groom in Bihar today commands anywhere between forty to sixty lakhs in dowry. It has led cynics to dub the service IDS or the Indian Dowry Service. A middle-class father of a bride has to gather resources, beg and borrow, if he wants an IAS son-in-law. Only those who themselves have amassed illegal wealth, whether through 'lucrative' government jobs or by other means, can acquire such grooms. For the upper middle classes, a five-star wedding reception and a honeymoon in Thailand or Singapore are today reasonable expectations.

Education seems to make little difference in outlook. Interviews with young men at Calcutta University revealed that most of them were satisfied with or resigned to the idea of dowry. Their main aim was to get a good job and their anxieties centred around the job search, not around who they would marry or whether they would take dowry. They preferred to leave the decision to their parents. When asked whether they supported 'dowry demands', most of them replied in the negative but added that they would accept whatever the girl's side gave in marriage.

'Why should I look a gift horse in the mouth? If they want to give, I will take. After all, I also am struggling and if her parents can help, why not?' was the reply of a pragmatic middle-class student who planned to join the army of computer professionals. Another young man accused girls' parents of indulging in a spending spree on weddings for status and prestige. He said he knew of cases in his family where the girl's father was 'foisting gifts and favours' on the groom to show off his wealth and connections. The group of twelve students that I talked to didn't seem to know the extent of the dowry problem or that women could be harassed and killed for dowry. They were too busy dreaming the new dreams fostered by the changing urban scenario. After all, the opening of the economy in the 1990s had transformed the face of urban India, making it a frenzied blur of new images. If the middle class was convulsing with change, the very rich, including politicians with their ill-gotten fortunes, were establishing new records in lavish and grotesque displays of wealth. Mobile phones, Coke and Pepsi advertisements, designer labels – there were a million messages a minute. The dreams came via television, which rapidly sold a lifestyle anchored in new products, certified by new icons of the advertising world. The blinding razzle-dazzle gave many more choices to the consumer, fed his greed and fuelled his buying instinct. He could now wear a Rado watch for seventy-five thousand rupees, don an Italian suit for slightly less and run in Nike shoes for five thousand rupees. He could buy a flat screen television and watch his regulation Hindi film on DVD. Every time he went to the market, he saw another swanky store and a whole range of new appendages he desired. What quicker way to get things than simply demand them as dowry?

A dowry for the wealthy was not just a car for the couple but a fleet of cars to be distributed to the boy's family at the milni ceremony. They built temporary theme cities for weddings, paid film stars to dance and created designer dowries. They gave and spent in multiple of crores. The chief minister of a southern state established new records in spending when her foster son got married. Weddings became an assertion of power, an occasion to indulge in one-upmanship and an opportunity to spend black money.

A young Marwari businessman told me of a case in his community where the bride's father promised to give two crore rupees in cash as dowry. He simply invited the prospective son-in-law to a game of teen patti and put the stakes sky high. He then proceeded to lose every hand and sent the groom off with suitcases filled with cash.

If demands are unmet or expectations grow despite a lavish dowry, harassment of the daughter-in-law can follow. The final outcome can vary depending on the class although any generalization is dangerous. Poor and lower-middle-class women are more likely to be killed – by burning, by poisoning or even by electrocution – while their upper-class sisters may be able to escape the fiery end by moving back to their parents' home. The upper classes have more options in today's India, including separation and divorce, although the conservative rich encourage neither. The overarching concern is izzat and not happiness of the daughter.

Cases of dowry disputes and torture among the rich and powerful are usually hushed up. Families use their 'influence' and contacts among the police to suppress information. Most cases do not reach the public domain but even a casual inquiry reveals that dowry is as much a painful reality in the upper classes as it is for the others. But harassment and torture are less than for their less privileged sisters. Veteran politician Arun Nehru's daughter suffered at the hands of her husband over dowry until she walked out and filed a case. The latest and most startling case to come to light involves that ever-suffering mother of the Indian silver screen – Nirupa Roy. She and her son Kiran allegedly harassed daughter-in-law Una for more money. Una filed a case in Mumbai in June 2001, and fled to Panchkula in Haryana to escape them[14].

But women who can actually walk out and start anew are few. The New Woman of the media revolution is a limited edition – you may see her as she grills corrupt politicians on TV, treks fearlessly in the mountains, stokes fantasies on MTV and makes mincemeat of villains in films. She may walk down the ramp sassily in a fashion show to assert her right over her body in public. She belongs to a thin layer of society where real choices are available either because of wealth or enlightenment. But a vast majority of women in urban and rural India are still without real choices, real means.

The Burden of Tradition

From the day a girl is born – if she is lucky enough not to be aborted via the many sex determination tests available today – she is perceived as a burden on the family. Discrimination begins early and thousands of baby girls die in the race for nutrition against their brothers. A girl child is not allowed to feel that she belongs with the parents and nothing describes the transient nature of her life than the words 'paraya dhan', or another's wealth. 'It not only establishes the very notion of (a woman) belonging (to a man) but also that a girl is wealth which ultimately belongs elsewhere,' writes Malavika Karlekar of the Centre for Women's Development Studies. From the idea of 'wealth', it is easy to see how women can be regarded as 'property'[15]. When a girl is ready to leave for her husband's house she is told: 'We are sending your doli (bridal palanquin) today. Let only your arthi (bier) come out of your husband's house.' Whatever comes in between doli and arthi is part of the deal. The steel frame of social conditioning clasps her m
and she believes that physical abuse, if it takes
natural offshoot of marriage.

A survey done in the year 2000 by the Mumbai-based International Institute for Population Sciences (IIPS)[16] revealed that 56 per cent of the women polled accepted and justified wife-beating on grounds such as neglecting the household or children, infidelity, disrespect for in-laws, *and* inadequate dowry. Economic independence seems to have made little difference because 62 per cent of the employed women also justified wife beating. The acceptance cut across religious lines in the survey of 90,000 women in the 15–49 age group who were married or had been married earlier.

Sanction for the subordination of women comes from old Hindu social and legal texts which still rule common thinking. According to the shastras, a woman's job is to perpetuate the family line and produce male heirs. She is deemed unfit for any religious sacrament save marriage because of her inherently 'weak' character. She needs male authority to shepherd her through life. With Brahminism becoming the dominant strand of Hindu religious thought in the post-Vedic period, some of the benefits women had earlier were slowly taken away. Brahminism has been seen as a religion that exalts the cow but degrades the woman.

The process of transformation was slow. In the Rig Vedic period[17], India was characterized by a pastoral society with the people organized along tribal, not varna, lines. Men were busy fighting tribal wars and dying in the process. Women were important as child bearers and producers of future fighters. The household was an important unit, ensuring a secure place for the women. Stratification along class and gender lines was yet to happen although the stirrings were there. Little is known about pre-Vedic marriage ceremonies but hymns in the *Rig Veda* and the *Atharva Veda* give some hints. The allegory of marriage of Surya, the daughter of the Sun, and Som is described in the *Atharva Veda* in these words:

'The bride started for the house of her intended lord in a canopied chariot accompanied by her friends. The kosa (treasure chest) containing her dowry was also placed in her chariot.'

Scholars believe that women had a high status during pre-Vedic and Vedic times. They were given the same training as men and both partook of the upnayana ceremony or the process of initiation into the world of knowledge. Gargi was a famous dialectician who locked horns in philosophical debates with the sages of her times. Some of the old Vedic hymns were written by women and women even guarded kings. Early marriages were not especially encouraged. But with time religious education got more and more complex, ritualistic and rigid, requiring long periods of absence from the house. Severe condemnation followed if any mistake was made in the performance of the rituals. Women gradually began moving away from Vedic studies and the upnayana ceremony began losing its importance because they gave up their studies after marriage. Finally, Manu pronounced the upnayana ceremony unnecessary for a girl and instead declared the marriage to be her Vedic sacrament. The declaration barred women from spaces they were accustomed to and gradually confined them to the service of husbands and home.

The society was undergoing other changes which had a bearing on women. By the first millennium before Christ, strict divisions and caste structures had developed alongwith the concepts of pollution and purity. A social order based on varna rules and maintenance of caste purity unfolded, creating a struggle between the old and new tribes. The complexity of the emerging social stratification created a need for the codification of law, which clearly defined lines between various castes. Thus came the Dharmasutras, which also established the Brahmins as the arbiters of the law[18]. They gave the rules on marriages, adultery and succession. With caste differentiation came class stratification, affecting the role and status of women. Women from the higher castes began to be confined within the house. Social hierarchies created their own pyramid of power with those on the top developing an interest in their perpetuation. The huge body of Brahminical literature prescribed hundreds of rules for women, the concepts of stridharma and pativrata being just two of them. It was the age of the Buddha by then and the patriarchal family had become firmly established.

The transfer of movable and immovable property to women became an issue as patriarchy became entrenched. As in other parts of the world where patriarchy took root from an agrarian society, such transfers took place at the time of marriage. But soon daughters were simply excluded from inheriting land to keep immovable property with the parental family. But they were permitted to take a part of the father's movable property with them as dowry. Thus, dowry could be seen as 'compensation' for forfeiting the right to family land. As the Brahminical influence grew, eight distinct types of marriages were listed in *Manusmriti*, which were graded from the ideal to the acceptable to the abhorrent according to prevalent norms[19].

The first four types, considered the dharmya or socially acceptable, gave the father of the bride the central role. He decided her destiny and if he performed her marriage properly, he earned spiritual merit in the process. The last four were termed adharmya or against socio-cultural norms and decadent. The top of the list and the most 'ideal' form of marriage – unsurprisingly – was called the Brahma type which till today is the dominant form.

The Brahma rite was characterized by the gift of a daughter (kanyadaan) by the father, after adorning her with costly garments, to a man learned in the Vedas and of good conduct whom the father himself invited. A son born of such a union was believed to purify ten ancestors and ten descendants.

The Daiva form of marriage was the next best and it involved the gift of a daughter decked with ornaments to a priest who duly officiates at a sacrifice during the course of its performance. A father would invite accomplished priests to his house for a long period to perform sacrificial rites during which he and his daughter would observe them and select one. This form was later disapproved by *Smriti* writers who said any thoughts of marital bliss during religious sacrifices were not a good idea. Such a marriage purified seven ancestors and seven descendants.

The Arsha rite involved the father giving the gift of a daughter after receiving from the bridegroom a cow and a bull or two pairs in fulfilment of the sacred law. The son born of this union would only purify three ancestors and three descendants. There is a hint of a bride price in this form.

The Prajapatya rite was marked by the father making the gift of a daughter after he has addressed the couple with the text 'may the two of you together fulfil your duties' and has shown honour to the bridegroom by offering him a honey mixture.

The next four forms of marriage were condemnable and they produced sons who were cruel and didn't respect the sacred law. Instead of a pure 'gift' of a daughter, there were monetary considerations and outright purchase of a woman. They were considered appropriate only for the lower castes. They denied the patriarchal norms and there was no role for the girl's father or rituals.

In the Asura rite, a bridegroom gave as much wealth as he could afford to the bride and her kin according to his own will. The next was the Gandharva rite, a voluntary union of a maiden and her lover when they joined in sexual union out of desire. In the Rakshasa form, a maiden is abducted from her home after her family and relatives have been slain and their houses broken open. The worst is the Pisacha rite when a man by stealth seduces a girl who is sleeping, intoxicated or disordered in intellect. It is the most base and sinful rite.

The importance of marriage as a sacrament of great religious and spiritual merit grew historically and it became binding on all castes and classes. The many rituals deified the gift of the bride and the act of gift-giving itself. Ancient scriptures eulogized these acts which also came to signify improved social status. The giving of gifts was a visible sign of prosperity, which in turn led to greater prestige in society. But, as Dipankar Gupta points out, 'In the kanyadaan system the bride giver is always inferior to the bride taker and this situation remains over generations. In some cases, as among the Sarjupari brahmins, the father of the bride worships his son-in-law's feet. It is called paon puja.'

The earliest references to large dowries are found in the epics and the Puranas where Sita, the ideal for many women even today, and Parvati, Lord Shiva's consort, both brought considerable assets with them, from cows and elephants to jewels and clothing, to say nothing of the armies of attendants.

To be sure, dowry is not unique to Indian society but its institutionalization and evolution into a modern-day monstrosity seem to be. Dowry practices and the custom of bride price have existed in Africa, China, Southeast Asia and even pre-modern European societies. The reason that dowry is found in many societies is because it is undeniably connected to patterns of inheritance and to the shift from the tribal to agrarian social structures. As family structures changed from the matriarchal to patriarchal, dowry began making a definite appearance. Large dowries were used to build political alliances in European society. The city of Bombay itself was 'gifted' as dowry by Queen Regent of Portugal when her daughter Catherine of Braganza married the English king Charles II.

Evolution and Apathy

The Indian patriarchal system has, over the years, spawned such anti-women institutions as child marriage, ostracism of widows, female infanticide and sati. Dowry deaths are only the latest blow. Violence against women is deeply rooted in Indian society and tied intimately to their low status. Women are unwanted but necessary burdens.

What better measure of where Indian women are today than the latest census figures on the declining male-female ratio. In 1992, there were 945 girls for every 1000 boys in the 0-6 age group but that number dipped to 927 girls in 2001. And the worst figures, ironically, were thrown up by the prosperous state of Punjab, showing that poverty was not the only reason for rejecting daughters. With all the other reasons for their lesser status, dowry demands have reduced their desirability even further.

A random sampling of news reports shows the extent to which some men can go to extort money and gold from the bride's family. In August 2000, Gogi Devi[20] escaped from her husband Ram Singh's house in a village in Rajasthan where she was kept chained to a bed for almost two months. Her crime: inability to bring more dowry. National dailies published her photograph with iron cuffs on her feet in a grim testimony to the cruelty and abuse suffered by women.

She was able to escape when one night her husband forgot to put the padlock chain through the cuffs. Gogi walked all night to the next village, took the bus to Jodhpur in the morning and went to a police station to lodge a complaint. Married for two years, she was constantly harassed by her husband and in-laws for more dowry.

Thirty-year-old Shalini Aggarwal[21] was allegedly shot dead by her husband, Rahul, in Delhi in April the same year because she couldn't rustle up enough money from her parents to buy him a Honda car. This was after her parents had already given the couple an Opel Astra at the wedding but the car was registered in Shalini's name. The husband sold off the Opel and bought a Honda in his name. This being a more expensive car, he demanded that she arrange the differential. Shalini's end came after two-and-a-half years of marriage during which she was constantly abused and harassed for more dowry. Her mother had secretly been borrowing money from relatives and funneling it to her daughter in the vain hope that things would settle down.

The end for Shallu Jain[22] came after her cries for help went unheard. She burnt in June 2000 in the confines of her husband Yash Jain's house in Delhi. The police arrested her mother-in-law but Yash fled the scene. Two days before she died, Shallu had tried to contact her parents but their telephone was out of order. She then called the marriage broker who had arranged the marriage and asked him to save her. She begged him to come over but he refused and instead advised her to go to her parents' house. She said she couldn't because she had been tied up. She was taken to the hospital with 90 per cent burns where she succumbed to her injuries a few hours later. Shallu's mother told reporters that her daughter's body was reeking of gasoline, as was the room where she was burnt. She had been married for two-and-a-half years and had a daughter. Her husband constantly demanded that she bring money for him to start a business.

If a woman is lucky enough to be taken to a hospital, the law requires that the police record her statement. But a majority of women in their 'dying declarations' repeat a chillingly familiar narrative dictated by their in-laws. They say they were cooking and their clothes caught fire. Husbands and in-laws have been known to threaten the woman that if she implicates them in any way, they will simply abandon her children or 'ruin' her parents or both. Since death for her is a certainty, she complies with their demand hoping to safeguard her children's future. Often the police record the statement in front of the husband and in-laws whose presence is hardly likely to inspire confidence in a dying victim.

K. Janardhan, an experienced public prosecutor in Bangalore, says that despite many Supreme Court judgments directing the police on how to record a dying declaration, they fail to observe the most basic rules. 'Even today the callous manner in which it is recorded makes me ashamed as a prosecutor. The dullest constable may be sent to record the dying declaration and most often at night. If the victim gives her statement in Tamil, the constable records it in Kannada because he doesn't know Tamil. During the trial the defence counsel demolishes the veracity of the dying declaration by "proving" that the constable didn't have working knowledge of Tamil to understand what the victim may have said.'

Doctors and nurses in government hospitals in major cities have seen so many young women come to them clinging to life with their charred bodies that they are matter-of-fact about the sequence. The women are brought in terminal stages, they tell the police the same story, the police record the statement without questioning, they live for a few days in agony and then die. Even though a doctor is required to certify that the victim is coherent and able before the dying declaration is recorded, he may look the other way while a policeman concocts a statement, takes the woman's thumb impression and leaves. Doctors casually sign the papers and move on and rarely stay to ensure the procedures are followed. What was meant to be an additional check on police complacency and callousness is today a failed idea. Overworked and underpaid doctors in crowded government hospitals are not flowing with sympathy for the victims. They may overlook obvious signs of abuse and assault while performing postmortems, robbing the families of crucial evidence.

Male bonding takes place at the scene of crime, resulting in casual and perfunctory investigations by the police. The policeman may or may not choose to record statements. He may ignore crucial testimony from neighbours. He may take as long as a week to bring the police photographer to the scene of crime, giving enough time to the accused to destroy evidence and clean up. It happened in Calcutta to Vishnu Dayal Dhanuk[23] whose daughter burnt to death in 1998 in the tiny one-room hovel she lived in with her husband and their infant daughter. The police investigation that followed was laughable. The police didn't seal the house immediately, took photographs after twenty-five days and then claimed the photos got spoilt. They failed to seize the dowry, instead sending the Dhanuks to get court permission. The court said the police already had the power in a dowry death case to seize dowry items. When they went to the ACP with the court's opinion, he sent them back to the investigating officer who in turn said: 'Where is the written order? If I do something, I will get a phone call from above. Will you save me then?'

At every step the investigating officer obstructed, delayed and ignored potential witnesses and evidence of the crime. He didn't interview the neighbour at whose house the husband had left his daughter on the night of the crime, probably to clear the way before knocking out his wife and burning her. The police also 'failed' to interview the neighbour who ran to tell the Dhanuks that their daughter had died. After all this the investigating officer had the audacity to tell the victim's mother: 'I know your daughter was burnt. The whole mohalla says so but what can I do?' The Dhanuks persevered, bringing pressure from where they could. The husband brought counter pressure and in the middle were police officers eating their share of the pie. The husband was freed after an ill-prepared public prosecutor put on a pathetic show in the courtroom.

Today this apathy is laced with resentment and contempt for the new pro-women laws. Study after exhaustive study of police attitudes reveals a shocking resistance to registering cases, filing chargesheets, interviewing witnesses and going after the culprits. It is a rare policeman or woman who breaks the mould.

Backlash

If the 1970s brought dowry deaths into national consciousness, and the 1980s brought legal reforms and awareness, then the 1990s were the decade of the backlash by the male establishment, the many police and judicial watchdogs notwithstanding. It was a reaction so severe that it mocked the laborious strides made earlier. Men began to feel women were getting the better of them because they were filing cases and seeking intervention from the NGOs. And that they must be stopped in their tracks. So the men spread new myths. They blamed them for collapsing marriages. They blamed them for showing greater awareness and vigilance.

Women today are being maligned and demonized for 'using' the law. They are being condemned for going to courts against husbands to get their dowries back. They are being branded as opportunistic and irresponsible. Their use of the law is being termed 'misuse'.

Several lawyers practising in the lower courts told me repeatedly how the anti-dowry laws had led to an alarming rise in lawsuits from the girl's side, choking the system. As if that in itself were a crime. Women, they said, had become 'too aware'. They were running to the courts at any hint of domestic discord. Vengeful parents were roping the groom's entire family in their complaints without a thought to the efficacy of the case.

The subtext: the women are not adjusting enough.

An up and coming, cellphone-toting lawyer told me with a straight face: 'The stress is too much these days. Women can't take the pressure. They expect a lot from marriage and when their dreams don't come true, they are disappointed. A woman who is not satisfied in her parents' house gets another chance to settle down so the pressure is double. A man *knows* his circumstance, a woman expects hers to change and improve with marriage. I don't agree that men kill their wives for dowry. In most cases it *just happens*.' When I pressed the issue, he conceded that mothers-in-law and sisters-in-law may harass the wife but he did not name husbands in the same list.

True, there is some misuse of the law as there is of any other law. But why in the case of dowry laws alone has the misuse become an issue? Don't murder laws get misused? Aren't property laws twisted daily to deny legitimate owners their rights? Aren't anti-corruption laws a weapon in the hands of the unscrupulous? But lawyers rarely shed tears over those. Why in the case of pro-women laws alone does the establishment get jittery? It does, because it feels threatened. It wants to shore up its ranks and stop this minor assault on its authority. Therefore the exaggerated myths.

Another highly successful Delhi High Court lawyer blamed the intense pressures of modern life for the increasing numbers of suicides among married women. For these lawyers, dowry demands were a mere ruse used by desperate parents looking for a reason to 'explain' their daughter's death in the community. Several other lawyers told me how tired they were of women bringing wrongful claims and of parents using the law as a tool of reverse harassment.

The sympathy from the system is clearly flowing in the direction of the men.

Since most of the lawyers I spoke to represented the accused, a certain amount of rationalization of the crime was expected but for them to be in denial of dowry murders was surprising. The statistics are for all to see. It was uncanny how similar was the language used, how similar the logic in dismissing reality and how depressing ultimately it was to listen to them. To them it seemed perfectly acceptable that a healthy woman should commit suicide. Facing these highly paid, sharp lawyers are the victims and their families who are at the mercy of government prosecutors. Underpaid and overburdened, public prosecutors generally show little interest in building a case, hampered as they are by inadequate and tardy police investigations.

Janardhan, a public prosecutor himself, was harsh on his tribe. He said public prosecutors in general lacked the zeal shown by defence counsels. 'They submit meekly to the court even when it is not necessary. A government prosecutor is recognized by his tired, hackneyed and lacklustre performance. If he is sincere, he can make things happen, but only to an extent. As the case progresses and comes to trial, he is more and more isolated because the witnesses have moved on or turned hostile. Or the investigating officers have been transferred to other districts and are not available to give evidence. The defence has all the resources at hand – to keep tabs on witnesses, to bribe them.

'Another problem is the procedural law in India which is too loaded in favour of the accused. In a civil case, if a party proves his case by 51 per cent, he wins the case. But in a criminal case, you have to prove the guilt a 100 per cent and beyond reasonable doubt. The other side may take a fanciful defence, but the prosecution has to stand on its own two feet.'

You can guess who wins most of the time despite the feeling that dowry laws have tilted the balance in women's favour.

It is true that the dowry death law as worded in section 304 (B) of the Indian Penal Code *appears* to shift the burden of proof on the husband but it also has conditions that must be fulfilled *before* the courts will actually convict a man. The law says:

(1) 'Where the death of a woman is caused by any burns or bodily injury or occurs otherwise than under normal circumstances within seven years of her marriage and it is shown that soon before her death she was subjected to cruelty or harassment by her husband or any relative of her husband for, or in connection with, any demand for dowry, such death shall be called "dowry death", and such husband or relative shall be deemed to have caused her death.'

(2) 'Whoever commits dowry death shall be punished with imprisonment for a term which shall not be less than seven years but which may extend to imprisonment for life.'

Prosecutors find it difficult to prove that the cruelty or harassment occurred '*soon before her death*'. The Supreme Court through various judgments has tried to define 'soon' but there is ambiguity. A woman may have faced degradation a month before she is killed but her case may not establish that she was harassed 'soon' before her death. Sujata Mehra, a Delhi-based lawyer who has advised NGOs and written a manual on laws for women for a legal literacy campaign, says the prosecution is required to prove a nexus between dowry demands and the unnatural death. A continuum must be established. It is only after the prosecution has established a tight case that the presumption of guilt kicks in. But experienced prosecutors question the need to shift the presumption of guilt to the accused if it is not going to help in establishing the crime. Janardhan has been advocating deleting the clause 'soon before her death' at legal conferences and has repeatedly written to the law ministry but received no response.

The male establishment may harbour beliefs about how women are 'running' away with the dowry laws, how their parents are bringing wrongful suits and how the police are arresting husbands first and asking questions later, but the reality is different. Courts tend to be lenient in granting anticipatory bail to the husbands and police do not easily register 304 (B) cases.

Let's look at another law dealing with dowry – section 498 (A), which defines cruelty towards a woman by her husband and his relatives. Without concrete proof either in the form of letters or receipts of goods delivered or corroboratory testimony from witnesses, it becomes difficult to establish such cases. Most parents do not meticulously catalogue expenditure for weddings despite the law exhorting them to do so. They also tend not to keep the bills for big dowry items beyond a certain time because they don't anticipate a calamity. But these days dowry demands, torture and deaths are being reported even several years after marriage, requiring parents to be ever vigilant.

It is not surprising that in 1998, the highest rate of acquittals/discharge was for 498 (A) cases dealing with torture and harassment. More women went to the courts but came back disappointed. The courts granted acquittals in 80 per cent of the cases and convicted only 20 per cent. The average rate of conviction for most crimes in India was around 37 per cent.

The judiciary, albeit indirectly, is also a part of the patriarchal backlash, taking the inaction further where the police leave off. A low rate of conviction and a high rate of acquittal for dowry-related crimes shows the extent of its rigour and response to crimes against women. Of the thousands of dowry cases filed every year, only a fraction see completion and fewer see conviction. In 1998, there were 22,055 cases of dowry deaths pending across India in various courts. Of these, 173 were withdrawn or compounded, leaving behind a staggering 21,882 cases. Trial was completed in 3359 cases, resulting in 1080 convictions and 2279 acquittals.

The few cases that are investigated travel slowly up the judicial ladder and end mostly in acquittals. Reason: lack of clinching evidence. Despite a Supreme Court verdict granting greater importance to circumstantial evidence in dowry death cases, lower courts still insist on the 'smoking gun'. Since the daughter-in-law dies inside the house, there are few witnesses. Neighbours maintain a conspiracy of silence either in perceived self-defence or for purely lazy reasons. While the police fail to ask the most fundamental questions during investigation, the administrators of justice allow the defence to seek repeated delays. 'The legal system is flawed and one is not supposed to question the judges because of the sanctity attached to the judiciary. But is it really correct to say that judges are infallible?' asks Donna Fernandes[24] of Vimochana, a Bangalore-based activist who has been in the forefront of the anti-dowry movement since the 1980s.

Since cases go on for decades, the victim's family often gives up in frustration or reaches a 'compromise' with the groom to get the dowry back in exchange for withdrawing the police complaint. Janardhan, after years of watching the system up close, says, 'Corruption is not limited to government servants but even the girl's parents bargain. Before the girl's death, the groom's family harasses her for money and after her death, her parents settle for monetary gain. They can compromise for just twenty thousand rupees. They say they are not going to get their daughter back, so what is the point in fighting on?' The bitter truth was tinged with sadness and an acceptance of the Indian reality where life has little value and a girl's life even less.

Delays and defence lawyers' tricks to derail the case also sap the energies of the girl's family. A monetary compromise is seen as a good way out since most of the cases in court are from poor and lower-middle-class families – every court hearing is a daily wage missed. In some cases, the victim's family may give another daughter in marriage to the same man because they 'believe' his story. The man may offer to marry the second daughter for a discounted dowry. Such are the compulsions of an Indian father. Janardhan told me he personally knew of seven cases where another daughter had been married into the same family where her sister died an 'unnatural death'.

If the natal family shuns daughters and can unwittingly send them to their death, police apathy or casual tolerance on part of the judiciary should hardly be surprising.

If there is a rare police officer who wants to probe further in search of the truth, he or she is faced with a deaf and dumb system. Suman Nalwa[25], assistant commissioner of police in Delhi, told me how difficult it was to engender sensitivity among lower ranking police officers who tended to be less educated. As a senior woman officer in charge of the special cell dealing with crimes against women in the late 1990s, she saw hundreds of cases of harassment, torture, cruelty and murder. Nalwa is known for her sensitive handling of cases but instead of getting encouragement she was cautioned by her colleagues and well-wishers not to be 'overenthusiastic' about the job. She sounded pessimistic when I talked to her about bringing criminal husbands to book for dowry murders. Her reasons for why there is failure on part of the police:

'We, as a society, are insensitive. I come across so many cases of dowry harassment that it pure and simple disgusts me. It is very frustrating for me when I am unable to help a woman feel secure in her own house and it doesn't help to tell her how the judicial system works. She just wants an end to her suffering and comes to the police as a last resort, contrary to popular belief that a woman goes to the police these days at the drop of a hat. Small incidents get accumulated and become unbearable. But the police tend to see things in black and white and for most policemen mental torture is an alien concept. The next step of quantifying it and deciding to act is even harder for them, especially if cruelty has not manifested itself in an obvious manner.

'We face a lot of constraints. First, it is the woman's word against her husband and no outsider will testify in the matter or be present during those situations. Secondly, the propaganda about women "misusing" the dowry law (because they are filing cases) has really succeeded which has led to a more insensitive criminal justice system as a whole where a single individual judge, no matter how hard he or she tries to deliver justice, can fail.

'Our investigative officers lack empathy and we tend to be case-centric rather than victim-centric. We are so bogged down by rules that we hesitate to do anything different or be enthusiastic in case our enthusiasm is questioned. Also, we are often not detached and impartial in our investigation. We tend to look at all cases with the same eyes when each one is different. Although everyone thinks that dowry cases are cut and dried, it is not so. It is often said that women exaggerate their claims by including all members of the husband's family in a complaint but nobody tries to ask why they do it. Aren't the relatives who arranged the marriage, received all the gifts, demanded more dowry and lived in the same house also responsible for facilitating torture by their silence?'

There are not enough officers like Suman Nalwa in the country but there are some who are not numb to the crimes in front of them, who still have the courage to keep their eyes open and who can cut through social slush to find the truth. At least one young woman is alive today because of Nalwa's zeal and her story is included in the book.

The Response

Some of the initial anti-dowry demonstrations were organized in Hyderabad in 1975 but the problem caught national attention in 1979 when several women's organizations in New Delhi joined hands under the banner of Stree Sangharsh to protest the murder of Tarvinder Kaur, a twenty-four-year-old newly married Sikh bride[26]. In her 'dying declaration' Kaur clearly said that her mother-in-law and sister-in-law had set her on fire. Yet the Delhi police registered a case of suicide, not murder. Women activists took to the streets and demonstrated outside the house where Kaur had died, demanding justice and a new investigation. Several other protests followed over the next few weeks with college students actively participating. Street plays were organized to take the problem to the heart of the city as the campaign spread to other Indian cities. Media coverage helped bring dowry deaths centrestage, jolting the nation towards action.

A memorandum of demands was presented to the government with a list of urgent reforms needed in the existing dowry legislation – the Dowry Prohibition Act of 1961, a toothless and vague piece of legislation. Years after dowry deaths had hit the headlines, the government appointed a committee in 1980 to suggest ways to deal with the menace. The committee submitted its report two years later, blaming the 'Frankensteinian growth' of the dowry system on modernization, urbanization and industrialization. It recommended expanding the definition of dowry to include gifts given before and after marriage, excluding the 'givers' of dowry from punishment since they were victims, setting up of family courts, appointment of dowry prohibition officers and instituting a National Commission for Women. It also suggested making inheritance rights for women equal to those of men as an important step in empowering women.

But Parliament ignored most of the recommendations while adopting the amendments in 1983. Outraged women activists termed it a 'defeat' and several organizations jointly prepared a new memorandum pointing out the lacunae in the half-hearted measures. The window dressing had failed to impress anyone. The continued anger on the streets and pressure from civil rights groups forced the government to adopt further amendments in 1986 which increased both the fine and the minimum punishment for accepting dowry from six months to five years. It expanded the definition of dowry to include gifts given 'after marriage or any time after marriage'. Most importantly, it inserted a new section in the Indian Penal Code – section 304 (B) – which defined a dowry death. It made the crime a non-bailable offence, which meant that only a court could grant bail not the police. But over the years the courts tended to be lenient in granting anticipatory bail to people accused of dowry-related crimes, as the defence lawyers successfully argued that their clients were falsely implicated. Once out on bail, the accused often went and remarried – a fact which he then exploited to seek further bail. His lawyers argued that the new family was not at fault and should not be penalized. They needed the accused to earn a living and feed them.

The government has tended to see dowry in isolation rather than as a manifestation of the low status of women in India, thus treating the symptoms not the disease. It has made few attempts to make real changes in the existing patriarchal system. Its attitude has been ambivalent at best and inimical to women's rights at worst. The parliamentary debates leading up to the enactment of the Dowry Prohibition Act in 1961 and the various amendments in 1983 and 1986 showed a political class desperately trying to maintain the existing family power structures dominated by males. Dowry was seen as a daughter's share in parental wealth and endorsed as a practice coming down from ancient times. Sons stood to inherit property and daughters got jewellery, clothes and kitchen gadgets. Any tampering of the system would strain the very fabric of Indian society, the parliamentarians argued. Once married, a daughter's ties with the parental family were deemed severed. As long as dowry was voluntary, it was acceptable in law.

But the law spoke with a forked tongue, reflecting the confusion of Parliament. On one hand, the law tried to make dowry solely the woman's possession by trying to stipulate the return of gifts in case of death, divorce or harassment. On the other it tried to stop the 'demand' for gifts. In essence, the government maintained the existing patriarchal system which implicitly acknowledged men as inheritors and successors and locked the women into a mother-wife role.

Once dowry becomes an issue for the woman's grasping in-laws, the house becomes her jail. Basically a dependent, a daughter-in-law is a sitting target in her new home with nowhere to run. Her sense of self is constantly assailed, her identity always under threat from the family power structures. Her parents' home is virtually closed to her because they have discharged their 'duty' by getting her married. It is bad enough to have to relay new dowry demands to the parents, returning to them would mean acknowledging that *they* failed. A rejected daughter is a taint on the family and parents so fear losing social status that they risk their daughter's life. The family izzat is more important. They chant the mantra of 'adjust, adjust, adjust' and the woman has little choice but to stay in the hostile environment while parents scurry around to feed new dowry demands. Mothers- and sisters-in-law often make life a living hell for them, tormenting them and treating them as bonded labour. Women become women's worst enemies.

Why does that happen since, to use a cliché, saas bhi kabhi bahu thi (a mother-in-law was once a daughter-in-law herself)? Gender affinity takes a backseat to 'status' enhancement. Dipankar Gupta explains the disturbing phenomenon thus: 'Once the bride becomes the mother of a son, she can slowly convert her status from being a woman who came from a bride giver family to a (potential) bride taker. When her son eventually marries, she is a full-fledged bride taker. The gender does not matter that much. This is a status she always aspired to and she has got it at last. If she had given birth only to girls, she would not have been able to elevate herself.' The new identity is often linked to oppression of new female entrants to the family.

Divorce is still not a valid option for most middle-class women not only because of the social stigma attached to it but also because of a lack of job opportunities. A battered woman would rather live with a bad husband than no husband at all even if it means continued physical torture and abuse. If children are involved, the decision is more perilous because of custody battles. Even if a woman considers divorce, her parents may not be supportive and she may have to start out alone – a near-impossible task unless she is earning well. Only the grittiest go down that path. A divorcee is open to harassment in a hundred different ways by other men. Shelters for battered women are few and far between and many do not allow children, thereby shutting the door on women who may want to leave with their children.

Madhu Kishwar[27] raised some pertinent questions about the persistence of dowry deaths despite introduction of new laws and public condemnation throughout the '70s and '80s. She stressed that dowry harassment continued because its primary purpose was to 'degrade and victimize a woman' so she felt perpetually insecure and recognized her subordinate position in the household. She argued that the harassment of wives was 'related to the utterly dependent and powerless position of women in our present family structure, which concentrates economic and decision-making powers in the hands of men.' All this happens because daughters are unwanted to begin with. Trying to abolish dowry was like trying to get into a room with the wrong key. To ask women to resist marriages with dowry, as the women's movement demanded in the early stages of the campaign, is to put the onus on the wrong person. Kishwar said the focus of the fight should be on empowerment of women through equal rights of inheritance. 'What we need to fight is not a phoney symbol such as dowry but the power relations within the family,' she wrote in *Rethinking Dowry Boycott*.

'Under the existing family structure, giving up dowry does not entail any alternative advantage for a woman. She loses the little she would get, and gains literally nothing. And yet, we the social reformers have shied away from this simple answer, and have continued to demand that women, as proof of their "liberated" thinking, should refuse to take dowry. Most women see their dowry as the only share they will get in their parental property . . . To suggest that women refuse dowry and go empty-handed to their marital homes is to suggest that they make even greater martyrs of themselves than society makes of them. Until we can ensure inheritance rights for daughters, we have no right to ask them to sacrifice the inadequate compensation they get by way of dowry,' she wrote, stirring a debate among women activists.

Many did not agree with Kishwar who seemed to mitigate the ills of the dowry system as it exists today while making her case for better inheritance rights for daughters. Her opponents said they had no quarrel with the contention that daughters should get their rightful share in parental property, but no one could ignore the exorbitant dowry demands and the resulting violence against women. The two problems had to be tackled simultaneously. Dowry is not 'only a symptom of her fragile rights' as suggested by Kishwar, but a reality which often envelops other forms of oppression. Dowry and other cultural practices together degrade women, and one is not exclusive of the other. Kishwar's argument outraged many feminists who said she was mistaken to treat dowry as a woman's inheritance when it is mostly a transaction between men.

The sad irony is that in the husband's home a woman rarely exercises control either over her dowry or her streedhan – her personal jewellery, clothing and other belongings. The jewellery is deposited straightaway with the mother-in-law while other items are grabbed for use in the dowries for daughters of the husband's family. In many cases even clothes for daily wear are locked up and given out on a rationed basis. The dowry cash transactions are done exclusively between male members of the two families – the bride's father to the groom's father. Even though dowry may be her legitimate share, a woman cannot enjoy it.

But she is made to die for it.

Mother Courage

Satyarani's Story

When I first met Satyarani Chaddha, she was seventy-eight years old and very angry. She had good reason to be. She had been ricocheting through Indian courts for twenty-two years for justice, trying to put her daughter's murderers behind bars. She was bone tired from the fight and at the end of it she had only a sad story to tell. Her hair had greyed, her gait now faltered and her steely demeanour was perforated with pain. When she tried to remember the past and talk about it, her anger bubbled and gushed out like lava lighting a fire of memories.

When it had all started, she was much younger and even hopeful of sending her daughter's tormentors to jail for good. Shashi Bala had died of 90 per cent burns in 1979 within a year of her marriage. She was six months pregnant at the time.

Satyarani's pain was still raw and seared with living images, each one alive in some corner of her mind and waiting to spill out. She wondered if the long years of perseverance were worth it. Yes, she had fought and fought for a long time. She had continued against all odds, neglecting her family and grandchildren in the process. But after two decades of legal wrangles and court appearances, she was more despairing than hopeful about dowry victims finding justice. Her son-in-law was convicted not of murder but of a lesser crime of abetting Shashi Bala's suicide. He went to jail but only for two months. He was sentenced to seven years' rigorous imprisonment but was quickly granted bail by the

Delhi High Court when his lawyers – some of the best in the city – successfully raised questions about the conduct of the trial and application of law. They argued that the conviction was based on the testimony of one principal witness, that of Satyarani's, and that she 'improved' on her statements through the years. They listed twenty-three reasons for appeal – a year more than it took Satyarani to get the conviction by the trial court.

'What did I get in the end for fighting for so long? People are laughing at me. I spent my life in courtrooms but what do I have to show for it? A two-month jail holiday for my daughter's murderer?' she asked, her sharp voice piercing the room, her sad sarcasm biting.

Satyarani had seen enough life to shred middle-class illusions about social change by the minute. She flung details of her long struggle at me like so many grenades, mocking me with information bombs, shattering my collected wisdom. She had little patience for words like 'courts' and 'justice'. She spat them out like they were bitter pills of uncertain benefit. 'I can't tear my chest to prove to you how singed I am inside. This is the justice a helpless mother gets in our system.' Police and judges, judges and police – they were two faces of the same problem for her.

'What kind of laws do we have that you bring a bride home with fanfare and then burn her alive? The husband simply marries again even while the court case is on? Tell me, tell me why this is?' she would ask, her eyes glistening with tears. Her son-in-law Subhash Bhasin had remarried and had children even though he was accused of burning his first wife. 'Don't ask me any questions. Go ask the Supreme Court judges why our girls continue to die. No, I don't have time for all this.' She shut me out vehemently and picked up the telephone. 'Yes, yes, we will get the dowry back. Don't worry, we are with you,' she told someone on the other side who needed help.

It was November 2000 when I first met Satyarani in New Delhi. Subhash had recently been granted bail and she was a bundle of emotions – enraged that he got away with so little and fatigued from the burden of her long fight. She was trying to decide whether to appeal the Delhi High Court decision to grant him bail. She was sitting in her modest two-room office in Jangpura in south Delhi from where she runs Shaktishalini (Women of Courage), an organization she launched to help dowry victims such as her daughter so they may live. Her daughter did not and Satyarani can never forget that. Leaning back on her chair behind a desk, constantly answering distress calls from victims, parents and lawyers, she remains very much a fighter. I could see why senior police officers grudgingly respected her while beat constables were in awe. She could barge into any police station and ensure that a dowry victim got a fair hearing.

It took me a while to draw Satyarani out of her angry shell and go beyond her all-consuming cynicism. She kept evading my phone calls and entreaties under one pretext or another – 'I am not well', 'too busy', 'have to go to court', 'have important meetings'. When she finally relented, she was brutally frank about the futility of talking to journalists and filmmakers, the two types of people who had hounded her periodically. 'What good will it do for me to tell you how I feel? I am tired of talking and listening. If things had changed, it would be different. Even now I am ready to face bullets and enter the arena if things will improve for our daughters. But nothing changes, it only gets worse,' she said. No sugar coating or political correctness there. I swallowed hard and listened each time she put my tribe and me in place. It was difficult not to get defensive and come roaring back with some justification about the 'need' for her to spread awareness by talking to the media. But I knew it was futile because Satyarani's truth and experience were her own and she had more ammunition to defend her position than I could ever hope to muster. If she were willing to tell me a little of her story – her daughter's story – even in bits and pieces, it was fine by me. Age and bitterness had to be respected in her case.

Satyarani spoke in Hindi and Punjabi, her voice alternately rising in a crescendo and dropping sharply as she lost her breath. She paused often to take a gulp of water, her few front teeth gripping the edge of the stainless steel tumbler. She obviously hadn't bothered with the formalities of dentures. In her life, there was no time for distractions. She was Spartan, and so was her office because the scarce funds had to be spent on lawyers' fees, telephone bills, taxi fares – not on frills. She was under pressure from the landlord to agree to a rent hike.

Shaktishalini is run jointly by Satyarani and Shahjahan Khanum who is popularly known as Aapa or elder sister. Both women have lost daughters at the altar of greed, having failed to fulfil dowry demands in time. But instead of suffering their grief privately, they created an organization to help other victims and their families fight back. They have filed hundreds of court cases, pressured police to investigate unnatural deaths of brides and recovered dowry items from reluctant in-laws. They started a shelter for young women who wanted to escape from the torment but had nowhere to go. 'But no man has yet been hanged for burning his wife,' Satyarani says, summing up the truth pithily.

Satyarani struck me as very different from other women activists I had met until then. She was a grieving mother whose personal experience had drawn her to the picket lines and she had stayed. Unlike some of the bandwagon liberals and activists who thrive in major cities now, she didn't dress in chic ethnic saris or wear fashionable tribal jewellery. She couldn't speak English nor flaunt a degree from one of India's pedigree colleges. Her friends didn't run influential government offices or media organizations and you wouldn't find her at city gatherings where her fellow travellers mingle with powerful bureaucrats and foreign representatives of donor agencies, trying to impress upon them the need for change. She is the Warrior Mama who cares little about her accoutrements. Very much an average middle-class woman, she is driven by her past, not by seminars and books. She says it as it is, bludgeoning egos because she has no desire to please. At the same time, she seems to revel in the prominence she now has, exhorting decision makers of the capital towards action but also blasting them at every opportunity.

Beneath Satyarani's efforts is a desire that dowry victims do not end up merely as statistics in government files. She made sure that her daughter Shashi Bala did not, although she had to devote twenty-two years of her life for that. In the process, Satyarani herself transformed from an average Punjabi housewife into a grassroots activist and remains one of the few on the national scene who continue to shine the light on the ugly sore of dowry. Her story is a textbook example of how long and tortuous the road to justice can be. When she finally began telling me the story of her daughter, she seemed transported back into another world. She was on autopilot then, going smoothly from one incident to another. Her language was shorn of any frills and her memory remarkable even after so many years.

Satyarani and her husband Suraj Prakash Chaddha had nine children but only five had survived. Shashi Bala was the middle child with a sister and a brother before her and a sister and a brother after her. The family lived in a modest house in the Old Gupta Colony in Delhi. Life was comfortable but not luxurious for the Chaddha family. Apart from facing the daily problems of water shortages and power cuts common to all Delhi residents except the VIPs, the family was managing well within its means. They were together and that is what counted. Shashi was in the process of completing her bachelor's degree from Laxmi Bai College. She seemed content doing just that and helping her mother at home. She was everything a 'good girl' in the Indian context is meant to be – she was obedient, she could cook, and she could sew and embroider well. 'She was also beautiful. Our relatives used to say that only a lucky man who had done good deeds in life would get Shashi,' Satyarani remembered. She was 'clever at all the household work' and never said 'no' to any request, however outrageous. She would run to the kitchen to cook something new if anyone complained about the food.

'If I scolded anyone at home, it was Shashi who cried. She would give her brothers and sisters her pocket money. She was full of love for everyone. I don't know how they could kill her . . . ,' Satyarani's voice trailed off and she was lost for the next few minutes.

When Shashi completed her BA, the whole family was excited. It was the summer of 1978 and her future seemed full of promise. A 'BA pass' girl in the family was something to boast about in the community. Satyarani herself hadn't gone beyond sixth grade because the times were such. She had wanted better for her children. Besides, a college degree was a sure value addition in the marriage market. But when Shashi expressed an interest in studying law, Satyarani balked a bit. Wouldn't marriage be a good idea now?

Shashi did not push and just let time glide by. She was enjoying her newfound status of a 'graduate' in the community. She wanted to go to the gurdwara to offer prayers of thanks for passing her exams. After all, she needed the benediction if she wanted to pursue her dream of becoming a lawyer. It was a mellow summer's day when the mother and daughter set off for the gurdwara. On the way they met Savitri Bharadwaj, a casual acquaintance, who, after exchanging pleasantries, asked Satyarani about the young woman next to her.

'She is my daughter,' Satyarani replied.

'Aren't you going to get her married?' Savitri asked without further ado.

She had come straight to the point, experienced as she was at matchmaking. Satyarani's daughter standing in front of her seemed ready for the market – she was good-looking and fair. Savitri had seen her walk and had noticed no limp.

'I don't have a boy in mind right now,' said Satyarani.

'Well, I have someone who will be suitable for your daughter, so tell me if you are interested,' Savitri said, throwing a bait. She knew any parent with daughters is by definition interested in a prospective 'match'. Satyarani was no exception. Ignoring Shashi's misgivings about an early marriage, she decided to follow up on the offer immediately.

'What about studying law? Couldn't marriage come later?' Shashi asked hesitatingly. Something in her felt it was all happening too quickly. She did not like the hurried nature of the discussions, the quick meetings. She had 'seen' Subhash but only over a cup of tea with parents hovering around. But Satyarani persisted and quickly cajoled her daughter into submission. Who knows what moral pressure she brought upon her but Shashi agreed to marry Subhash Bhasin, the boy recommended by Savitri. Shashi knew that there was another sister to be married off after her. Any delay in her own marriage would mean an automatic delay in her sister's and that could set tongues wagging in the community. She had to do the 'right' thing and the 'right' thing defined by years of conditioning was to accept the proposal. Besides, her mother really seemed to like Subhash. She thought he was a good prospect and one must not miss this 'godsent' opportunity.

'I told Shashi that we won't find such a boy again. Indeed, we wouldn't have found a murderer, a killer so easily!' Satyarani recalled bitterly. By now she had tears streaming down her furrowed cheeks. I asked her what was so special about Subhash that instead of looking around for a few prospective grooms, she wanted to hitch her daughter to the first man who came along. After all, most parents cast a wider net. They advertise in the matrimonial columns, spread the word among relatives, talk to friends and only then the process of selection begins. What was the big hurry, I asked. 'Was he very rich?'

'No, in fact, not at all. He had four sisters,' Satyarani said, quickly giving me a perspective on his debt-asset ratio. He was earning but being the eldest son he had the responsibility of helping his father marry off his four sisters. That meant four dowries and four wedding receptions. It was an onerous burden. Satyarani was aware that Subhash was only scraping through. His large family was spread over three cities and three different households. His father, two sisters and the youngest brother lived in Kanpur. His mother, two sisters and a brother lived in a suburb of Delhi. He himself lived in Mathura, about two hours from Delhi, where he worked as a salesman in a Bata shoe store. It was an unusual family situation.

But Satyarani was taken by Subhash's sweet-talking ways, she recalled. 'He was very handsome. He was fair. I was just mesmerized by his manner. He spoke so well.' She reacted as many mothers might – eager to find a good man for her daughter, she projected on Subhash qualities that she wanted to see in her son-in-law. There was no talk of dowry during the initial meetings between the two families before marriage. Among the Punjabis, the groom's father customarily doesn't ask for dowry but says he will take the daughter-in-law in 'three sets of clothes'. But just because families don't openly ask for dowry doesn't mean they don't expect it. They may not ask for even a spoon but still expect the whole kitchen. I heard this from several Punjabi families who later became victims of dowry harassment. Some other communities, by contrast, especially the trader castes, conduct dowry negotiations openly. Among the banias, the amount of the dowry is specified down to the last rupee and generally there is less confusion later.

'Subhash told me, "How can I ask for anything? I would have to ask for four of each article since I have four sisters. I have to buy four of the same," ' Satyarani remembered. 'I really liked his way of thinking.' He made it very clear that he was not demanding a dowry. But there were murmurs of trouble, nonetheless. Satyarani got a taste of it shortly after the engagement ceremony when Subhash's parents asked for a refrigerator, a television set and a scooter. The bickering started when the saris sent for Subhash's mother and sisters were not found up to the mark. The future mother-in-law wanted a better one. 'She complained about the saris and I offered to exchange them. But she said she couldn't return the saris given at shagun because that would be inauspicious.' The mother-in-law was simply asking for more saris. 'I said to her that tomorrow is the wedding and you shouldn't be talking like that.'

Perhaps Satyarani's antennae, now sharpened and honed after years of experience, weren't receptive enough at the time or she felt it was simply too late to change course. The family name would be mud if the engagement were broken and the wedding called off. After all, the invitation cards had been sent and everyone knew.

Shashi and Subhash got married on 4 May 1978 in a simple ceremony. It was summer time – not the best of times in Delhi. May, as usual, was brutally hot but preparations had to be made. The temperature was hovering between 42 to 45 degrees Celsius during the day and only partially less at night. Satyarani still remembers the steaming heat that made everything doubly difficult. Subhash arrived more than two hours late for the wedding, honouring the long tradition of tardiness shown by ladkewalas to establish who is boss early on. 'We were waiting and it was so hot. Most of my relatives left without having dinner because they couldn't eat before his relatives had,' Satyarani recalled. Since the wedding was being held outdoors and under a shamiana, the heat was oppressive. As a result, a lot of the wedding food went bad and had to be thrown away. 'I still remember how hot it was that day. Our relatives just drank Campa Cola and left.' Shashi left the next day after the vidai ceremony amid tears. But it was a temporary goodbye for her and she knew she would be visiting often.

Satyarani and her husband Suraj Prakash gave a respectable dowry to Shashi given their means, which had to stretch to cover the marriage of five children. There was a refrigerator, some cash, kitchen utensils, clothes, gold jewellery, and clothes for the groom and his family. 'We gave more than enough,' said Satyarani. When noises were made about a table fan, Shashi's parents decided to add that too. But they could not afford to give a colour television set and a scooter as the groom's family demanded. When Subhash wouldn't stop complaining, Satyarani agreed to buy a black and white set on instalments and deposited about fifteen hundred rupees for the first three instalments. But she was categorical about the scooter – she simply couldn't afford it. The expectation was actually for a car but when Satyarani's family flatly said they couldn't, Subhash's parents shot back with, 'If you can't give four wheels, at least give two.'

Shashi was taken to her in-laws' house in Delhi, not to Mathura where Subhash himself lived. To signify her arrival into a new home and her new role, her name was changed to Kanchan as is customarily done among some Punjabi families. It was as if she were being denied her earlier life. Satyarani continued to call her Shashi Bala, and for the purposes of telling her story I decided to stick to the name she was given at birth. Shashi started living with her mother-in-law, Krishnawanti, a brother-in-law, Naresh, and two sisters-in-law, Chanchal and Aruna, in their Gandhi Nagar house in Delhi. It was a small two-room place already cramped for the number of adults living there. Shashi, as the newest member of the family, was expected to 'adjust' – the necessary mantra for all daughters-in-law – to her crowded environment without a complaint. She did. She began taking on responsibilities around the house and was quickly made in charge of not only cooking meals but also cleaning the house and washing clothes. 'She was treated as a maid, nothing more. That is why they took her to the Gandhi Nagar house and not to Mathura,' Satyarani recalled. 'They wanted a free servant and they got my daughter.'

In the small claustrophobic house, the bickering and taunts sounded even louder. Shashi had no place to run, no corner to call her own. She could not escape into solitude, there was none to be had in those two rooms. She could not walk ten steps without bumping into a member of the family. Even when her husband visited from Mathura, they had little privacy. At night when they were alone in one of the two rooms, they were still within whispering distance of the rest of them. There was no opportunity for the husband and wife to share moments together or get to know each other under the many prying eyes.

Shashi wanted to move to Mathura with Subhash but he always made some excuse or another. His mother, now old and infirm, needed Shashi more, he would say. Besides, he didn't have a 'proper' house in Mathura for Shashi. He was living in a one-room place where he had to share the bathroom and kitchen with other tenants. This was not something he wanted his new bride to experience, he told her. He would visit her on weekends and she must learn to cope with the situation in his mother's house. Shashi found him strangely unsympathetic, and not very eager for her company. He left her after his brief visits with promises of finding a good house but he never seemed to find one.

Soon she began to dread his visits because he seemed different. He seemed to have joined forces with his mother and the two of them would berate Shashi about something or the other. It looked like he enjoyed prodding and poking her with jibes. The mother-in-law often made references to the scooter and how Shashi's family had failed to give a good dowry. 'We have been shamed,' she would yell. With biting anger, Krishnawanti would talk of her expectations for her only son but how they were belied. The message was clear – you are not good enough for our fair-skinned, able and clever son. Shashi would simply listen and try to ignore the verbal assaults. They were mounted almost daily but she learnt to live with them. Whatever her family had given as dowry had been confiscated by Subhash's family from day one. The kitchen utensils were kept aside to be used for his sisters' dowries, ditto for the saris. Only the refrigerator was being used by the family. Shashi had no control over her jewellery either – it had been taken away from her for 'safekeeping' when she first arrived at her in-laws' house.

When Shashi visited Satyarani, she stayed clear of the subject at first. She did not volunteer any information nor did she confide in her mother. 'When I asked her about her in-laws, she would say, "They keep talking and I keep listening," ' Satyarani remembered. Subhash would constantly taunt Shashi about how much money her family had but how unwilling they were to part with it. It was as if they were obliged to share it with him. 'You should ask them. Why don't you ask them?' he would berate her. The weekends with Subhash became something to be dreaded, not welcomed.

In her recounting of the terrible atmosphere in the house, Shashi would try to placate her mother and tell her not to worry. 'I know what you have and how much you gave me. Let them talk,' she often said. But Satyarani was beginning to get worried about the tenor of things. Her daughter wasn't happy no matter how brave a front she put up in front of her mother. Satyarani's instincts said there was going to be trouble.

Within three months of getting married, Shashi was pregnant. When she visited her mother's house, she always seemed hungry. 'They didn't even feed my daughter properly. She would crave things but they wouldn't allow her to buy them. She had no money at all,' Satyarani said. Every time Shashi came, her parents and brother would give her some money so that she would have something in her purse in case of an emergency. They didn't want their daughter to have to beg her in-laws for every rupee. But according to Satyarani, Subhash would snatch Shashi's purse and take the money the moment they left her mother's house and turned the corner. Once she got back home, her sisters-in-law would raid her purse to extract any goodies her mother might have given. Once her mother gave her a pomegranate delicacy meant for pregnant women, and they even snatched that from her.

But Satyarani and her husband still didn't think of calling their daughter back and when I asked her why, she was embarrassed. Like most traditional parents, she had believed her daughter 'belonged' in her husband's home and once Shashi was pregnant, there was more reason for her to stay with him no matter what the circumstances. It was centuries of conditioning and years of bowing to tradition. She would try to slowly fulfil the demands and buy her daughter's happiness.

The pregnancy seemed more a problem than a reason to celebrate. Shashi couldn't satisfy her cravings for different foods. Satyarani remembered Shashi telling her about a particular incident that had sent her blood boiling. It was the winter of 1978. Most women in the neighbourhood would sit around in the afternoons outside their homes on small charpais, exchanging gossip. Shashi's lane was no different. Once the lunch was over and pots and pans had been scrubbed clean, the women came out and enjoyed the sun. The hawkers and vendors came to catch the women at leisure, hoping they would be in a better mood to spend. The snackwalas, sariwalas, bartanwalas tried their luck.

It was one such October afternoon that Shashi's sisters-in-law decided to buy aaloo tikkis for themselves. They were savouring them as Shashi looked on. She also wanted some but they never offered. Krishnawanti was watching the scenario, her devilish mind working overtime. 'Do you want some tikkis?' she asked Shashi. 'They sure look delicious.'

Shashi nodded. 'Stop ogling at my daughters and get some for yourself,' her mother-in-law urged. Shashi said she would do just that. She went inside to get her purse and bought two tikkis for a rupee. She didn't know she was walking into a trap. The moment she paid the man, her mother-in-law burst into a violent tirade. She began abusing Shashi and raining blows on her. 'How can you afford to eat tikkis? You are wasting money. This is not your father's house,' she yelled. The only reason Krishnawanti had egged Shashi on to buy them was to find out whether she had any money on her. Because under her orders, her son was not supposed to leave any money with Shashi. He had obviously failed at his task and would have to answer. 'How will you build your house if you don't save your money? You are wasting my son's income. You are destroying our house, our peace of mind,' Krishnawanti shouted.

Shashi was stunned at the sudden turn of events. She tried to defend herself but her mother-in-law would have none of it. She just wanted to disappear, somehow, somewhere, away from all this. She cried a lot that day into her pillow – there was no place even to cry in peace. She wondered if she should tell her mother everything, spill her guts if only to relieve herself of the burden of pretence. It was becoming more and more difficult to live in the house. She wanted so much to go to Subhash in Mathura, and bury her face in his lap. She imagined Subhash would be a different man away from his mother. No son is quite himself around his mother, she thought. She was convinced that things would improve if only she had her husband to herself without all the meddling from Krishnawanti. But whenever she raised the subject, he deflected her pointed questions.

In despair, Shashi tried to contact her parents but could not talk to them on the telephone. Dejected, she decided to write a letter, which later became an important piece of evidence against Subhash during the trial. It helped establish that he had been harassing and neglecting her even in her pregnant state. In the letter, Shashi pleaded with her mother Satyarani to contact the friend who had helped arrange the marriage. She wanted the woman to mediate and talk to Subhash.

Dear Mother,

I tried to ring you yesterday but could not get through. The bell kept ringing but no one picked up. I thought probably no one is at home. Then I called up Pinka (her brother) *but he also did not call you. So I decided to write a letter.*

Mother do not worry about me so much. Just pray to God and remember him. God Almighty will set everything right. You must have heard from Bombay. How is my brother-in-law? Please let me know.

*Mother, please tell Savitri Bhardwaj (*who had introduced the two families*) to write a letter to Subhash in Mathura. She should ask him what he wants. She should ask him why doesn't he take me to Mathura? What wrong have I done? Whatever he wants to say, he should say to Savitriji. She should tell him that even he has sisters. He should be afraid of God. It is not good to harass anyone so much.*

Yours Shashi

The judge recording the evidence called it the 'most significant letter' because it showed 'how tortured and harassed' Shashi felt while living with her in-laws. The letter was a plaintive cry for help. Shashi wanted to leave her in-laws' house but she could not depend on anyone, not even her husband, for support. He was almost absent from her life. He hardly cared about her or the child she was carrying.

Satyarani was disturbed by the letter and immediately went to Savitri Bhardwaj, to ask her to intervene. She felt there was still time to patch things up and, like Shashi, she felt that moving out of the mother-in-law's house would solve most of the problems. Savitri wrote a letter urging Subhash to take Shashi to Mathura and to be more sensitive to his wife's needs. The exact contents of the letter are unknown because Subhash failed to produce the letter during the trial. While he was diligent about recovering letters written by him to others, especially those he wrote from Mathura to his mother in Delhi and his father in Kanpur, and producing them in court, he conveniently 'lost' many letters that others had written him. Judge R.L. Chugh of the district court, who heard the case and finally sentenced Subhash to seven years' imprisonment, said in his judgment that Subhash was 'very selective' in producing the correspondence between him and others.

'He produced whatever letters should not have been in his possession but in the possession of other family members,' the judge observed. Even though the letter written by Savitri Bhardwaj was unavailable, Subhash's reply to her was found and produced in court by Satyarani. His letter was revealing. He claimed he was passing through great difficulties, which no one seemed to appreciate. His melodramatic language only served to create a cloud of confusion instead of suggesting a way out for Shashi. An excerpt from the letter:

I am feeling ashamed that I am not following your suggestion. But I told you the reason. If a mother won't understand her children's difficulties, who will? I can't tell you what hardships I am going through because you seem to see only others' difficulties, not mine. Shashi is living happily at Gandhi Nagar and I have explained everything to her. But I don't know why everyone wants to mock my helplessness . . . Just wait for sometime and everything will be all right. Have faith in me. I am not a bad person but people have started thinking of me as one.

Subhash's 'difficulties' – real or imagined – seemed to block out Shashi from his mind. Her needs were irrelevant to him because he found a new reason every week for not taking her to Mathura. There is not enough space, he told her. He lived in a single room in a bad area. As if Shashi lived in a palace in Delhi. She was confined to two small rooms with four hostile in-laws and no one to turn to for comfort. Her husband was the only soul she could call her own even though he too harassed her about dowry. But the tragedy – according to the trial judge – was that Subhash simply did not care enough for Shashi to want to rescue her. He did not seem to care where or how she lived. It is clear from the exchange of letters that he often did not know whether Shashi was at his mother's house or her mother's. She felt neglected and abandoned by him, a pattern noted later by the judge in his verdict.

Satyarani was getting increasingly alarmed about her daughter's plight. Shashi was pregnant and she seemed to be suffering from emotional trauma. She was not even eating well. 'They kept her hungry. She did not even get full meals,' Satyarani said. She decided to call Shashi over for a few days, and no sooner had she arrived than the floodgates opened. Shashi told her mother that each day spent at her in-laws seemed as long as a year. It was unbearable.

But there was no talk of a separation or divorce. After a round of mediation, Subhash took Shashi to Mathura around November 1978. During the meetings, he once again raised his demand for a scooter and Satyarani once again expressed her inability to buy one. He ominously reminded Satyarani about it in a letter a month later. '*You should bear in mind whatever I had told you*,' he warned. Now that he was going to be a father he really 'needed' a scooter. He said the birth of his child deserved the gift of a scooter.

Subhash and Shashi barely lived together for two months in Mathura before she was once again brought back to her in-laws' house in Delhi. The new year came but there was no reason for Shashi to celebrate. It was during early 1979 that Subhash and his family closed in on Shashi, as it slowly became clear that she was unable to extract a scooter from her family. The resentment mounted, the daily insults became more vulgar and hurtful and the taunts sharper. Shashi felt helpless but apart from occasionally confiding in her mother, she could do little else. Each day became a mountain she had to climb, each night a short rest and a chance to cry. She felt trapped. She felt she would not survive her ordeal. It was so surreal. She was asked to write letters on blank pieces of paper, saying how everything was going fine and how happy she was. They were addressed to Subhash's grandmother, his mother and his father in three different cities. The in-laws seemed to be preparing for their defence as far back as that. But when the letters were produced in court, the judge dismissed them without much discussion, saying they seemed to have been written under duress.

Something was going on but Shashi didn't know what. Nor did Satyarani read the warning signs closely. Everyone was trying to placate Subhash and his family, hoping that the situation would improve. It was wishful thinking. It was almost March and the festival of Holi was approaching. Winter was fading and there was an air of excitement around the city. Satyarani had invited Subhash and Shashi to her house on Holi for a meal. It would be the last time she would see her daughter alive and the date is etched in her mind. It was 15 March 1979. She welcomed them home but the visit turned sour almost immediately. Shashi took her aside and told her in detail how they were abusing her day and night about the scooter. Satyarani felt helpless and didn't know what to do. As she struggled for an answer, Subhash came into the room and bluntly asked about her promise of a scooter now that Shashi was getting closer to her delivery date.

Faced with a direct question, Satyarani gave a frank answer. 'I can't afford to give you a scooter right now because I have some other things to take care of first. As soon as I have the money, I will buy it for you.'

'You are only trying to avoid the issue. You are not being honest. But let me just say, you may regret it. You may cry for the rest of your life,' he said. Satyarani could hardly believe her ears. She was suddenly jolted into full consciousness. His threat sounded so real. Until then she had thought that she could handle Subhash and his family and still work something out. Compromise seemed possible. But after listening to Subhash that day, she realized that matters had gone beyond control. In her mind the scooter suddenly seemed like a gigantic pincer closing in on Shashi. Satyarani was scared, very scared that day. Sensing real and present danger, she asked Shashi to stay back with her until she could work something out.

Shashi said she would rather go back with Subhash because she had decided to fast for sixteen Mondays in a row and she should do the puja at her husband's house. She wasn't an overly religious woman but perhaps her situation had made her turn to God. Satyarani did not argue with her daughter nor insist upon her staying lest she be accused of 'breaking up' the marriage. She watched her daughter leave with a heavy heart.

Two days later the telephone rang and Satyarani was told that Shashi was dead. It was around 9 p.m. on 17 March 1979. Shashi had died of burns, nearly 90 per cent burns. Satyarani rushed to the house in Gandhi Nagar in a taxi. It was dark and the streetlights were few and far between. A thousand thoughts flooded her mind. Very soon she was blaming herself for it. If only she had insisted that Shashi stay back with her, fasting or no fasting, if only she had acted with more conviction, her daughter would be alive. She knew they had burned her. No one will ever be able to prove that but she knew it deep down in her heart. When the taxi stopped in front of the house, she ran in breathlessly, her dupatta flying in the air. Her hair was all over her face, sticking to her cheeks. She saw her daughter lying in the courtyard tied up in a piece of cloth as if she were a log. She was horrified at the sight. Shashi's body was as black as tar, her face contorted in pain. She looked ugly, not the pretty girl who married Subhash. Satyarani ran from one side to another, from one person to another as if looking for answers. She was crying, screaming, hurling abuses, all at the same time.

There were no police on the scene, only a few neighbours. She yelled out to the neighbours at large: 'You Gandhi Nagar residents, if you have daughters in the house, for God's sake call the police.' Someone did and the police arrived.

After this point, Shashi's story gets sadly entangled in conflicting versions given by Satyarani, the police and Subhash himself. Satyarani said, and continues to say after all these years and after a court judgment, that her daughter was murdered. 'It was not suicide. It wasn't. My daughter would never do that. She wasn't like that and especially because she was pregnant,' she insisted when I met her.

When Satyarani reached the place that night, she found Subhash and his family members but there was not a tinge of remorse on their faces. 'You can carry the garbage away,' said the mother-in-law, according to Satyarani. 'They were not crying. They were not even sad that Shashi had died.' The truth of what happened that night may never be known because there were no eyewitnesses but there is enough circumstantial evidence to point to murder. Satyarani is convinced that Shashi was doused with kerosene and burnt to death in the tiny kitchen of the house by the family. She told the police that Subhash was in Delhi that night and not in Mathura as he claimed. 'I saw them all there. They were all in the house at the time.'

The police recorded her statement at about 11 p.m. in which she accused the family of murdering Shashi but she failed to mention Subhash's presence in her statement. This gave the defence a good escape hatch during the trial. Discrepancies between the first statement and subsequent ones in court are always exploited by the defence even though it is humanly impossible to think of every possible detail at the time of the tragedy. The family members pleaded innocence, saying they had no idea how or why Shashi burnt to death. 'She committed suicide,' they said. They insisted there had been no quarrel in the house and everything seemed normal. Subhash said he was not even in Delhi at the time and had rushed to his mother's house after his brother phoned him with the news. On 18 March 1979, when Shashi's body was sent for an autopsy, the doctors said she had died due to shock resulting from 100 per cent burns.

Shashi's painful death left more questions than answers. The slow and lumbering investigation by the police and a lacklustre prosecution only added to the pain of the unknown. Satyarani alleged that the police had been bribed.

Shashi died in 1979, before 'dowry deaths' had become a national embarrassment, forcing changes in the law and laying down rules for how deaths of women under suspicious circumstances were to be handled. She died in the times when most murders by burning were termed 'kitchen accidents' and dismissed by the police.

The case file reads like a record of an amateur's fumblings. Even the trial judge was forced to point out that the 'case had not been properly investigated right from the beginning'. Judge R.L. Chugh of the sessions court, giving his verdict twenty-two years after the case was first filed, was damning in his indictment of the way investigating agencies treated Shashi's death. He felt the case for murder was weakened because of the way the police handled the initial evidence. 'There were circumstances suggestive of the fact of murder,' he said in his twenty-seven-page ruling but the prosecution failed to build the case. For a judge to record his impression in this manner was significant.

We will never know how that fateful day unfolded for Shashi, because the only version on record is that of her husband's family who were hostile to her. According to a statement made in court by Chanchal, Shashi's sister-in-law, everything in the house carried on the same way as it always did. The milk was delivered in the morning, breakfast was made as usual and there was nothing out of the ordinary in their humdrum life. She herself had visited the tailor's shop in the afternoon and had come back home. After a late lunch, they were all watching TV and chatting. Her mother had bought oranges that day. Shashi asked Krishnawanti if she wanted a cup of tea because she was going to make some. When the mother-in-law said yes, Shashi picked up her clothes and went into the kitchen. She said she was going to change into her nightgown and prepare the tea. 'We again started watching TV,' said Chanchal.

At about 8.30 p.m. they heard their landlady shouting 'Fire, fire' from the floor above. The family thought the landlady's gas cylinder had burst and caught fire. 'My sister and I ran outside and woke up our brother who was taking a nap. My mother did not go out with us.' The sisters then ran to an aunt's place nearby and when they came back with her, they saw a small mob of people outside their house. 'We came to know that the fire was in our house. My sister-in-law's body was covered with cloth and then I came to know that she was burnt,' Chanchal said in her statement.

If her statement sounds incredible, the failure of the prosecution to ask her questions is astonishing. In a small house of two rooms and a kitchen, how could its residents fail to notice that the fire was in *their* house, not somewhere else? Also, why would the two sisters flee leaving their mother inside when there was a fire in the vicinity? Couldn't it spread to their house given that the two-room tenements are stacked like sardines in Gandhi Nagar? It strains credibility to think that someone would leave a mother and a sister-in-law inside and rush to an aunt's place before ensuring the safety of all members of the household.

According to the police, Raj Kumar, a tenant who sublet a room in the same house, discovered Shashi's body that night. Raj Kumar heard his landlady shouting 'Fire, fire' and ran in her direction. The landlady said that Subhash's kitchen was on fire. The doors were closed and Raj Kumar kicked them open. He immediately rushed to get a taxi to take Shashi to the hospital. But someone called a doctor home and he declared her dead. It was the landlady who noticed the fire, it was a neighbour who kicked the kitchen door open and who rushed to call a taxi and it was Satyarani who asked for the police. No one in Subhash's family seemed to care or took any action. There was an able-bodied young brother at home, two sisters who were old and competent enough to take charge of the situation but who say they ran out. No one in his family wondered 'Where is Shashi?' when the first cries of 'Fire, fire' were heard. No family member ran to look for her. No family member tried to ensure her safety.

Satyarani remembers with bitterness that no one from Subhash's family came for Shashi's funeral. 'They always wanted her dead. They couldn't be bothered.' The police did not arrest anyone until 1 May 1979, more than forty days after Shashi's death. Only after the women's organizations had rallied behind Satyarani and decried their inaction did the police arrest Subhash, his mother and his sister. But on 8 May they were granted bail by the Delhi High Court on grounds that there was no clear evidence of murder. Section 304 (B) defining a 'dowry death' was yet to be added to the Indian Penal Code. Satyarani immediately filed an application in the Supreme Court of India for cancellation of bail and she even made an application to the highest civil authorities of Delhi. But the matter was referred back to the lower court.

The police finally registered a case of murder under section 302 but dismissed it after a preliminary investigation for lack of evidence and eyewitnesses. Satyarani says the police never tried hard enough to recover evidence from the scene of crime. No formal charges were filed as a result. A civil case under the Dowry Prohibition Act 1961 – before the law was amended in 1986 – was also registered against Subhash but it didn't go far. The 1961 law, inadequate and full of loopholes, said only valuables given in 'consideration' of marriage were considered dowry. Gifts, cash, ornaments and other articles that were given voluntarily were not 'dowry'. The 1961 law made it difficult to distinguish between voluntary gift-giving and extortion since it was impossible to prove what was extorted and what wasn't. Predictably, in *State vs. Subhash* the magistrate ruled that the demand for a scooter before marriage and repeated days before Shashi's death could not be seen as the same demand. Besides, the demand made before her death was to celebrate the upcoming birth of her child. It did not amount to a demand in 'consideration' of marriage and therefore the provisions of the Dowry Prohibition Act did not apply. The letter of the law was followed, not its spirit. Satyarani appealed to the Supreme Court but the order of the magistrate was upheld. It was not a 'dowry case', the highest court in the land told her.

Her Kafkaesque journey had begun.

She wrote letters to Members of Parliament, she visited senior officials in the home ministry and she ran around to various police stations. Because of her persistence and the pressure from various women's organizations, the police transferred the case to the Crime Branch. But even the Crime Branch investigation concluded that it was not murder mainly because the special branch sleuths did not cover new ground but rehashed the old files. Satyarani was not satisfied. When she raised doubts, the investigation report was sent for 'scrutiny' to the Criminal Bureau of Investigation (CBI). The CBI affirmed the initial results. Satyarani felt depressed at the bureaucracy's time-tested tactics – no agency would go against the other or take a different stand. They clamped shut like a huge oyster and repeated each other's findings. They took refuge in the various court judgments – after all the Supreme Court had said a dowry case could not be made. There was little reason to stick their necks out for a desperate mother. She had raised an alarm by writing letters but there was no political heat on them, just polite inquiries.

Satyarani had seen her daughter suffer and she knew it was not a simple case of suicide. She fired off another set of letters, this time to the speaker of the Lok Sabha, Balram Jakhar. She thought a senior politician's intervention would get results. She had tried dealing with the system in a straight manner but the system was unmoved, indeed immovable. She needed someone with 'influence' to nudge the bureaucracy.

Jakhar wrote a letter in August 1980 to the home ministry, asking about the progress in Satyarani's case and four other cases of dowry deaths. A senior bureaucrat replied – as only a bureaucrat can – 'Shashi Bala's case was scrutinized by the CBI who found it to be a clear case of suicide.' The able bureaucracy had delivered its judgment, the oyster was shut again. No doubts, no ambivalence, only a crisp reply.

Jakhar had inquired about five cases, presumably because other distraught parents like Satyarani had besieged him with petitions about police inaction and apathy. But the home ministry bureaucrat had no trouble deciding their fate and shooting off a letter. Of the five suspected cases of dowry deaths that the speaker demanded a status report for, four were deemed suicide and one an accident. The home ministry reply was a fair indication of how the police handled suspicious deaths and how easily they were dismissed as suicides. The reply was dutifully mailed to Satyarani. A copy found its way to the defence lawyer, making Subhash's case stronger. The police, crime branch and the CBI had all said Shashi committed suicide. Even prominent politicians and all the media attention could not force a fresh investigation or a real re-examination of evidence. In the end, the police only filed a case under the

Dowry Prohibition Act which did not stand the test of trial because of the inadequacy of existing laws.

The act defined dowry as any property or gift given by one party to another 'at or before or after the marriage as consideration for the marriage'. It had to be proved that a particular gift was 'in consideration for marriage' to be considered dowry and for the act to apply. A good defence lawyer could easily prove that a demand for a scooter was not 'in consideration' for marriage since the man had already married the girl. Therefore, it was not technically a 'dowry' demand, only a demand. Satyarani alleged that Subhash's family had paid off the local police – a common complaint by dowry victims even today. A few hundred rupees could do the job which any family can muster in times of crisis, she alleged. Today, the bribe amounts are in thousands.

Satyarani began doing the rounds of police stations but met with a wall of resistance. It was a lonely trek. Her ailing husband and two sons felt she was wasting her time running around. Nothing would come of it really, they told her every time she returned home from an exhausting day. But she wanted justice and nothing was going to stop her, not even her own family. She had heard about 'bride burning' and dowry deaths. She had been reading the Hindi newspapers after all where reports of young women dying 'accidental deaths' in kitchen fires were all too common.

She then heard about a huge street demonstration by women's groups in Model Town in north Delhi, which was to become seminal in the anti-dowry movement. Hundreds of ordinary people joined women's groups to express anger at the peculiarly horrific crime of bride burning. They were brought together by an appalling tale of police complicity and apathy. A young Sikh bride, Tarvinder Kaur, had been burned alive in Model Town for failing to bring enough cash in her dowry. The police called it suicide even though in her

'dying declaration', she clearly said that her m
and sister-in-law had set her afire. Outrage and anger
streets rose as the news spread, resulting in one of the largest anti-dowry demonstrations in India. Satyarani found out about it two days after it was over but she still went to Model Town looking for women leaders to help her.

The year was 1979 and the month was June. Hot and unforgiving. The wound of Shashi's death raw in her heart, Satyarani asked people for names and addresses of the organizers. No one seemed to know where they came from but a helpful soul did produce a leaflet the protesters had distributed during the march. There was an address for Karmika, one of the first groups to launch an anti-dowry agitation. It was in Jangpura, the same area where Satyarani would later open her own office for dowry victims. She took a bus and finally tracked down Subhadhra Butalia, one of the leading figures of the anti-dowry movement. She related her story and the two women started a long association and friendship. Several women's organizations came forward to help and added their voice. If it weren't for them, Satyarani's case would have got lost. They helped her organize her thoughts and devise a strategy for the long road ahead.

Frustrated and angry at the casual attitude of the police and the dismissal of the dowry case by the magistrate, the women's organizations advised Satyarani to file a private complaint, which anyone can in a magistrate's office in case the police fail to act. Based on the merits of the complaint, the court can then direct the police to investigate. On 4 October 1980, she lodged a complaint under section 302, accusing Subhash, his mother, his brother and two sisters of murder. When she started making the rounds of courts, she didn't know it would go on for the next twenty-two years. Her complaint had to be examined by a magistrate who would decide whether the case was worth sending back for trial. There was one adjournment after another for some reason or the other. Satyarani would go trudging up to the court on the appointed day for a hearing only to be told of some lawyerly trick pulled by the defence causing a delay. On other days, the magistrate was indisposed. It took the magistrate years to summon the accused. He chose to examine several other witnesses first and in the end he summoned only Subhash and his mother. He was merely recording evidence, not allowing arguments to start.

All the while, Satyarani was represented by public prosecutors whose interest in her case waxed and waned almost with seasonal regularity. Her activist lawyer friends were in an 'advisory' role and couldn't appear in court on her behalf. Satyarani couldn't understand why it was taking so long. Her friends – by now she was a part of the women's movement and often out on the streets for protest marches – advised her to keep at it. She was encouraged by their voluble support, especially on days when she despaired and wanted to forget it all. Her family had lost patience with her. She was frequently gone from the house when her husband needed attention. He was often ill and doctors had to be called. But Satyarani felt she must stick to her resolve – their suffering was nothing compared to Shashi's who had died a violent death. She couldn't forget Shashi's charred body. The image always made her restless and angry. Something should be done, something must happen, she thought and carried on. She kept her faith in the process – she had no choice.

Women's organizations filed a special petition on Satyarani's behalf in the Supreme Court against the manner in which the magistrate was proceeding on her complaint, hoping to send a few tremors through the system. The petition also pointed out that the magistrate adjourned the matter for long periods at a time, causing undue delays and hardship for Satyarani. The women's groups were trying to exert pressure on the lower courts any which way they could to get them activated. The Supreme Court must intervene, the leaders thought, or the defence would keep playing the magistrate for time. Subhash was represented by D.C. Mathur, a criminal lawyer who went on to become one of the topmost in New Delhi. Mathur stayed on with Subhash over the years because the case became high profile and attracted media attention.

The Supreme Court did issue a notice to the State to expedite the case. By the time the notice came, the magistrate had begun hearing the case. Witnesses came and went and Satyarani grew older as she waited. Waiting had become an integral part of life by then – waiting for court dates, waiting for legal advice, waiting for police to produce reports and waiting for justice. After five years of waiting, the magistrate gave his order. On 10 January 1985, Metropolitan Magistrate R.S. Arya announced that there was no case against the sisters-in-law. He sent the case back to the sessions court after deciding that Subhash and his mother Krishnawanti should be tried for abetment to suicide under section 306 of the penal code, not murder. It was a shock for Satyarani who had hoped for a favourable verdict but what she got was another go at the system. She would have to begin again at the lowest level, start the slow climb and relive the agony.

The session's court finally began hearing the case five years after the crime – a real travesty. The police officer who had investigated the initial complaint in 1979 was long gone from the thana, his memory dimmed and burdened by a hundred other cases that came after Shashi's. The records were difficult to obtain despite the media attention and continuous pressure from women's organizations. There were delays, adjournments, court holidays and other unfortunate interventions. Satyarani felt like giving up – her husband's health was failing and her sons had begun questioning her wisdom. Who goes to jail for dowry death, they would ask her. 'No one,' they answered before she could say anything. She was also tired but since the women's groups were actively pursuing the case, she felt emboldened and encouraged to carry on.

Rani Jethmalani, one of the leading women lawyers in the country at the time, was helping her. Rani came from a family of distinguished lawyers. Her father Ram Jethmalani was prominent on the national scene not just for his legal acumen but also for his political affiliation with the Bharatiya Janata Party (BJP). Despite all the help, the case moved at a snail's pace. But that it moved at all was thanks largely to the efforts of the activists and their legal networking in the city. They kept the hot light of attention on Shashi's tragic death, making the case a cause célèbre in the larger struggle against dowry deaths and harassment.

Once Satyarani's case was sent to the sessions court in 1985, it took another six years for charges to be framed under section 306 (abetment of suicide) and a public prosecutor to be assigned. The exact date is imprinted in her memory – 8 January 1991. More than a decade had passed but she was no closer to getting Subhash behind bars now than when she first started. While she was traversing the web of the legal system, arguments on amending the old dowry law were raging in the Parliament, which had little choice but to listen. After lengthy debates, some key amendments were adopted in 1983 and 1986, and Satyarani's case had gone on long enough for her to benefit from the changes. In fact, according to Rani Jethmalani, her case contributed to the amendments and sharpened the debate in Parliament. The new law expanded the definition of dowry, put the onus of proof on the husband if his wife died an unnatural death within seven years of marriage and tightened the Evidence Act to help the prosecution.

While there was cause for optimism for Satyarani and the prosecution, the defence had not been idle. Subhash's lawyer filed a 'revision' petition in the Delhi High Court against framing of the charges, causing further delays. The high court put a stay order against the proceedings pending in the trial court. Several months passed and Satyarani did not have a clear memory of exactly how long each delay was. Even the many lawyers who helped Satyarani did not remember the various legal entanglements the case went through since there were so many at every stage. The case file kept growing thicker by the year, fraying at the edges. When I looked at the files, it was difficult to decipher some of the old court orders and statements because the photocopies had faded with age. It was the same story on Subhash's side. His lawyer occupied a plush office in a prestigious southern suburb of the city but even his records on the case were less than organized. Many papers were torn or illegible and there were many missing sections.

The trial court began examining witnesses in the mid-nineties – more than fifteen years after Shashi's death. The prosecution called five witnesses –Satyarani; Dr L.T. Ramani, who conducted the autopsy; Ramesh Lal, who said he was in the vicinity at the time Shashi died; Jiwan Kumar, who also happened to be passing by the scene of the crime; and Sub-inspector Bachan Singh who investigated the case for the first two months before handing it over to the next sub-inspector. Ramesh Lal and Jiwan Kumar were both dismissed by the judge as unbelievable witnesses. Lal, a vendor of animal feed, deposed in court that he was passing by Subhash's house around 8.15 p.m. on the night of Shashi's death when he heard noises about a woman being burnt. 'I was going to my customers near there. When I heard that a woman had been burnt, I went to see. I saw the body lying in the courtyard of a house and the relatives were standing. They were saying, "It's good that the cause of our daily problems is over." ' He also testified that he saw Subhash there.

The prosecution made an error by producing Lal because his testimony was full of holes – each exploited gainfully by the defence. The State counsel had been lackadaisical about crosschecking Lal's claims before producing him in court. Some may call it negligence. The judge found Ramesh Lal 'wholly doubtful' and threw his testimony to the side. 'He did not produce any record that any amount was due from any of his customers residing nearby the place of occurrence. He did not even name the customer from whom he was going to collect the dues. His statement is so unbelievable that further comment is withheld,' wrote Judge R.L. Chugh, who concluded the case and sentenced Subhash to seven years in May 2000. He found Lal's statement about Subhash's presence at the house 'irrelevant' since he was being tried for 'abetment to suicide' not for murder as originally demanded by Satyarani.

Similarly Jiwan Kumar, another prosecution witness, was dismissed by Judge Chugh as unreliable. He was produced to establish that Subhash's family might have killed Shashi because they showed no remorse. Kumar, a passerby who was going to meet a municipal corporation councillor, heard commotion on the street about someone dying of burns.

Since Delhi was full of talk of dowry deaths, his curiosity was aroused. He went in the direction of the house and heard an old woman saying, 'Now her family will know what it means to break promises' – a reference apparently to the demand for the scooter for Subhash, which remained unfulfilled. Kumar testified that he stayed there for fifteen-twenty minutes and moved on. The police did not arrive in his presence. He also testified that he had no discussion with Satyarani. But Judge Chugh found Kumar's testimony unconvincing and set it aside.

As another year passed, Satyarani began to feel despondent about the fast-crumbling case mounted by the constantly changing cast of characters. In desperation, she contacted Lawyers' Collective, an organization of eminent lawyers who provide *pro bono* services to deserving candidates. She wrote a letter to Indira Jaising, the director, asking for help. The group immediately responded, assigning V.K. Ohri, a young energetic lawyer, to the case. He helped to link the harassment with the suicide, thereby tightening the noose around Subhash's neck.

The primary investigating officer Sub-inspector Bachan Singh testified that on the night of 17 March 1979, he had gone to the residence of Subhash and registered a formal report. He seized several articles from the house and got the police photographer to take photographs. But the photographs were inadmissible because the police failed to produce the negatives in court. There was no explanation in the court documents as to why such a lapse occurred but lawyers who helped Satyarani over the years felt the State-appointed prosecutor and the police simply did not take the case seriously. Reading the judgment by Judge Chugh, one gets the feeling that it was the judge who put two and two together for the prosecution. He found a pattern of cruelty in Subhash's behaviour towards his young wife – a crucial factor that proved the charge of abetment to suicide. The judge noted with alarm the fact that even four months after marriage Shashi was living away from her husband.

'It is indeed torture of the severest order that a newly-wed should not get the physical, social, psychological and sexual support from her husband in the first few months of her marriage, more so, when she is carrying a child,' wrote Judge Chugh. He zeroed in on Shashi's torment; how for her each day was a burden and how her husband seemed oblivious of her agonized state of mind. He concluded that Subhash just did not care for Shashi or her company and that is why he left her in Delhi. He found that the requirements of section 498 (A) of the amended Dowry Prohibition Act which defines cruelty had been met.

The act defines cruelty as:

(a) any wilful conduct which is of such a nature as is likely to drive the woman to commit suicide or cause grave injury or danger to life, limb or health (whether mental or physical) of the woman or
(b) harassment of the woman where such harassment is with a view to coercing her or any person related to her to meet any unlawful demand for any property or valuable security or is on account of failure by her on any person related to her to meet such demand.

The judge then went on to carefully examine the evidence to see whether requirements of clause (b) had been met. He noted that Satyarani right from the beginning had claimed that Subhash had demanded a refrigerator, a television and a scooter. She gave the refrigerator and a few instalments for the television but could not give a scooter because of financial constraints. He noted that letters exchanged between the two sides in 1978–79 showed that Satyarani's family had only one earning member – her husband. Her son was unemployed. She had mentioned the demand for a scooter in the first report she registered with the police after Shashi's death. During the trial Subhash denied making any such demand, especially two days before Shashi's death, when he visited her. But the judge said that Satyarani's statement 'in this regard has a ring of truth and was not an afterthought'. That there was harassment was also apparent from her conduct when she reached Subhash's house after getting the news. She created a scene because she had anticipated something might happen.

The most important element in the judgment was the linking of Shashi's suicide with Subhash's indifference. Judge Chugh found it curious that Subhash had no explanation as to why Shashi committed suicide but noted that he was not obliged to under the law. 'She was in the prime of her health. She was quite beautiful if one looks at her photo. She was able to conceive within three or four months of marriage. Subhash would have us believe that everything was normal and she was happy.' By implication, Shashi had no apparent reason to commit suicide. There was no hint, even a frivolous one, that she was depressed or was chronically or terminally ill or had other reasons unconnected with her husband to commit suicide. 'Healthy brides do not commit suicide for nothing or for the fun of it, particularly when they are likely to bear a child within a couple of months,' he wrote. Therefore, the evidence of mental torture and her letters to her mother become important. They showed she wasn't happy and was constantly harassed for the scooter. This agony led her to commit suicide and in that her husband was complicit.

Judge Chugh convicted Subhash for a seven-year term for abetment to suicide under section 306 but acquitted his mother Krishnawanti because the prosecution was unable to link her with the demand of the scooter either through oral or documentary evidence.

Judge Chugh delivered his judgment on 11 May 2000 – a full twenty-two years, two months and four days after Shashi's death. Satyarani had tears in her eyes as she heard the sentence. She had finally been proven right, albeit partially – the police, the various investigators, the many lawyers, the endless courtroom debates and the many judges decided it was not murder but suicide. For her it was a victory but not worth celebrating. It seemed like a vindication of her stand but only partially. To her, the law had seemed too literal, the interpretation too narrow and the punishment lenient. She had seen many more like Shashi die in the meantime. Before she had a chance to think about the judgment and savour her victory, Subhash's lawyers filed a petition in the Delhi High Court asking that Judge Chugh's verdict be set aside and the sentence be suspended because it was 'erroneous both on law and facts'. They requested and got Subhash out on bail after he had served just two months of his seven-year jail sentence. They argued that he had gone through a 'trial by media' and that Satyarani was unnecessarily harassing Subhash by entangling him in multiple lawsuits.

It was the harshest slap on Satyarani's face. She could not fathom the workings of the system – not even after her long struggle. She told me she wasn't sure whether to go back to court and file an appeal against Subhash's bail and start the fight again.

Wasn't one lifetime in courtrooms enough?

Trapped in Hell

Jyoti's Story

The room was closing in on Jyoti. It was so small she could stretch and touch the walls. But she was afraid to kick the water pitcher, the only other object in the room and her sole companion. The sound of water sliding inside the earthenware pot and hitting the contours sent her into a fantasy world. She imagined herself running fast in the bright red sunshine. Bright enough to burn the skin. Or walking along the dusty roads of Delhi, gazing at movie hoardings. Just simple things, nothing complicated. Straightforward dreams are better, more peaceful, she thought. For Jyoti, dreaming was a full-time occupation, not a mere escape or an occasional detour. She dutifully did so from morning to evening, cataloguing her dreams with clinical precision. Every morning she decided which dream she wanted and then divided it into segments to fit her long day. Today it was the turn of the 'sunshine dream'. She had just felt like it.

She suddenly heard a familiar sound, the sound of a key turning inside the lock. She wanted to crawl to the other side but there wasn't much distance to travel – only about six feet – before she met the wall again. The other side of the room smelled a bit more.

The door opened and she got a glimpse of the fading sun. She tried to store its brightness inside, to fill herself with ten seconds worth of sunlight so she could slowly let it out of her later, particle by particle. She could make sunlight last, she had to. It could be three days or four or maybe even five before Vinay would remember to come and feed her. And throw some stale chapatis at her after a drunken orgy of beating and kicking. He would lock her up again and go back to his mother. There was a small window in the room, which opened on to the narrow, crowded lane below but she couldn't look out. Vinay had boarded it up and locked the stairs to the terrace. Right below her second-floor prison room was the hustle and bustle of life – street vendors, small shops, children running around and the general confusion of any narrow lane in a poor colony. But she was cut off, sealed inside the hole of a room with mosquitoes buzzing in the summer and dankness in the winter.

Jyoti tried to swallow a portion of the dry chapatis, kept some for the next day and tried to sleep. She slept a lot. A lot. Sleep was her entertainment. It did not come easy on the cold, damp floor, and on a growling stomach. But when it came, it soothed her body a bit. Today had been a particularly difficult day – even by her own grim standards. Vinay had come in very drunk. He blabbered on about how she had ruined his life and brought him bad luck. He began kicking her and abusing her in gutterspeak. He threatened once again to 'fix' her brothers if they tried to go to the police again. 'Who do they think they are? They had better not mess with me. They will pay a price they will never forget,' he yelled, spitting out each word.

The threat was unmistakable. He was capable of anything. Last year he had put her on the streets – literally – to beg to feed herself. She remembered how for three long months she sat outside a temple in Raghuvir Nagar in northwest Delhi like any of the hundreds of beggars who converge around holy places for alms. They gaped at her in disbelief when she told them that her husband was a cable operator and owned two small houses in Delhi. Why was she on the streets then? They thought she had lost her mind.

He kicked Jyoti again. Her spine jangled as if a thousand bricks had hit her. Her back felt like jelly, it had been assaulted so often. She tried to crawl out of his range but those damn walls – they always came in the way. In her dreams she imagined a network of tunnels and secret passages from the room crisscrossing their way across Delhi to her mother's house in Kashmiri Gate. That was her action dream with lots of drama.

When I met Jyoti for the first time, she was twenty years old. It was late 2000. She seemed to exude a certain calmness even though her life had been anything but calm. She talked in soft tones, always looking down at her toes. It was as if she was more embarrassed than angry at what had happened. She would sit on the bed, pull her legs in and hug them tightly with her arms. I felt she was trying to shrink because she still imagined herself in that tiny hole being beaten. She remembered everything vividly . . . in fact, in excruciating detail. She grew more vocal and open with each meeting. Every time she recalled a particularly appalling example of her husband's brutality, I was left wondering if he needed institutional help more than a jail sentence. He would hurt Jyoti by flaunting his extramarital affair. 'He would constantly talk about marrying her and keeping me too. He even showed me that girl,' she recalled. It seems he was coerced into getting married to Jyoti by his mother. 'He would take out his frustration on me.' Jyoti prayed a lot, reciting whatever holy scriptures she could remember from her memory. Every time she heard a noise on the stairs outside, she worried if someone was hiding there.

'You bitch, you are going to die. I will see to it. You think you can run away from me. You think your brothers can rescue you?' Vinay had bellowed that day. Another kick, another and then another landed on her knees. 'Why did your family go to the police? Why, why? They think they can help you. Never. You will rot here until I divorce you. Then I will throw you out.'

Jyoti was stunned. He would divorce her and simply get a new wife, a new dowry, another colour TV, another washing machine. His plans had changed recently after the police had appeared on the scene. The local Station House Officer had been calling and insisting that Vinay produce Jyoti in the police station for her to meet her family. Jyoti's mother Devi Bai told the police that she feared for her daughter's life. She knew something was very wrong. Jyoti had not been back to see her mother very often even though they lived in the same city. Since Jyoti got married in December 1995, she had seen her mother barely six or seven times and only when the police arranged the meeting.

Until the police entered the picture, Vinay had planned to simply starve Jyoti to death in that little hovel. He would simply say she was weak and infirm and it was a matter of time before God beckoned her. No one would be suspicious since Jyoti herself had never complained about him to anyone. He had made sure of that. And there would be no 'kitchen fire' or kerosene. No smell. Not a shred of incriminating evidence. Anyway, who cares these days, neighbours wouldn't say anything. He never encouraged any interaction with the neighbours even when Jyoti was staying at his family house. And they never bothered either. Besides, they wouldn't want to mess with him.

Her family was a different story though. Her mother had been more persistent than he had anticipated. She had filed complaints demanding to see Jyoti. Now the police were involved and he couldn't just get rid of her. Therefore, the divorce plan. He would get Jyoti to sign papers for a 'mutual consent' divorce and send her back to her parents' home and that would be that. He barked a few more obscenities at Jyoti before locking her up again and walking off.

The door shut, the key turned and Vinay's heavy steps moved down the dark, mosquito-infested staircase and off. Jyoti was alone once again with her matka, her water pitcher, her lifeline. She clutched it with all her might, and cried some more. She could hear the traffic buzzing by. Marutis, Ambassadors, three-wheeler scooters, buses. She could not believe that Vinay would divorce her after all that she had suffered at his hands. Wasn't that part of the bargain – that if she kept quiet, did as she was told, took the beatings without a word, then she would get to stay at his house? That she would continue to be his wife in the eyes of the community and not become a burden for her mother once again?

She didn't want to add to Devi Bai's already swollen bag of woes. The small two-room place she had called home was overflowing with lives unhinged by circumstance. Her mother struggled with her Rs 3,000-a-month salary from the post office with seven mouths to feed. There was food on the table but just about. Her two brothers, although grown and married, were unemployed. Sanjay bhaiya's wife was mute and incapable of doing much in the house. Even their son had severe speech problems. They all lived in her mother's small house. Devi Bai made ends meet with the help of relatives and her fellow workers at the post office. They had been kind to her after her husband's death in 1984 and had arranged for her to get his job. Their kindness had sustained Devi Bai through her ordeal. She was the glue of the family, taking care of the six children, getting them married one by one and fulfilling her responsibility. She kept at it, day and night. How could Jyoti go back and force a redivision of the pie once again? No, that wouldn't be right.

A vegetable hawker called outside with his wares: 'Tamatar, bhindi, pyaaz, aaloo le lo.' She slid down and lay flat. Her back was hurting too much. It was a shooting pain, going up from the last vertebra to the middle of her spine. Like a raging bullet. She wanted her mother. She wanted to tell her the truth. Finally. All these years she had been pretending that all was well with Vinay and her. Even when her mother could see through her lies. Otherwise, why would Devi Bai run to the police and beg them to intervene? Each time the police asked Vinay to allow Jyoti to meet her mother, he would unlock her and throw some clean clothes at her. His sister Chanda would dress Jyoti up, dab some rouge on her cheeks, put a bindi on her forehead and bring her to the police station. They couldn't hide the bruises but they didn't care. If anyone asked, Vinay just said: 'She fell down.' He had so many ready lies. The charade carried on in the police station. Jyoti would stay mum even as her mother tried hard to talk to her, pleading with her to tell the truth. But instead of the truth, Jyoti told lies – lies that were forced upon her by her husband. She told the police that Devi Bai was interfering in her marriage and that she was 'happy' with her husband. He had blackmailed her into silence. Very effectively. The police, distracted by thousands of other cases that were less ambiguous, didn't look deeper.

Devi Bai could see Jyoti's diminishing shape, her emaciated body, the bruises on her arms and she didn't need her daughter to tell her what was happening. But try as she might, Jyoti wouldn't talk. It was December 1998 when Devi Bai went to the special Crime Against Women cell in Delhi's Nanakpura police station. She pleaded with the officers but they expressed their inability to get Jyoti out since the victim herself claimed all was well. They said their hands were tied.

Jyoti had already spent nearly a year in solitary confinement. She was rapidly losing weight and the use of her legs because of the constant beatings. Crawling came easier than walking around the small room. She hardly believed what was happening to her. She always dreamed that Vinay would one day turn from a monster into a human being. That was her fairy-tale dream. He had seemed like a decent person and his mother had seemed so keen to have Jyoti as her daughter-in-law. There were no demands for dowry when the two families began discussing the plans.

Devi Bai recounted the exact sequence of events to me several times during our meetings in her small, overcrowded two-room home near the Red Fort. She always sat on the floor, giving me the pride of place on the bed, which filled up the tiny room. She would touch my arm and hold my hand to emphasize her points. Everything was fresh in her mind, fresh enough to bring tears to her eyes as she remembered and talked.

Jyoti was only fifteen years old when Vinay's mother, Darshana, spotted the pretty girl during a chance encounter. Devi Bai and Jyoti had gone to meet an aunt in Raghubir Nagar, a lower-middle-class Punjabi neighbourhood in west Delhi. Little did Jyoti know that those tiny, cheek-by-jowl houses would soon become familiar. Just as they were having tea, a woman came to deliver milk to the house. It was Darshana who owned a small milk delivery business in the area, providing door-to-door service. She noticed Jyoti at once. She could not take her eyes off the young girl. Jyoti was indeed pretty, fair and sharp-featured – all valuable assets in the marriage market.

'Who is this girl?' she asked the aunt. Darshana had seemed so inquisitive, so much in a hurry even then. She stayed to have tea with them, all the while dropping details of her family business to impress Devi Bai. She was laying the ground for a possible future alliance. Two weeks later, Darshana had appeared at Devi Bai's doorstep. The family was surprised at the visit but did not object.

'Arre behn ji, I just thought I would come and say hello,' she said cheerily, standing at the door. Devi Bai welcomed her in and offered her a cup of tea. Without further ado, Darshana said she had come to ask for Jyoti's hand in marriage for her son Vinay. 'I have only two sons and a daughter. We are a small family and by God's grace we have plenty,' she said. 'My older son Ram Prakash is already married. Vinay is my younger son and he has a small business. My daughter Chanda will soon be married and believe me Jyoti will be the queen of the house.' Devi Bai had protested at this verbal onslaught. She was taken aback at the speed at which Darshana was moving.

'I really can't agree to the marriage yet. My older daughter has just got engaged and we have planned the wedding for the winter. I really can't afford two weddings right now.' That was that. As it is she would have to take loans, depend on neighbours, relatives and office colleagues to meet the expenses of one wedding and she certainly didn't want to double them. But Darshana was unfazed. She was so slick with her tongue.

'Don't worry. You just come and see my boy and meet our family. I really like Jyoti. Please promise her hand for my son. We don't want anything. We will take her as she is – in the clothes that she is wearing. You don't have to worry about all the give and take.' She was saying she didn't want any dowry – no lena dena, no give and take. Jyoti remembers the words clearly – 'We don't want anything. Only the girl.' Devi Bai sighed and said she would think about it and let her know. But Darshana wouldn't leave without a promise or a hint that she was in the fray. She wanted to register her interest in Jyoti with a small ceremony and give her 101 rupees as a token. Devi Bai balked at the tactic and motioned to Jyoti not to accept. 'There is no need for all this just yet,' she said firmly. But the seed had been planted.

That evening Devi Bai told her son Sanjay about Darshana's visit. The family decided to call the eldest son Vijay from Rajasthan for consultations. Vijay came with his wife and everyone decided to go and at least meet Darshana's family and see the prospective groom. There was no harm in meeting the family. Who knows it may be for the better? Jyoti must be lucky that the boy's family was pursuing her instead of the other way around, they thought. Their keenness was certainly a plus point.

A meeting was set for 25 June 1995 for the two families to assess each other. Darshana invited them to come to her house but Devi Bai, trying to retain her independence in the negotiations, declined and suggested a neutral place. She said they could all meet at the Raghuvir Nagar gurdwara – since it was a house of worship, the gods would hopefully watch over them. Marriage negotiations can be a tricky business: you need everyone's blessings. On the appointed day, Devi Bai escorted her clan to the gurdwara as Darshana did hers. The families met and Vinay and Jyoti saw each other for the first time. Everything seemed fine – Darshana's family was financially stable and Vinay had a good business as a cable operator. He was a good-looking young man, fair and light eyed. The elders on both sides decided that an auspicious date should be set for the engagement after consulting the pundit. But the marriage would take place only after two years once Devi Bai had recovered from the expenses of her older daughter's wedding. She was firm about that. A long engagement was necessary not only for practical reasons but also for Jyoti's sake. Jyoti needed time before being sent off into the adult world of responsibility. Darshana did not object, nor did Vinay.

Jyoti and Vinay were engaged on 12 July the same year, less than a month after they had set eyes on each other. The evening of the engagement, they talked to each other for the first time. Things had gone off fairly well. Gifts were exchanged, some money was given but no dowry demands of any kind were made. Jyoti was happy that she would be going to her 'own' house. Like most women she felt her real place was next to her husband, rather at his feet and in his service. Her parents' home was but a temporary stop on the way. The excitement of getting new clothes and jewellery was beginning to tickle her fancy. This was the one time she felt she could rightfully ask for things and not be snubbed.

Two months later, the date for Jyoti's elder sister's marriage was set for November and Devi Bai was frantic with worry about the wedding arrangements. She began informing her relatives about the wedding and also called Darshana to invite her. A few days later, Darshana visited them again and this time with another request. She said that even Jyoti and Vinay should get married soon.

'What are you saying, behn ji?' Devi Bai asked, her face white with shock. She tried to fathom the full implication of the demand but couldn't. It seemed beyond her imagination – just the expense of the wedding. Forget everything else. She simply couldn't and she had been very clear about it. So what was this all about? 'I told you before that we had to wait two years after the engagement,' she said, summoning the courage to speak up. She was the girl's mother and the 'seeker' not the 'giver'. Her position would always be lower in the scheme of things.

'I know, I know. But Vinay is after me for an early marriage and even our relatives think that it would be a good idea. You know how it is. People might start talking,' Darshana said. The veiled threat was too obvious to miss. Either do as we say or we might have to break the engagement. All the ignominy of a broken engagement would obviously fall on Jyoti. It is the girl who carries the burden. Always. Jyoti would get branded and her chances of finding a groom in the community would diminish. It would be a blow to Devi Bai's standing in the samaj, a real blot on her prestige. Her world started to rattle around her. She simply could not afford two weddings on her meagre savings. Two weddings, two dowries, two dinners, two sets of expenses.

'No, no. Jyoti is too young,' Devi Bai insisted feebly. 'I simply can't manage two weddings in one year. I don't have the means and you know it.'

'Did I ask for anything from you except for Jyoti's hand? We don't want any dowry,' Darshana insisted. Those words are so clear in Jyoti's mind, even today after four years and the endless beatings.

Devi Bai kept quiet and somehow sent Darshana home that evening. She was confused and distraught at all this hurry, the insistence. She asked her sons their advice and everyone said the family should wait. Of course, Jyoti was never asked, consulted or otherwise included in any significant way in the discussions about her marriage. That is how things were. She didn't expect to either. She was brought up to think that a girl's duty is to bear in silence what fate and family had to offer. She never thought of complaining or participating, she said later. Her only aim was to make things easier for her mother who had so many burdens to bear.

Jyoti could see that her family was stretched emotionally and she didn't want to add to the tension. She was a girl and one of six children in the family. She always thought that girls were meant to be married off. Isn't that how life was supposed to be? She had studied only until fifth standard because her family couldn't afford it after that. Her sources of inspiration were Hindi movies and television soap operas – all reinforcing the suffering of women. She knew her world would be designed and determined by her family and her future husband. All girls must marry. Otherwise where will they go? Her mother, bless her heart, was a kind woman and only doing the best she could under the circumstances. Struggling, always struggling to make ends meet.

A week later Darshana came again to Jyoti's house, this time with a new twist in the tale. Devi Bai had begun to look at her frequent visits with dread and didn't know how to evade her fast-expanding grip on her life. After a cup of tea, Darshana dropped the latest bombshell. 'Behn ji, we want the marriage to take place this year because Vinay is insisting on it. What can I do?' she said casually as if the full import of her demand was lost on her.

'He says if he marries, it has to be this year or he won't get married for the next five years. He says, "We are not asking Jyoti's mother for any dowry. So what's the problem?"' Darshana continued. Devi Bai swallowed hard, nearly choking on her syrupy tea. This was outrageous even by Darshana's standards, especially after she had made it amply clear that the marriage would have to wait.

'Please, you have to give me a quick answer. Your daughter is eating two chapatis here and she can eat the same at our place. What's the difference?' Darshana said. 'We want the marriage solemnized this year.' The finality meant that it was an edict coming from the boy's family, no longer a request for compromise or consideration. The tone had changed completely but still they had not demanded any dowry. Devi Bai was stuck between Scylla and Charybdis – if she succumbed to their demand, she would be going against her own best instincts and if she resisted she would risk breaking off the engagement. Both ways Jyoti would suffer. She was at her wit's end and even her sons had no answer. They advised her to consult relatives and seek their advice. Devi Bai decided to ask her own sister Santosh who was close to the family.

The two hadn't met for a while but there was a real strong bond between them. Santosh and her husband Manohar had always regarded Jyoti as their own. They had six sons but no daughters. Their sons were looking after small businesses and the family was financially secure.

'I feel so helpless. Tell me, what should I do?' she asked Santosh. 'The boy's family is after me to marry Jyoti off this winter. Darshana keeps coming here every week and now she has begun to threaten me.' Santosh gave her elder sister a good tongue lashing. 'What kind of nonsense is this? Have you lost your mind? Jyoti has just turned sixteen and you already want to marry her off. Go ahead if you want to spoil her life.'

Devi Bai knew the truth of her sister's tirade. Santosh was right but what could she do? She couldn't hold herself together any longer. All her strength seemed to drain from her and her world seemed to crumble. She felt she couldn't do anything right. That day she desperately wished her husband were alive. So many big decisions about her children's lives and so little guidance. 'I felt there was a mountain before me and I had to climb all by myself,' she told me.

Overcome by a feeling of helplessness, she cried a lot that day. Santosh wanted to help her sister who clearly was under a lot of pressure – both mental and financial. She went home and discussed the situation with her husband Manohar and together they decided to pitch in. They went back to Devi Bai's house and offered to bear the expense of both marriages. 'My heart says you shouldn't send Jyoti away so soon but I know if the engagement is broken, people will talk,' said Manohar. 'Don't worry about your daughters' wedding expenses. We will help you but try to have the ceremonies on the same day so we can save on some of the cost.' Practical and sensible, Manohar had stepped in and Devi Bai was grateful. They selected 18 November 1995 for the twin marriages of the sisters.

But Darshana had other ideas. When informed about the date, she insisted on consulting her pundit who found another more auspicious date. The second of December. Darshana was playing a not-so-subtle power game where, as the boy's mother, she wanted to set the agenda. She felt it was her right and society sanctioned it. And Devi Bai was forced to organize the two weddings on two separate days.

Darshana came for Jyoti's elder sister's wedding and the family got the first real hint that she meant trouble. She saw the dowry Devi Bai and Manohar had collected for the older sister and immediately began whispering about it to others. Obviously, Devi Bai heard about it. As she was leaving after dinner, Darshana said: 'Now you must take good care of our Vinay's baraat.' Another blunt message that they expected more. Devi Bai replied: 'We will do what is within our means. We will give what we can.' There the matter rested for the time being. Soon enough, Jyoti's wedding day arrived.

'I was excited. I got ready in the evening in my wedding sari and jewellery. It was such a special day. I was going to my husband's home,' Jyoti said while talking about that fateful day. Her eyes twinkled a little at the memory. Vinay was dressed in the traditional headgear or sehra, his face hidden behind a curtain of flower strings. He was also wearing the ceremonial sword. He looked distant as the family prepared to bring the bride in. Just as Jyoti was being escorted up to the platform for the jaimala ceremony, Vinay began shouting and creating a fuss. 'Why is there no ring for my brother? Do you think he is not important?' He then took his sword out of the scabbard, enacting a fantasy straight out of a Hindi movie. He was the displeased 'hero' and the people should have quaked in fear. He refused to participate in the ceremonies. 'We were so shocked. We didn't know what hit us. He insulted us in front of the whole community, that man,' remembered Devi Bai, her voice bitter and angry.

Status, honour, importance, propriety, the quality of food and how the groom's side is welcomed on the wedding day can and did become points of dispute. An oversight here, a missed cue there – the boy's family can read a whole book into it and decide that it was an insult. It is as if the all-important groom's party is waiting for the other side to slip. The slip, whether real or imaginary, becomes part of the packet of insults that will be recalled and repeated at every family occasion as a way to remind the girl of her family's lack of etiquette and its lowly position. Of its inability to meet expectations. Taunts would come flying in the future whenever the bride needed to be cut down to size. After all, taunts as verbal weapons are razor sharp and, like missiles, can devastate the other side. They may ride on the basic vehicle of sarcasm but they rise higher and drill deeper. A new bride knows just how deep.

Vinay's behaviour on the wedding day should have been enough for Devi Bai to call the whole thing off but she didn't.

It was too late as far as she was concerned. Besides, she didn't have the mental strength to take such drastic action. She felt beaten and withdrawn. Her daughter could have been saved from Vinay by walking out but not from the whisper campaign that would immediately start against her. All the 'talk', the speculation, the guessing games would viciously engulf Jyoti and permanently force her out of the marriage market. She would be branded as 'trouble' and even unlucky or inadequate. Who would marry her then? Devi Bai was trapped and so was her daughter on the tightrope of tradition and honour.

The ceremony was somehow completed and at about midnight the two walked around the fire, tying themselves to each other in its sanctity. The next morning Jyoti was sent off to her husband's house after the vidai ceremony. Vinay's elder brother Ram Prakash and other relatives carted away the dowry in a hired van. Her dowry was larger than what would be expected from a Class IV government employee, thanks to the generosity of her relatives. The family's list of dowry items was impressive. Jyoti was given two gold necklaces, four pairs of gold earrings, a gold bracelet, four gold bangles, two gold rings and several pieces of silver jewellery. There were gold earrings for Darshana, her mother-in-law, a gold ring for Vinay, and one for his brother. All the gold jewellery was 22 carat and given Devi Bai's economic background, what she gave her daughter was well beyond her means.

Apart from the jewellery, Jyoti was also given the following dowry items:

1 colour television
1 almirah
2 mattresses
1 dressing table

1 table
2 suitcases
1 sewing machine
2 wrist watches
1 iron
1 soda-making machine
1 stainless steel dinner set
Various kitchen utensils
21 sets of clothes for Jyoti
21 saris
5 suits for Vinay
5 saris for Darshana
2 suits for Ram Prakash
Clothes for other relatives
Sheets, quilts and a blanket

Jyoti went to her in-laws' home in Raghuvir Nagar, trying to forget the scene Vinay had created during the wedding. She was apprehensive but felt the dowry problems would be sorted out between the two mothers. Somehow she and Vinay would be immune from the messy accusations and counter-accusations. The first day itself shattered her illusions. She made the mistake of taking away Vinay's gutka – a kind of tobacco he was addicted to – and throwing it away. He went into a rage and slapped her in front of the whole family. Mortified and horribly shaken by his behaviour, she didn't know what to do except do as ordered – apologize. She was made to beg forgiveness and she never forgot the insult. 'I was humiliated. He was my husband and he was treating me like this,' she recalled. The next morning Vinay took her back to Devi Bai's place for a ceremony but she didn't have the courage to tell her mother about the welcome she had received.

'What could I say? That you have married me to the wrong man? What would she do? Ask me to leave him? It doesn't work like that, didi,' she told me. Devi Bai remained oblivious that her daughter was physically abused on the very first day of her married life.

Within two days of moving to her husband's house, the complaints about dowry started. Jyoti's family had failed to meet the standards. 'Doesn't your mother have the intelligence to know what makes a proper dowry?' Chanda, the sharp-tongued sister-in-law, screamed.

Jyoti, the new bride couldn't resist and snapped back: 'My mother has given more than she could afford.' The mother-in-law stepped in and taunted Jyoti with words that seared her. Five years later, they still burned. 'Even a pauper's daughter brings what you have brought,' Darshana had said to the young bride. Jyoti listened in silence for it was not a daughter-in-law's place to answer her mother-in-law back. It would only add to her problems – to be labelled as rude and brassy. But she was smarting from the verbal assault. It had come too soon. She hadn't even got a chance to settle in when it all started. That night she told Vinay what had transpired and how his family had accused her of not bringing enough dowry. She wanted sympathy. She wanted to know that her husband was on her side.

'You have to listen quietly to whatever my mother and sister say. If you ever dare to answer them back, you will be sorry,' he said.

'I could not sleep that night. I was so worried,' Jyoti said, remembering the night four years ago. She felt her world cracking around the edges. She felt alone and she wanted her mother. It was as if she had been thrown into a snake pit. Her Hindi movie dreams of bliss where girl meets boy, marries, finds love and lives happily ever after seemed out of place. The next day was worse. She was asked to cook a meal – a test of sorts to see whether she would serve well in the household where a daughter-in-law is often just a glorified maid. 'I thought I made okay food but Vinay threw a bowl at me, screaming there was too much salt.' She longed to go back to her mother's house and start all over again. If only everything could be erased and rearranged. Just like a cassette, she wanted her life to rewind to the days before she met Darshana and then follow a different story line.

The abuse began getting worse with each passing day. After about two months of marriage, the demands for more dowry got specific. 'One day my mother-in-law sat me down with other family members and said: "Your mother gave you a sewing machine but why not a washing machine? She gave a colour TV but did not give a refrigerator," ' Jyoti recalled. She made the mistake of reminding them of their own promises that they did not want dowry. 'If you wanted dowry, why didn't you say so before?' Jyoti asked, bewildered at the turn of events. After all, they had been quite clear about 'no dowry'. No sooner was her impertinence registered, the whole family pounced on her. Vinay started hitting her. His mother and sister pulled Jyoti's hair and slapped her. Vinay's brother watched the show but did not participate. He marked his presence by saying, 'Better make her understand her place in this house. If she wants to live here, she must not open her mouth so much. She must live like my wife does.'

His wife Ashu lived in the house like a sad shadow, moving about quietly and never saying much. She was the second wife of Ram Prakash, the first one having left him because of incessant dowry demands. Ashu too was often beaten and abused for not bringing enough dowry. Jyoti and Ashu, both victims of abusive in-laws, had become close to each other. They often talked about their 'bad luck' that they were married into this cursed house. They found some comfort in sharing each other's pain.

That day Jyoti was told to ask her family to buy a scooter for Vinay and give fifty thousand rupees in cash so that he could start a new business. She was speechless at the absurdity of the demand. How would Devi Bai ever be able to give so much? Not in this lifetime. Her mother was already weighed down by debt and it was impossible for her to stretch her means any more. Jyoti made the decision not to ask her mother for anything more in dowry because she knew it was unrealistic. She refused to be a conduit. Her forthright manner irritated Darshana a great deal. The more Jyoti refused to succumb to pressure and ask her family for more dowry, the more she was beaten and abused. Now Darshana, Chanda and Vinay hardly needed an excuse to beat her. Anything could trigger a rain of kicks. She was being shown her place in the house. The violence was meant not only to teach her a lesson for her daring but also to establish the unalterable power equations in the house. Daughters-in-law as outsiders had little or no status, especially if they were not a source of constant income.

'Hardly a day passed when I wasn't beaten for some reason,' Jyoti said with a resigned air. 'Whatever I had imagined about marriage was being proved wrong daily. I felt so trapped.'

Four months into the marriage, around April 1996, Jyoti found she was pregnant. She didn't know whether to be happy or sad. She was confused about it all. She hadn't expected motherhood so soon and she wasn't prepared. She was wondering whether to tell her husband when her confusion became irrelevant because she lost the child in the violence of the house. After an especially brutal verbal assault by Chanda in which she called Jyoti a 'whore' and worse, Chanda kicked her in her stomach and pushed her. They were standing near the stairs and Jyoti, unable to keep her balance, tumbled down. She landed at the bottom with a thud, yelping in pain. Chanda simply gaped and did not budge. 'No one came to help me except Ashu. She helped me change my clothes. Vinay didn't even take me to the hospital,' remembered the young bride, her wounds still raw from horrible turn of events. Jyoti had lost her child.

Ashu herself was five months pregnant at the time with her second child and like Jyoti, a victim of violence and torture. The household treated daughters-in-law as bonded labour–cum–baby producing machines. They had no rights, only duties. The abuse was gratuitous at times and at others it was clearly to subjugate and humiliate the women. They were never allowed to feel they had a legitimate stake. Ashu was not allowed to spend time with her first child, a son, who was deliberately kept away from her by Darshana. Whenever she complained or pleaded for spending time with her son, she was beaten. Just kicked and beaten. The family wanted to claim the son, the carrier of the name, the perpetuator, the future breadwinner. He wasn't allowed to develop deep emotional bonds with his mother, the outsider, who might take him away if the going got too tough.

Jyoti had watched all this in horror but didn't know a way out. In August 1996, Ashu gave birth to her second child, also a son, and the family was pleased. But Jyoti was not allowed to hold the child. Every time she played with the baby, her mother-in-law would snatch him away, saying even her touch was inauspicious because she was unlucky. After all she had lost her child. 'You will be childless. You will never bear children. You have ruined my son's life,' Darshana would rant. Jyoti usually listened quietly and went to cry in a corner away from their prying eyes. But she never confided in her mother during those occasional visits. She felt it would only make things worse for Devi Bai.

In March the next year, Ashu's second son died after a prolonged illness. His death became a new reason for Vinay to abuse Jyoti. He blamed her for the tragedy, saying she brought 'bad luck' into the house. She harbours a witch inside, they all shouted. Her 'shadow' must have fallen on the child. She was packed off to her mother's place with an explicit warning: 'Get a scooter and fifty thousand rupees or don't come back.' Vinay asked her to ring him up once all the money was arranged and left her at Devi Bai's house. After about eight days, Jyoti rang him up and pleaded with him to take her back, all the while hiding the truth about her marriage from her own mother. She felt it would create problems for all sides. Besides she felt he would see the light one day and reform his behaviour.

Vinay came to pick her up but instead of taking her home, he dropped her at a gurdwara and told her to live there. It was 1997 and the two had been married for a year and a half by then. Most gurdwaras have temporary accommodation for itinerants and holy men who move about. A woman on her own in a gurdwara was odd for the temple caretakers. They would see Vinay sometimes coming to 'check' on Jyoti but she was mostly by herself. They took pity on her and allowed her to stay for a while. But after about three months they began questioning Vinay about his plans and warned him that he couldn't leave his wife there indefinitely. Instead of taking Jyoti home, Vinay took her to a temple some distance away and dropped her there. She was told to fend for herself and beg, if necessary.

In the winter of 2000, Jyoti and I revisited some of the places where she had been confined. It was seven months after her rescue from Vinay's jail but she still shuddered at the sight of the gurdwara where she had slept in the big hall. The Sikh priest in charge recognized her at once when we walked in accompanied by her brother Sanjay who had helped in her rescue. The priest hadn't heard about Jyoti's plight or read her story in the newspapers but he remembered her clearly and how her husband used to mistreat her. He kept nodding his head as Sanjay showed him the articles and photographs from the papers.

When I asked the priest why he hadn't intervened, he was quiet. For him the question was too absurd to deserve an answer. It was not *his* job to meddle in marriages and that's why he had never considered calling the police. All he wanted was that Jyoti should leave the gurdwara premises, which she did when Vinay dragged her to the sprawling, imposing temple nearby and dumped her there.

Vinay's cruelty was like a Siberian winter – never ending. Why did he marry her if he wanted to reduce her to this, Jyoti thought. If she sat on the street to beg, surely it was an insult also for his family? Wouldn't people talk about them and condemn them for all this?

She survived for about two months near the temple, but never thought of running away to her mother's house. Not once. Vinay always threatened to 'wipe out' her brothers if she dared complain or go home. He kept a strict eye on her, telling people around that his wife was 'sick' and needed to be protected. The temple was just a ten-minute walk from his house and while he went home once a day to clean up, and take care of his business he forced her to use the public toilet.

'I used to wonder why I got married. He never let me have any money because I might make a phone call. He did not even give me a pen so I wouldn't write a letter.' He always talked the language of violence – how he would 'take care' of her brothers, how he would beat her if she ever thought of running to her mother. He knew some of the local goons because of the competition in the cable business. He was one of the two main cable operators in the area and nearly every family crammed in those tiny hovels had a television blaring. But no one wanted to mess with him, such was his reputation. Raghuvir Nagar looked shabby and crowded but there was enough turnover for Vinay to make at least ten thousand rupees a month – a comfortable income.

Jyoti begged him to take her home. She could not bear it any longer – sleeping out in the open and sitting all day staring at people go by. It was around September and the nights were getting cold and she didn't even have a proper blanket. He said he would 'ask' his family's permission first. After a few days he took her away but not to his house. Jyoti was taken to a room near the family home and dumped there. There was no kitchen, no stove, no gas connection. She was dependent on whatever food Darshana brought for Vinay who stayed with her off and on. Darshana treated her with contempt, making it plain that she would rather Jyoti was gone, somehow, somewhere. 'She treated me like an animal. One day she even said that she feeds me because she would also feed a dog,' Jyoti remembered.

The atmosphere in the room was suffocating. Fights went on daily, followed by beatings and kicks. Vinay often drank and savagely beat her. One day things went to such an extent that he poured kerosene on her. She thought this was the end. She knew about bride burnings and dowry deaths. She started screaming and crying loudly, with all her might. She wanted to alert the neighbours. Vinay went out and saw some people had gathered. He came back in and told her ominously, 'Today I will not burn you.' He left her there and went to his mother's house. So terrified was she that she slept in the kerosene-soaked clothes. It was as if he had stilled her senses. She was so afraid of him. She didn't dare contact her mother because of his threats. After about three months in that place, Vinay announced he would take her somewhere else.

She couldn't understand why she was being moved so frequently from place to place. What was he trying to do? She didn't dare protest because it would only make him angrier. He took her two streets away to a small room in the '12 gaz' colony. The name of the colony – '12 gaz' – described the precise dimensions of the tiny hole of a room Jyoti was to call home for the next two years. She shuddered when he opened the door to it. She knew immediately that he would keep her prisoner here until he got 'rid' of her. There was no toilet, no place to bathe. Even in her worst nightmare she hadn't imagined living like this.

She thinks it was sometime in January 1998 when he took her there but she had lost track of time. She remembers it was cold. She had lived in so many different places since Vinay had brought her back from her mother's last March. The taunts about the scooter and the money had continued. She hadn't seen her mother all this while. She wanted to but Vinay had threatened to kill her brothers and ruin her family's name if she ever asked them for help. Now she was locked up. He would leave her locked up for days, visiting sometimes in a drunken stupor only to abuse her. As for food, it all depended on his generosity. He would throw a couple of dry, stale chapatis at her twice a week. There was never any vegetable or dal to help swallow them. There was a raw onion sometimes.

'Did your mother give me money to buy you vegetables? Who do you think you are?' he would yell at the top of his voice. Jyoti drank water from a pitcher that was kept in a corner. Her list of possessions in that room wasn't very long. She had a few clothes but couldn't wash them very often because there was no water. She had to even beg for water. 'My clothes were always dirty. I had to plead with him once a month to get me water,' Jyoti told me when we went back together to Raghuvir Nagar.

'Why should I carry water buckets for you? What will people think? They will laugh at me,' Vinay said as she clutched him. She remembers going without a bath for nearly two months once and she felt repulsed herself. There was a public facility nearby but he wouldn't allow her to go there regularly. Her degradation was complete and she had to live with the constant odour in the room. 'I was always thinking whether I would ever get out. If I died there, would my family even get my dead body for cremation? I had not met my family properly for years,' she said.

It was very hard for me to listen to Jyoti's story, but she seemed calm and just grateful that she was alive. Looking at her tiny frame inside the wobbly taxi we were using, I wondered how she had survived years of abuse. Was it mental discipline or physical strength that carried her through?

Jyoti remembered praying and crying, crying and praying in the first few months in that dark room. She remembered pleading with the man who was supposed to be her husband to stop the beatings but it only got worse. The violence spiralled and he began using a stick. He often aimed at her lower back and knees. Her whole body hurt. She had to devise different ways to forget the pain and pass the time even if for a brief while. Dreaming and living mostly in her imagination seemed like a good idea. She created a separate world in her mind and safely lodged herself there. She would conjure up different sets of sequences about her life in which *she* exercised control. Vinay figured only as a suitor she rejected with aplomb and Darshana was shown the door after her first attempt to lure Jyoti. That was the end of them. They never entered her new world again. Her mother often did.

It had been nearly a year that Devi Bai had seen Jyoti. Whenever she went to Raghuvir Nagar to meet her daughter, she was told Jyoti wasn't home. 'We don't know where she has gone,' Darshana would say. Devi Bai began to suspect that something was wrong and decided to go to the police. She lodged a complaint in the Rajouri Garden police station that she wasn't allowed to meet her daughter and that she feared for her safety. The police went to Vinay's house and asked him to 'produce' Jyoti. Chanda and Darshana quickly went to the room where she was locked up. They cleaned her up and dabbed some rouge on her cheeks and brought her for her mother to see. Devi Bai knew Jyoti was suffering but whenever she asked, her daughter wouldn't say anything. She saw Jyoti six or seven times with the help of the police but her daughter maintained a thick wall of silence, refusing to answer her mother's probing questions. Devi Bai was desperate with worry, unable to understand what was going on. Without a complaint from the victim, the police said they were unable to do more.

'I couldn't say anything about my life to anyone because of Vinay. He said he would "finish" my family,' Jyoti told me. He had threatened to throw acid on her face if she ever dared tell the police the truth about her plight. But there was another reason, a diabolical reason for her stoic silence. Sometime during 1998 – she doesn't remember the month – Vinay came to the room with his whole family. He told her he had brought her some painkillers and she gratefully accepted them. She wondered about their sudden show of concern. Was it because they were afraid of the police? Or had they come to repent their sins? Maybe they were frightened of God? Whatever the reason, she wasn't going to refuse the pills. She quickly swallowed them and a few minutes later she could feel the effect. Her eyes began to close and her aches dulled. But she remembers Darshana and Chanda pulling at her clothes for some reason. She protested but she was too feeble. When Vinay came over the next day, he boasted that now he had the ultimate weapon against her. She would never be able to implicate him in anything. He had in his possession several 'naked' photos of her. She realized the painkillers were given to dull her resistance, not to ease her pain.

'If you dare to say anything to the police, I will send these to your mother's post office. I will show them to all the boys in your colony,' he had bellowed, flinging the photographs at her. Jyoti was frightened as never before. She felt a terror in her spine. She knew his threat was real. He could do anything. If he could lock her up without food or water, he was also capable of distributing the photographs, she thought. She didn't disbelieve him even for a minute. She couldn't bear to imagine the shame, the pain and the horror of his crime. She just wanted to curl up and die. That would be far simpler. How could she or her poor mother ever fight this man and his family?

He had thought of everything, especially after the police had begun showing up at his mother's house asking for Jyoti. He put a few cable wires and antennae in the room where Jyoti was confined to show it was his 'office' in case the police traced her. When I went to see the room in November 2000, I asked several people who lived next door if they knew about Jyoti. It seemed that the neighbours had been coached and prepared. Some of them were plain scared. Most of them denied ever seeing her or even knowing she existed. But they had erected a wall in self-defence. They didn't want to get involved in a police case. This was a narrow lane where overcrowding was a way of life and most neighbours would hear you even if you sneezed. A woman vendor of dry snacks squatting on the street right opposite Jyoti's room smiled benignly when I continued asking questions. No, she had never heard the shouting, the beatings, the crying. Never. She hadn't even seen the police when they came to rescue Jyoti. When I persisted, some of the more enterprising neighbours claimed they had seen Jyoti around and she came down regularly to buy vegetables. A shopkeeper even said she owed him money. In the end they were evasive. Who wanted Vinay as an enemy?

Vinay was the local businessman-goon who showed them pirated movies on cable and had recently thrown in the bonus of a free month. They didn't want to take him on. Most were indifferent, even afraid to take on Vinay and his brother. The brothers had 'connections' that, if activated, could spell trouble. Besides, who wants to be part of a long court case? But they were not all heartless or oblivious. Jyoti told me that some of them would occasionally push food under her door. She was grateful even though she didn't know who they were.

Devi Bai and her elder son Sanjay had been to the police station again to plead with them to rescue Jyoti. Worried sick about her daughter, she had been pursuing the police to follow her case. On 8 December 1998, she went to the Crime Against Women cell in Delhi's Nanakpura police station – the headquarters for tackling dowry complaints. The cell was established in the late 1980s to arrest the rising graph of dowry deaths and give victims a separate channel to contact the police. Today most major cities have anti-dowry cells. Victims of dowry harassment had repeatedly complained that policemen were unreceptive and often refused to take the case seriously. Vinay's family was summoned to the Nanakpura police station and they showed up in force. Jyoti too was released from her lockup for the visit but she was under strict instructions not to say anything against her husband's family. When the police officer asked her how things were going, Jyoti began abusing and criticizing her mother. She said she didn't want to go home to Devi Bai. That she wasn't her mother and that Sanjay wasn't her brother. She couldn't tell her mother that Vinay had blackmailed her and how.

Devi Bai started to cry, listening to her daughter mouth such untruths. She told the police that whenever she went to see Jyoti at Vinay's house, she was never around. Why was she always missing? She planted a serious doubt in their minds about Jyoti's statements. She told them that Vinay had not allowed her daughter to visit and there were signs of physical abuse. The police promised to investigate and even went to interview her a few times but they expressed their inability to extract Jyoti from the house against her will. They had no choice but to 'honour' Jyoti's statement that she wanted to live with her husband.

'That day I felt completely helpless. I just said a prayer and left her to God,' remembered Devi Bai. 'What else could I do under the circumstances?' Sanjay and she returned home dejected and frustrated.

The police made Vinay promise that he would send Jyoti to visit her mother from time to time and especially for festivals. He agreed but it was an empty promise. Jyoti was taken back to the room and locked up as before. Months went by and she continued on her starvation diet. Her condition was deteriorating fast. She was slowly losing the use of her legs because of the pain from the constant beatings. Every time she tried to walk, her legs felt like jelly. She had to crawl around the room. Her degradation was complete. 'I used to try to sleep a lot because then I didn't feel as much pain,' recalled Jyoti, her hands nervously playing with the edge of her scarf. She wanted an end to it all and if that meant her end as well, that was just fine. She knew Vinay wanted her to die. At least her agony would end.

What she did not know was that Vinay was growing impatient with the whole thing. Now that the police were involved and he was suspected of dowry harassment, he had begun to panic. He was determined to get rid of Jyoti but no longer by the method of starvation and slow torture. A new way had to be found to avoid suspicion by the police. He found one soon enough and it seemed foolproof. Its simplicity charmed him. He decided to divorce Jyoti quietly and send her back to Devi Bai. He would do it swiftly before anyone was wise to the plan and, of course, the divorce would be by 'mutual consent'. It was sometime in the middle of 1999 when the idea struck him. He went about looking for a lawyer who wouldn't ask too many questions and found Ashok Rohtagi.

Rohtagi was told that it was a straightforward case of 'mutual consent' divorce and that he could represent both husband and wife. As for Jyoti, she was asked to sign the papers quietly or face the humiliation of public distribution of the photographs. The divorce petition claimed that the couple had been living separately for a year as required under law and that all her dowry had already been taken back to her mother's house. Vinay had thought of everything.

Vinay filed the divorce papers in the court of M.S. Sabharwal and on the appointed date both the husband and wife appeared to sign the papers in his presence. The judge asked her, 'Do you want a divorce?' Jyoti replied: 'I am giving him a divorce of my own free will.' Those who saw Jyoti that day in court still remember her terrible state. She looked so fragile as if she would break into pieces any moment. She was thin as a stick and covered with bruises. She weighed less than thirty kilograms.

Rohtagi, the lawyer, too saw Jyoti and was shaken. He felt something was very wrong. It was not a straight case of divorce. Jyoti's condition was pathetic and she could hardly walk properly.

'I felt maybe there is some deception going on. The girl looked almost handicapped,' Rohtagi recalled. He asked her several times whether she indeed wanted a divorce and she said yes. But he had a lurking suspicion that she was being coerced and that he was being used as an instrument of a devious plan. She was bruised and in obvious physical pain. He felt he needed to inform her family so at least they could take action if they wished. Since it was a joint divorce petition, he represented both the husband and wife. He went to the Kashmiri Gate post office, found Devi Bai and broke the news to her. He told her that Vinay and Jyoti had already appeared once and signed the papers but the divorce would be final only after the second motion. He gave her the date of the second appearance and advised her to get a lawyer. Devi Bai was grateful for the information and she immediately filed a petition with the help of a lawyer. If the divorce went through, Jyoti would be thrown out like a piece of used tissue. Once divorced, it would be very difficult to prove anything against Vinay even if she wanted to. Her own statements exonerating him would be just one of the many hurdles. It would be a long and difficult process to recreate the past four years of her life, find witnesses and prove in

a court of law that she was tortured. And that the di
meant to get rid of her.

Rohtagi's timely intervention was like a boon. When I asked him as to what prompted him, he said simply: 'Even I have daughters. I felt from the beginning that something was wrong because Jyoti was always very quiet. She never answered my questions in any detail. I just didn't want to be party to any fraud.' He also found Vinay's reasons for divorce confusing and contradictory. 'Some day he said he wanted to go abroad, some day he said he wanted to marry someone else. Sometimes he said he wanted to keep Jyoti in his house.'

When Vinay learnt that Devi Bai had found out about the divorce plan, he went into a terrible rage. 'How did your family find out? He beat me a lot that day and kept saying that I must have told them,' Jyoti recalled. On the next court date, Devi Bai was present but there was no sign of Vinay. The divorce proceedings were halted but there was still a question of rescuing Jyoti and filing a case against Vinay. Desperately worried about Jyoti's life, Devi Bai and Sanjay approached Nari Niketan, a government-run women's organization, to intervene. Caseworkers from the organization questioned Vinay and decided the situation was serious enough for action. They forced him to take Jyoti to the hospital for a complete checkup and recovery. They kept the pressure on but he was not in a mood to comply. Once in the hospital, Jyoti was not allowed to see anyone but Devi Bai persisted. She remembers standing helplessly by Jyoti's bed when Vinay ordered her daughter to sit up and 'show your mother that you are fine'.

'She could not even sit up. Her back was giving up on her. She leaned on her elbow and somehow sat up,' Devi Bai remembered. Although not strong enough to support her weight, Jyoti was frightened enough of those photos and she once again abused her mother. 'Why have you come to see me? Go away,' she said to her mother and brother.

She spent about ten days in the hospital in January 2000 while the Nari Niketan workers pursued her case. But whenever they called the two sides for counselling Vinay never showed up. When they went to his house he refused to meet them. He wasn't interested in working things out. The social workers closed the case because they didn't have the authority or the powers to rescue Jyoti. Besides, she was still unwilling to tell the truth. The police already knew about the case but seemed uninterested in taking the final step of rescuing Jyoti.

Next month, Devi Bai again went to the police and lodged a new complaint against Vinay. She accused him of wrongfully confining her daughter. Her elder son, Sanjay, who had stood besides her like a rock through the ordeal, was once again with her. Fortunately for the distraught mother, a very able female police officer Suman Nalwa had taken over as the head of the west Delhi's Crime Against Women cell. Nalwa, an enthusiastic and sympathetic officer and not yet cynical about life and her job, listened to Devi Bai and Sanjay with care. They showed her a thick file of various complaints and representations they had made over the years to the police. They told her Jyoti might die if she wasn't rescued soon. Nalwa was touched and felt there was a lot of conviction in the mother's voice. She was especially taken by Sanjay's determination to help his sister. Here was a brother who did not want to abandon a sister in distress, even though he had done his 'duty' of getting her married.

Nalwa told me that it was a rare sight to see a brother 'so ...ate for the well being of his married sister'. Usually ...f the brothers help their sisters in distress, it is more to satisfy their own egos and to show another man down – the groom.

Nalwa immediately got into action and summoned her inspector. But the inspector told her that Jyoti was happy with her husband and in fact had given statements last year to the police to that effect. Jyoti had told the police that her mother was interfering in her life. According to the inspector nothing could be done. But Nalwa was not convinced and she decided to examine the case more closely. 'What touched me was the persistence of the mother and the brother for more than two years, that too when Jyoti had for all purposes rejected them in front of the police and others,' Nalwa told me. She inquired about Jyoti's health from various police officers who had seen her and was told that the girl could hardly walk the last time she was brought to the police station for a meeting. This set Nalwa thinking and she called the assistant commissioner of police for Rajouri Garden. She told him that there was something very wrong about the case and they needed to reexamine the whole situation.

Nalwa decided to raid the house to see for herself what was going on with Jyoti. After making some inquiries she found out about 'Jyoti's jail' and ordered her rescue. Her officers went to the room and broke open the door. What they saw shocked them – Jyoti's condition was so fragile that she could not stand up on her own. Her brother had to carry her out in his arms like a child. Nalwa took her to the hospital for emergency treatment and after a few days of rest, she began regaining her strength and told her real story to the police. Hardened policemen who see death and destruction on a daily basis were speechless. They couldn't believe that a husband could do this to his wife. Jyoti weighed only twenty-one kilograms when she was rescued.

'When I saw Jyoti, I was shocked by her physical condition. She was just skin and bones. She just wanted to thank me and when I asked her what had happened, she told me how she had been surviving,' Nalwa recounted. She was hanging by a thread and another week might have been too late.

Jyoti came home on 8 May 2000 after more than four years in hell, a domestic hell from where she felt she could not escape. It was a sad homecoming for all. Emaciated and gaunt, she walked slowly with a lot of effort. Devi Bai was crying but she felt relieved that her daughter had finally been rescued. Jyoti was soon telling her family the painful story of her marriage, her bondage. She told them about the blackmail, the falsified divorce papers, her forced signature, the order to denounce her own family, the threats to finish them off, the threats to throw acid on her brothers, and on and on. No one could believe that she had survived the ordeal – she wasn't meant to by her husband's calculations. Her face had aged but her body seemed to belong to a child, not a woman. So emaciated was she.

'Our main aim was to get Jyoti out safely and then came the case and evidence gathering,' Nalwa said. The local police post worked round the clock and recovered the photographs from Vinay's house, including the negatives. So confident was Vinay of duping the system that he waved Jyoti's medical reports and test results in front of the police and said he had been taking good care of his wife.

'He had the temerity to laugh about the whole thing even after being caught,' Nalwa remembered. He had all the papers and receipts from the pharmacy – many of them false – to show the world that Jyoti was seriously ill and therefore her emaciated condition, a line of defence his lawyers would pursue later.

Even though they had earlier treated Devi Bai's complaints with routine interest, the police showed extraordinary coordination at this stage, thanks perhaps to Nalwa. She felt that at the very least the police needed to independently establish the veracity of the case so that Jyoti's mother would have the satisfaction of knowing the truth. Nalwa took the matter all the way up to the police commissioner, forcing the police machinery to work. Four days later, she ordered the arrests of Vinay, Darshana, Ram Prakash and Chanda on five different charges including abetment to murder, wrongful confinement, cruelty and dowry harassment. Jyoti's story made the front pages of almost all the newspapers, prompting several women's organizations to come forward with offers of help.

The police filed a chargesheet soon after based on Jyoti's statement and medical reports after an independent examination.

The court case is on but it may be years before a verdict is given. Vinay is lodged in New Delhi's Tihar Jail but Darshana, Ram Prakash and Chanda were released on bail within months of their arrest. Darshana was released on grounds of health and Chanda on grounds that she is a minor, even though she looks anything but underage. Ram Prakash was set free after his lawyer successfully argued that as the sole earning member of the family, he needed to look after the cable business and take care of his sick mother. The easy manner in which they all got bail cast a pall of gloom in Devi Bai's house. But as long as Vinay is incarcerated, she will feel a degree of satisfaction.

I saw Vinay for a few minutes during a hearing in the sprawling Tees Hazari courts in Delhi. Accompanied by a heavily armed guard, he sat quietly waiting for the judge to call out the case. He had come in a police van surrounded by policemen. He wore a saffron tika on his forehead – his family had obviously visited a temple in the morning to invoke divine assistance. I tried talking to him, but he refused to say anything. Instead he kept asking me to convey a request to Jyoti that he wanted to talk to her one last time. His brother, Ram Prakash, who bore a striking resemblance to him, hovered around, wanting to know who had sent me. Suspicious and furtive, he ordered his sister not to talk to me. Even though Jyoti sat a few seats away from Vinay and his family outside the courtroom, she still shuddered at the sight of him. 'Can you see how he looks at me? He told me last time he will take care of us as soon as he is out on bail,' she said.

The court hearing was of a preliminary nature and the case was adjourned for another two weeks. Neither the government prosecutor who is fighting Jyoti's case nor the lawyer named by a local NGO to help keep track of the case was present at the hearing. Sanjay said that they weren't there even the last time. On the other hand, the defence was represented by an aggressive young lawyer who talked confidently about getting Vinay out. He blamed the media for 'making these cases out to be bigger than they are'. I was speechless as he revealed his strategy. He hinted darkly that Jyoti was getting all the treatment she needed but because she may have contracted HIV, she was not responding. He then dropped a bombshell – the notorious photographs, which frightened Jyoti into silence, were taken with her consent. He claimed she was smiling in them. I left Jyoti at her mother's, wondering if Vinay's lawyer might succeed in his manoeuvres and mitigate the case against his client despite all the efforts of Devi Bai, Sanjay, Suman Nalwa and the other police officers. The judicial system with its own inherent problems will now have to shepherd Jyoti for the rest of the way as she tries to rebuild her life.

Jyoti is back in the compound of the Kashmiri Gate post office in old Delhi close to the majestic stone walls of the Red Fort where she grew up. The streets are hard to navigate for the uninitiated but finding an address is not difficult. People live so close, they know the rate of each other's heartbeat. Most of Jyoti's neighbours, like her mother, are class IV employees at the post office. They are the cleaners, the carriers, the packers and they are able to survive mainly because of free government housing. When I asked for House No. 1784, the local cobbler gave me a quick look up and down. 'Are you looking for Jyoti beti?' I hesitated to say yes, afraid that the neighbourhood might have turned hostile to intruders looking for new ways to torment Jyoti.

But he sent me down a narrow lane stacked with the backs of what would be two-room houses. Some women returning from their daily shopping trip to the vegetable market noticed the 'outsider' at once and personally escorted me to Jyoti's house. Everyone in the small square of cheek-by-jowl homes has shared her pain. She is *their* Jyoti and they feel protective towards her. I first met Jyoti in September 2000, four months after the police had rescued her. There she was sitting on a bed, back in her mother's house, ironing clothes. She looked up and smiled in anticipation. 'Namaste didi,' she greeted me, making room on the bed and unplugging the iron. She got down from the bed but she had difficulty standing straight. Her tiny five-foot frame seemed even tinier because she couldn't straighten her back. The room was crowded with the many members of the household – Sanjay, his wife, their two children, Jyoti and Devi Bai – all living in the two rooms. Jyoti settled down on the bed, trying to find a comfortable position for her fragile back. It wasn't easy because she needed something to lean on.

When I again met her in November 2000, she looked much better and healthier. She was getting ready to go to the court for the hearing. She looked like a young girl ready to embark on a new journey. 'Do I look as if I have TB, as he used to say?' she asked with a newfound confidence in her voice. I talked to her again two years later in May and learnt she had begun working at a garment export factory while pursuing her case. Meanwhile, Vinay had secured bail from the high court albeit with several conditions attached. He was not to harass her, come close to her house or trouble her in any way.

But Jyoti was still afraid. 'Didi, he can do anything. He always told me he would "take care" of us if we went to the police.'

Perhaps her ordeal is not over yet.

Driven to Suicide

Tikka Preet's Story

The wedding preparations were in full swing. The peach-coloured shamiana was ready and flowers peeked from everywhere, pinned to the many corners, hanging from the crisscrossing wooden beams. Gladioli, roses, lilies and of course marigolds tied delicately together so each could have a window to the world. Vases, bunches, arrangements, torans – the flowers dominated. The tables and chairs were dressed in white and tied with a bow, gently off-setting the peach of the shamiana walls. Fluorescent streamers covered the trees in the Defence Services Club, fluttering in anticipation of the celebration. It was February 2000, the millennium year. The winter sun presided with aplomb except for an occasional distraction by a stray cloud weaving its way through the blue sky. But it was comforting enough, just like a well-worn blanket, soaking the women in languid warmth. They could shed their shawls to show off their shimmering salwar-kurtas, their newly acquired kundan sets. They enjoyed the gentle breeze as it spread the mix of their sophisticated perfumes and manly smells over the gathering.

The setting was almost perfect: a tastefully decorated venue, guests bustling about exchanging gossipy tidbits, waiters fussing behind counters laden with delicacies, children adding that bit of chaós essential to Indian weddings, music wafting across and the Himalayas standing guard right behind them all. On a good day you can see the peaks of Kasauli from Chandigarh and it was a good day. The wide roads of Chandigarh seemed wider, the green trees greener and the air cleaner. The city of gardens was in full bloom, its sprawling homes buried under bougainvillea and rose vines. Guests were arriving by the carload, in Zens, Hondas, Maruti Esteems . . . it was a veritable parade of what was best in the market. Relatives, friends, colleagues, retired army officers, they were all there to celebrate. After all, it was their darling Tikka's wedding.

Tikka Preet looked lovely in her red lehnga-dupatta, embroidered heavily with gold, and all the bridal finery. She hadn't wanted too much make-up, she hated the fussiness of foundation and eyeliners. A bit of colour on the cheeks and some lipstick and that was it. She was luminescent with an inner peace that had always been the envy of her friends. It was her big day, she had supervised the arrangements herself – selecting the menu, the décor, the music. She had plunged herself into the whole idea of marriage with such gusto that her brother Ishpreet was a little surprised. But he wasn't going to question her unbridled enthusiasm. 'Main vyaah poore shauk naal karna hai (I want to get married with all the pomp),' she had told him. She was happy like a child out to buy a new toy. The family was enthralled to see the transformation – she had seemed almost afraid of marriage until now.

She had said no to all the 'offers' in the past on one pretext or another, and her fear of marriage had only grown with time. She saw bad marriages all around – some of her best friends were struggling. She didn't want to volunteer for an experiment she felt had a high probability of failure. She was happy working as a teacher at the Institute of Tourism and Future Trends and didn't feel any real compulsion to follow in the footsteps of her girlfriends. They were all married and seeped in the drudgery of daily life. What is the hurry, she would ask her parents, and then joke about their eagerness to turn her out of the house she loved. She was strong enough to resist social pressures and fortunate enough to have parents who respected her wishes not to rush her into marriage just for the sake of ticking off the checklist of life.

But sometimes, only sometimes, she did wonder about staying single. She hated the whisper campaign, the sad but understanding looks from relatives, the steady gaze of older women. They all wanted to know why. At the age of twenty-nine, why was Tikka single? They never asked anything directly because she never allowed them the opportunity but like anxious spectators at a long show, they wanted an answer. And the answer could only be marriage. Without a man beside her, Tikka was only half there and noticeable for the wrong reason in family photographs.

She had seen a few prospective grooms but somehow something always kept her back. Whether it was her mother's ongoing battle against cancer or her desire to be a pillar of strength in the house where she was the only child left or just the enormity of the decision to spend her life with someone she hardly knew – she shied away from marriage. Her brother Ishpreet had moved to the US and had settled in New Jersey and her mother had really felt his absence. Tikka thought she had to be there for her parents, if for nothing else, for reassurance. Papa wouldn't be able to manage everything on his own – her mother's treatment, the household, his business, his voluntary work. Besides, no one had swept her off her feet yet so why bother? She was good-looking, bright, educated and a professional. Her beauty came from an inner confidence that sprang from a happy and loving home. She didn't feel the need to prove herself because her parents had never restricted her from anything.

But Tikka had finally said yes to Bhupinderjit Singh Gill, an MBA from Jammu University. He was working for Bridgestone Tyres in Ludhiana. She wasn't getting younger and obviously her parents – even though they never pestered or prodded her for marriage – must have felt a certain awkwardness, she thought. They would lace the occasional dinner conversation with hints or suddenly talk of some qualified boy they had heard about. Her mother desperately wanted to 'settle' her, see her as a bride before leaving for the US for cancer treatment. The two had been making the rounds of doctors and hospitals for the past several years, running to Mumbai whenever they heard about a new cancer specialist there. But the doctors had recommended that her mother Kamaljit Kaur go abroad for treatment. This was working on Tikka's mind. As long as she was single, her mother would stay on in India continuing her search for a suitable son-in-law. Her illness would breed, her chances of survival would lessen. It was a burden too heavy to bear and Tikka had said yes.

She met Bhupinder a few times before the wedding to try to get to know him a little. Just a little. At thirty-two years, he was in the prime of life. But he seemed a little odd, perhaps shy. He never wanted to come into her house somehow. He would come to Chandigarh to shop for the wedding but he always wanted to whisk her away from outside. He would later drop her at her gate. He never wanted to come in, sit and chat with Tikka's parents and brother. Hers was a small, close-knit family and they wanted very much to welcome him into the fold but he seemed to want to keep his distance. They found it strange but said nothing for fear of upsetting him. Sons-in-law are China dolls, after all, and need all the care they can get. Even when Tikka's family took him out to dinner, he sat sullen and quiet, munching his food. He never seemed to open up, not even with her brother who always made friends easily. They thought he was reserved and quiet – not necessarily flawed – although a certain lightness of being would have been welcome.

Her mother and friends helped her get ready in the morning for the anant karaj, the Sikh wedding ceremony in the gurdwara. The hours were blurring in her mind. She had got up early and taken a bath. Her house in Sector 34, an upper-middle-class enclave, was abuzz with activity. Servants and helpers ran around giving everyone a cup of tea, picking up plates of breakfast, ferrying baskets of fruit and sweets to the cars. She had to remember to put on all the jewellery in this commotion, ensure that no little frills were forgotten and look her best. So many details, so little time. The day had come too soon. It was 28 February 2000, when Tikka married Bhupinder.

'Mama, where is my bracelet?' she shouted across the house as her mother hurried over with a velvet-covered blue box of wedding jewellery. She was going to wear the 'amardeep' gold set and the diamond rings. She patiently resisted her mother's pleas to wear another gold necklace. 'Please, mama, I feel like a Christmas tree already. Why load more ornaments?' But Kamaljit, so delighted, so supremely happy that day, wouldn't listen. She just wanted her daughter to wear everything and shine like a thousand suns. She was thankful that Tikka had finally agreed to marry. It was God's grace and she must remember to go to the gurdwara and offer special prayers. Her daughter was a radiant bride, just like she had imagined. Her joys and sorrows were her own, the two were so close. Tikka had been the rock throughout her struggle with cancer, always trying to stay ahead of the curve. From the Internet, from books, medical journals, Tikka had accumulated formidable knowledge about cancer. She often stumped the doctors by her familiarity with the protocol, the latest medical breakthroughs.

Tikka's father, a retired army colonel, was running about taking care of the last-minute details. Sporting his smartest turban, Col. Nirbhai Singh Pandher was a man fulfilled. His daughter on whom he doted no end, was finally going to her 'own' house. He was a bit sad; no doubt, he had become so used to her cheerful presence, especially after his son had left for America. Tikka was the spark of his life and now she was leaving. But he banished those thoughts quickly, instead concentrating on the myriad details of the wedding. This would be the last wedding in the house and he had been lavish. No expense was deemed too high, no detail unnecessary for his darling daughter. She deserved every bit of it, he thought.

She was like a son to him and destined to go places. He had tried his best to find a good boy for Tikka, someone who would take care of his precious child just as he had all his life. He had searched with the discipline of an army man that he was. 'Not that one: his family background is not impressive. Not that one: he is in debt. Not even that one: he just pales in front of my daughter.' He broke off Tikka's engagement with a young man when he discovered the boy had lied about his background. Tikka had wanted to marry an army officer, perhaps searching for an ideal she saw in her father. The pomp and ceremony of the army had always appealed to her – the excitement of postings all around India, the social life – but Col. Pandher had failed in his mission. He could not find a suitable army boy, instead they had settled on a family from Moga. The boy was an MBA and his father had been with the Life Insurance Corporation. The family had land and the three sons were well settled.

Bhupinder and his family arrived at the gurdwara with a small number of friends and sat down for the ceremony. Col. Pandher didn't notice but there were hardly any relatives from the boy's side in the baraat. No chachas, no cousins, not even his grandmother came. But how was anyone to know that Bhupinder's father, Karamjit Singh Gill, had few *real* friends? Karamjit had fought with all his four brothers over land, filing suits against them, entangling them neck deep in litigation. He said he was wronged and was denied his fair share. Col. Pandher wasn't Sherlock Holmes but even if he had known about the court cases, what would he have done? He might have brushed them aside, so common are land disputes in Punjab – like the paddy that grows all around. No one is supposed to be awed by the smell of litigation. District courts are choked with cases, the judges buried under claims and counter-claims on pieces of ancestral land. Karamjit Singh in the past had tried to oust his own mother, who is now in her eighties, from the family farmhouse by harassing her and dragging her to court. The mother was forced to go public with her allegations.

Bhupinder and his two brothers had grown up in an environment of constant tension and turmoil. Their parents seemed to thrive on intrigue, living on high-wire acts of legal brinkmanship. For them no line was ever straight, no relationship without deception. They believed passionately in themselves, they thought nothing of filing yet another case, one more affidavit or complaint against anyone who dared to challenge them. Bhupinder's mother, Parminder Gill, was the headmistress of the junior section at Summerfield School in Moga from which she was later dismissed for gross misconduct. She dominated the family of three boys supremely and completely. They ran to her whenever there was a problem, whether office politics or marital discord – mama had the right answer. While she ran the family, Bhupinder's father, Karamjit, took care of the dozens of property cases crawling through the courts, spending his days rushing to the district court in Faridkot. Karamjit had been the source of most of the litigation, fighting his three brothers who were all on one side. He was the David against their Goliath – or so he imagined. But to others he was a man with a chequered record – he had faced charges of official misconduct as an LIC officer. He had been accused of perpetrating fraud on poor, innocent farmers, stealing their life savings in insurance scams.

But Col. Pandher didn't know any of this before Tikka's marriage. A typical army man, he was straightforward, uncomplicated and in many ways the exact opposite of the Gill clan. He hadn't a clue about their controversial antecedents and he hadn't checked as thoroughly as he might have wished with the benefit of hindsight. He had believed what he was told by the middle man, one Capt. Hardev Singh, who was a close friend of the Gills. 'I took them at their word. They seemed quite fine – a good house in Moga, land holdings, the boys were well settled. You don't go in suspecting the worst,' he told me later. When the truth finally came to him from one of Karamjit's brothers, a fellow army man, it was already too late.

Bhupinder was wearing a traditional white achkan with a sword dangling lazily by his side. Tall and fair, he had looked quite handsome in his wedding finery. A colourful scarf around his neck matched his red turban. He was a mona Sikh but in deference to his elders he had laboriously grown his beard for a few weeks for the wedding. On such important days, rules had to be obeyed especially if one had to sit in front of the Granth Sahib. Bhupinder had complied but just about.

Once the gurdwara ceremony was over, the wedding party headed for a lavish lunch under the peach shamiana. Col. Pandher led the guests to the Defence Officers Club where the real celebrations were to begin. It was the happiest moment in his life – watching his married daughter walk side by side with her husband. He was so proud. He had discharged his responsibility with honour, he thought. It was with this sense of relief that he began welcoming the guests. They came bearing gifts and flowers, saris and toasters, dinner sets and tablemats – all the things Tikka would need to set up her new home. But Bhupinder was nowhere to be seen. Minutes turned into hours but the groom failed to reappear.

'Where is Bhupinder?' Col. Pandher finally asked. His family said he was getting ready.

'But he was ready,' said Col. Pandher, under his breath, not wishing to annoy the all-important in-laws. What was taking so long? He had never taken so long even for the most formal army gathering where each brass buckle had to shine just so. It was getting embarrassing because the guests had been waiting since noon. No lunch could be served until the in-laws arrived and took the first bite. The caterers were ready but they could not serve until they got the green signal. Tikka was puzzled and a little miffed. Imagine making a bride wait on her wedding day. It seemed like a precursor of things to come.

Finally, after about two hours, Bhupinder and his entourage appeared. He had changed into a suit and shaved off his symbolic beard. He had also taken off his turban. He looked so different, the guests were stunned. Zoya Randhawa, a close friend of Tikka's, told me the transformation took everyone by surprise. 'We couldn't even recognize him. It was very odd,' she remembered. Was it the bravado of a small town boy trying to impress big city folk with his I-care-two-hoots-for-tradition attitude?

For Col. Pandher it was a 'bad omen' and he filed it away in his memory. Why couldn't Bhupinder keep up appearances just for a day? What was the big rush to go and shave? It was disrespectful and inconsiderate to say nothing of the sheer self-indulgence of the act. 'We Sikhs, we keep the beard for marriage. Some even grow their hair for a while if they are monas,' Col. Pandher told me when I met him in Chandigarh more than a year later to find out more about Tikka's marriage and her tragedy.

Bhupinder sat next to his wife on those throne-like seats that elevate the husband and wife to a demi-god status on their wedding day. He seemed self-conscious and ill at ease. Somehow, he was a bit out of his depth in the gathering – the people seemed more urbane, they chatted with his wife with an ease he found difficult to comprehend and everyone seemed just a bit too breezy. His parents too were feeling a little out of place – they stood grimly behind the newlywed couple, never smiling. This didn't have the air of familiarity that Moga did. There they knew everyone, at least everyone who mattered. Parminder's job at the school ensured that – parents desperate for school admissions always are a vulnerable lot. The school had given her a powerful perch from which to look at the world. But in Chandigarh it was different. It was a big city and they knew few people. They watched everything carefully, they filed away people in their memory cards – neatly stacked for a later occasion. It was important to know about Col. Pandher's friends. Karamjit's eyes were like giant satellite dishes, soaking in every signal, every detail, every nuance. Never for a moment did he let his guard down to enjoy the afternoon.

'Achcha ji, haur lijiye,' Col. Pandher was heaping one more helping of sweets on Karamjit's plate. The two seemed to display a healthy respect for each other. There was no choice really – they were relatives now, they had to get along. The lunch over, the bride and groom retired to change and rest. The next day was going to be another long day – there was a celebration in Moga. Col. Pandher along with his family and a few relatives went to Moga for the reception. They noticed that not many from Bhupinder's extended family had come. 'I still remember Bhupinder didn't really look very happy. It seemed that it wasn't his wedding we were celebrating but someone else's,' he recalled. But they drove back with a deep sense of satisfaction that Tikka had gone into a good family.

Tikka woke up in her new home with an uncertain feeling. She didn't know where she stood in the new dispensation of life. Things would be different, she knew, but how different, she couldn't fathom. She suddenly heard Bhupinder's voice in the room.

'You didn't behave well at the reception. You should have mingled more with my relatives,' he said. She was stung. The first thing she had heard from her husband was a complaint. She swallowed hard and listened as she packed for her honeymoon in Goa. She wanted to carry some jewellery with her but Bhupinder had locked it all. When she asked for it, he said there was no need to carry valuables in case they got robbed. Conmen hovered around newlyweds and it was better to be safe than sorry. He had taken all her jewellery for 'safekeeping'. She didn't like the idea one bit but felt it would be inappropriate to raise it at this time. I will deal with it later, she thought and continued packing.

'And by the way, tell your father he should pay half the cost for the Goa trip,' Bhupinder suddenly said.

'What did you say?' she asked.

'You heard me. I think he should pay something for the Goa trip,' he repeated himself. She couldn't believe her ears. Is this the proud Sikh who married her claiming to be a big executive? Which self-respecting man would ask his wife to foot half the bill for a honeymoon? Was this really a flavour of things to come? She was nauseated at the very thought. But when he persisted, she called up her father in Chandigarh.

'Papa, I don't know what to say but something really strange has happened,' she said haltingly over the phone. 'Bhupinder wants money from you for the honeymoon.'

Col. Pandher was just as stunned. He felt embarrassed for his daughter. He knew how difficult it must have been for Tikka to have to ask him for money. She had never had to do that at home. She was earning a good salary, and it was he who would put extra money in her hands every month for household expenses. He felt his feet getting glued to the ground as she spoke on the telephone. He mumbled yes and tried to put the best face on it before ringing off. But deep down he knew that something was seriously amiss. Had he and Tikka made the wrong choice? What was the meaning of this outrageous demand? More than the money, it was the crassness of the move that bothered him. Imagine humiliating a young bride who had just made a great leap of faith by walking into an unknown home and called it her own. He went to bed a worried man.

He had not scrimped for his daughter's marriage. No one could accuse him of cutting corners or pinching pennies. He had given an elaborate dowry, right from clothes for the entire family to gold karas for the groom and his father to kitchen gadgets to air conditioners to a washing machine and a refrigerator. He had even given three lakh rupees in cash for furniture and a new car. The gold jewellery for Tikka extended to twenty-two items with four complete gold sets. The expense on the wedding day itself was more than three lakh rupees. The total expenses, including the dowry and gifts for the family, ran into more than sixteen lakh rupees. Even though the Gills had repeatedly said they didn't want any dowry, the middleman would come calling with elaborate lists and demands. 'We just want a decent wedding,' was their refrain when the two families met. 'A decent wedding' was a code word for what was 'expected' and Col. Pandher understood it as any normal person would. He would obviously spend well on the wedding – she was his only daughter — and give her a good dowry.

'The vichaula (middleman) would tell us what all we had to give them and to their relatives. He had lists. They made sure it was a lot more than just "a decent wedding". But we didn't mind it at the time because we were so looking forward to Tikka's wedding,' recalled Ishpreet, her brother.

Col. Pandher fulfilled every demand, every whim that Parminder had dreamt of for herself and her son. 'I had some family land and other securities but otherwise I have retired from the army. You know how much we get and it is not a whole lot. Even my army friends said I had gone overboard at the wedding. But I have no regrets. It was for my daughter and I wanted to spend,' he told me sitting in the living room of his house in Chandigarh.

It was hard for me not to feel sympathetic towards a man who although extremely open and liberal in most ways was a traditionalist at heart. He sat there reminiscing, lost in memories, struggling to understand where he had gone wrong. He was vastly more cosmopolitan than an average Indian father; his interests were wide ranging, his activism in the human rights field admirable. He was the president of the All-India Human Rights Watch, an organization he had launched to highlight and combat persistent social problems of Punjab. He believed in going to the grassroots and was recruiting members in villages where female foeticide, abuse of women and police repression are common. But in some essential way, he represented his generation, its expectations and desires. He could not have lived comfortably with an unmarried daughter were she to decide never to get married. Few Indian fathers can.

Col. Pandher arranged for twenty-five thousand rupees quickly and called Bhupinder to go ahead with the honeymoon. He also arranged for an expensive hotel room for the couple, thinking he was doing all this for Tikka's happiness. They stayed in Goa for about five days and returned to Ludhiana to start their life together. It was a new challenge for both and it had to be faced. Tikka walked into the company flat Bhupinder had in the bustling city but was struck by its starkness. There was an empty feeling to the whole place. No signs of welcome, no flowers, nothing to suggest that he had thought even a bit about making her feel at home. There was hardly any furniture in the house. He had removed most of it and deposited it in his parents' house in Moga, perhaps in anticipation of the new things he was going to get in his dowry.

'There wasn't even a chair to sit on. She called me and I hired a Sumo and rushed to Ludhiana with some chairs and a table,' Col. Pandher remembered. He did not complain but counted it as a second warning. 'I had given Bhupinder three lakh rupees in cash to buy furniture and a car. He was soon telling me that the money wasn't enough.' Then, at the end of March, just a month after the wedding, Col. Pandher got a call from Bhupinder asking that he immediately come to Ludhiana.

'Something is wrong,' he said mysteriously, leaving Tikka's father breathless with worry. Col. Pandher rushed to Ludhiana, a three-hour drive on a good day, and knocked on the door. Tikka was surprised to see him, she didn't know he was coming because her husband hadn't bothered to inform her. But once she saw her father, she couldn't help herself. It all came tumbling out. 'She told me he wanted a bigger car, not the Maruti 800 for which I had already given him the cash at the wedding. We hadn't talked about the Mitsubishi or Honda. It was up to me what I wanted to give and what I could afford to give.'

She broke down and told her father how badly Bhupinder treated her. Whenever he talked to her, it was about dowry and what else her father could supply them. She found all the talk of dowry cheap and demeaning. She couldn't understand why he was so obsessed. He was demanding a second air conditioner – she had already brought one in her dowry. It wasn't her family's responsibility to fulfil every outrageous demand. They hadn't signed on to take Bhupinder as a 'dependent', she thought. Besides, where was *his* pride? Didn't it demean him to ask? But whenever she tried to talk to him, he snubbed her brutally. Then, when she became quiet to save herself from another harangue, he complained how she didn't talk to him. Slowly it was becoming chillingly clear to her that they had very different values. Their families were different, their upbringing poles apart. In fact, they hardly shared any interest. She also had the nagging feeling that he felt inferior to her in some way. She came from a more liberal, urban background having lived in many different parts of the country on various army postings. She had even studied abroad. She had gone to Britain for her MSc and worked towards her PhD. Bhupinder's parents had always lived in Moga and hardly travelled outside Punjab. It was clear he wanted to assert himself, compensate for his small-town background and show that he was boss. His behaviour reflected the worst in male aggressiveness.

In Punjab, men talk blithely about settling scores violently, be it a land dispute or a personal problem. Land grabbing has even led to NRIs hiring professional hitmen to get rid of rival claimants. During my trip to research Tikka Preet's story, I listened to several conversations at social gatherings where violence lurked in the backdrop. Prominent Chandigarh citizens held forth on the 'necessity' for quick action, calmly justifying their proclivities on their very 'nature' on the one hand and police inefficiency on the other. 'We are Jat Sikhs. We can't brook any nonsense,' was a common explanation. If it was not land, it was women. A Chandigarh journalist covering the city told me that it was common for sangeet ceremonies in and around Chandigarh to end in a physical fight. She had witnessed several herself. 'It is always about women and how someone looked at someone else's woman the wrong way,' she said. The Chandigarh police are on high alert every Valentine's Day and deployed in force all along the 'gheri route' where young men come to ogle at girls.

In the heady cocktail of prosperity, machismo, cultural sanction for aggression, drop the modern-day obsession with cars and it is a volatile mix. Chandigarh boasts of the highest car to people ratio in the country. For its nine lakh citizens, there are five lakh cars on the streets. Mercedes Benz has recorded some of its highest sales in the city while Ludhiana and Jalandhar are not far behind. The city administration and the police, weary of young men looking for 'action', do not allow 'late night' joints to stay open beyond 11 p.m. to avoid damage from drunken fights. A newly opened disco in Chandigarh decided not to serve alcohol at all.

Bhupinder wanted a big car, not the Maruti 800 which was considered downmarket. Col. Pandher listened quietly, wondering what he should do to help. He suggested to both of them to be calm and try to adjust to each other's personalities. After all, marriage was a compromise from beginning to end whether it was a love match or arranged by parents. He drove back with a heavy heart, his third trip to Ludhiana in two months. He had taken his pregnant daughter-in-law with him so she could give Tikka some comfort. But he had to bear his grief alone. His wife had left for the US for her cancer treatment shortly after Tikka's wedding. Besides, he didn't want to burden her with too many details of things gone wrong. Yet he needed support and counsel of a family member. He could not bear to see Tikka unhappy, but he had faith, the misplaced faith of many Indian parents, that things would work out.

It only got worse. Bhupinder treated Tikka as if she were an irritating fly, which needed to be swatted now and then. He demanded absolute subservience and when she resisted he got abusive. But resist she did. She had the spirit. It had been just a few months since she got married and she wanted to give it a chance. He laid down a hundred rules – sit here, not there, don't sit with the lights on, don't watch television, don't wear those colours, don't drive my car, don't sit in the verandah. She felt suffocated. It was as if she were in a dark tunnel and however much she tried she couldn't get out. When she rebelled, there was an ugly fight. Once she said that she was getting bored sitting at home and perhaps she could join a computer course. 'You need brains for that. Do you have brains?' he yelled. Tikka was crushed. Here was a woman who had topped in her BSc in agriculture from Ludhiana, had gone on a scholarship to Britain and had worked towards her PhD. She didn't need a certificate from him in the brains department.

'Can you imagine? Here we asked Tikka's opinion on everything, consulted her because she was such a mature person. She had so much dignity. There she was insulted like an illiterate. It was like she went from our home to hell,' Col. Pandher recalled, his eyes glistening and his voice choking with anger. Bewildered and helpless, Tikka thought she would seek her mother-in-law's help since Bhupinder was always calling her anyway. She trusted Bhupinder's parents, thinking they were decent, regular folk who happened to have a son with problems. She decided to confide in Parminder about Bhupinder's temper and his strange, secretive world. She thought she might learn something valuable and gain insights into his personality. But instead of a sympathetic ear, she got betrayal. Parminder promptly went and told her son that Tikka thought he was 'crazy'. Infuriated that she had gone behind his back, he took it out on her. It was a verbal lynching. Tikka slowly and painfully began to understand Parminder's game – it was her clever, manipulative, greedy mother-in-law who was running the show, guiding Bhupinder at every step. Not that it made him less guilty in her eyes but she saw the patterns more clearly.

The issue of the car was raked up often singeing whatever there was of the relationship. Col. Pandher told Bhupinder in no uncertain terms that he couldn't afford a Mitsubishi but Tikka was welcome to take her Zen over to Ludhiana which he had bought for her just a few months ago. Bhupinder reluctantly agreed. He made a good bargain – he not only got a car but also kept the cash Col. Pandher had given him for the very purpose at the time of the wedding.

Winter turned to summer and the heat slowly became oppressive. So did Tikka's existence. Should she walk out and not even give her marriage a year to work? She didn't want to be rash, now that she had taken the plunge. But Tikka was living like a prisoner in her own home. She had been barred from using the telephone, lest she call her father or the police. When Col. Pandher found out, he bought her a mobile phone. But Bhupinder would hide even that. He had turned their new home into the same joyless space he had grown up in – no friends ever dropped by, hardly anyone called. There was no laughter, no parties to attend, nothing to celebrate. When Bhupinder called anyone, he shut the bedroom door on Tikka so she won't hear anything. He locked himself in even to balance his cheque book. His wife was an intrusion, an interruption in the paranoid world he inhabited.

He had a Godrej almirah which he always kept locked. When Tikka asked why she couldn't use it, he said: 'I have kept my first wife's things in here. I even have a son.' It was as if Tikka fell from a high-rise. She tried to mumble something but the shock had numbed her. She choked on her own words, shouting and crying in anger. No response seemed adequate and he simply laughed at her misery. He told her they lived in Mumbai. She knew he had been posted to Mumbai with his company but no one had mentioned anything about a previous marriage. She didn't know if he was being sadistic or telling the truth. She called her father and told him about the latest kaand. Her life was becoming tragically episodic like Sita's in the epic. Col. Pandher was at a loss for words and didn't know how to comfort his daughter. He contacted Bhupinder's parents in Moga but they vehemently denied everything, saying it was a sinister plot to malign them. Surely, their enemies were spreading lies about their son.

But Bhupinder soon began getting violent. In the second week of August, six months after their marriage, he turned Tikka out of the house. She told her father the saddest thing he was to hear from his child's mouth: Bhupinder had beaten her. He had shoved and pushed her around, pulled her hair and hit her. Once he had even rammed her against the bedpost. Another time, when he seemed to have lost all control, she somehow managed to lock herself in the bathroom to escape the blows. Now he had thrown her out of the house with a warning that she could come back only if she brought more money.

This was unacceptable to Col. Pandher. Physical abuse? It didn't happen in his family and he wasn't going to tolerate it. He had never raised his hand on his children and this brutish treatment of his daughter just pierced his heart. He decided to call Bhupinder's parents for a meeting to tell them that their son had crossed the line. He asked them to come to Ludhiana and they all met in August. The meeting was held at a local community centre to maintain a sense of neutrality. Not much was achieved at the communal meeting except that lines were clearly drawn. Col. Pandher said with folded hands that he would not tolerate violence against his daughter, come what may. Bhupinder must respect certain basic norms of civilized behaviour and restrain his temper. After all, he was educated and an executive. Did it behove a young man to descend to such depths no matter what the provocation?

Bhupinder, for his part, unleashed a litany of complaints against Tikka, mostly of a petty, niggling nature. But to him they were slights to his large ego. 'She doesn't get up when I walk in. She doesn't offer me a cup of tea. She is watching TV all the time. She doesn't talk to me,' and so on. When it was Tikka's turn, she said he was violent, demanding and temperamental. She talked about the physical abuse and beatings. His violent behaviour dominated the meeting, not the dowry demands. Col. Pandher wanted to draw the line and tell him clearly that physical abuse simply had to end. After being challenged to confess the truth, Bhupinder did admit that he tended to go into a rage. 'I don't know what happens to me when I am angry,' he said in front of all the relatives.

'Then maybe you should go to a counseller,' Col. Pandher suggested. There was no shame in admitting one's problems and facing them squarely.

'Why should he go to a doctor? He is not mad. She is so rude to him. She even abused him,' Bhupinder's mother jumped in. Parminder was at her schoolmarmish best, hectoring and lecturing her audience. Tikka had called Bhupinder a haraamzada once as she tried to defend herself against his blows. Parminder deftly used the occasion to remind one and all that Tikka had actually abused her in essence. No matter that Tikka had little else to defend herself with. Physically she was no match for him, he towered over her petite frame. When he was in a rage, he seemed even bigger.

Bhupinder was unrepentant. At the meeting meant to reconcile the two sides, he bragged about being a 'terror' in his office and how he kept everyone in line.

'But why are you being one at home?' Col. Pandher tried to ask but he had no patience for the question.

'I don't know what he is made of. He thought no end of himself. Nothing that anyone said made any difference,' the dejected father told me. The meeting ended but there was no commitment from Bhupinder's side to improve his behaviour. He was defensive and belligerent. His parents were far from constructive – they didn't want to acknowledge their son's problems. To admit Bhupinder had a problem would be tantamount to admitting their own failure as parents. Besides, they were the boy's side, they were not required to bend. A thousand aggressions are forgiven a husband and this was just the beginning. Col. Pandher didn't raise the dowry demands because the issue of violence and abuse was more immediate. But nothing constructive was achieved and the meeting ended in bickering.

Col. Pandher had gone to Ludhiana with hope but he came back feeling depressed and anxious. He wasn't sure about Tikka's physical safety. He jumped every time the phone rang, fearing the worst. Still trying the sane approach, he suggested that they write each other's good and bad points and then try to emphasize only the good. But it seemed hopeless. The more he suggested counselling, therapy or other means of battling old demons, the more defensive Bhupinder got. Such ideas were an assault on his very manhood. He did not believe in this namby pamby, pop psycho nonsense. It was outside his ken and he wasn't bothered about widening his horizons.

Tikka was in Chandigarh, trying to understand the nightmare she had walked into. 'Bhupinder did not make even a little effort to get along. I wanted that their compatibility should increase and they should sit across the table and sort out their differences,' Col. Pandher would remember later. After one of Bhupinder's violent outbursts, even Ishpreet tried to intervene all the way from New Jersey, pleading with him to treat Tikka better. 'I tried to make him understand that she feels wronged and belittled but he didn't want to listen at all. He was argumentative and just kept harping about his petty complaints,' said Ishpreet later. 'I spoke to Gugu (Tikka's pet name) briefly and she was crying bitterly. I will never forget what she told me at the time. She said, "Ainhe to mainu kamla kar chadyaa hai (He has turned me mad)." '

Tikka went back to Ludhiana in late August after a two-week separation to try to give her marriage another try. It had only been six months since she had got married. Her father and family elders had persuaded her to return to her husband and she had agreed. Even though she was reluctant she knew she would be blamed for the failed marriage, not him. There was no space for truth in those pronouncements, they were made with such brutal casualness. It was the law of the jungle.

No sooner had Tikka set foot in the flat, Bhupinder assailed her with the same dowry demands. It was the same old refrain, no change of tune. She wrote to her father:

Dear Papa,

This is a quick note from me to say that all is not well here. After meeting his parents and making all sorts of promises, his behaviour still remains unchanged. He continues to threaten me by shouting and even raising his hand. I don't know what is to become of my future. I can only hope and pray that he improves.

Lots of love,
Gugu

Tikka also talked to some of her friends in Ludhiana and Chandigarh, confiding in them about how terribly wrong her marriage had gone. How he would slap her and shove her around. How Bhupinder would call his mother every time there was a fight in the house and complain to her. He showed signs of paranoia. She wanted signs of remorse. She just wanted to know if he had missed her even a little while she was gone. When she asked him if he felt he had wronged her, he said 'not at all'. She began to feel there was no space for a compromise. She didn't really figure in his world, except as a caretaker and a source of expensive gifts. She soon wrote to her father again. The letter was dated 4 September:

Dear Papa,

I am writing to you in a great hurry. Bhupinder is still being difficult. He continues to get violent every now and then and at the smallest of excuses. He does not let me talk at all. I open my mouth to say something, he snubs me back very rudely. Life is very unbearable with him. No matter how hard I try he is never happy. But is always finding faults and goes on expecting more.

I will pen off.

Bye,
Gugu

Barely a month had gone by when Tikka was forced to leave again after another awful episode. But she wasn't allowed to take her clothes, her purse, not even her driver's license. He told her, 'Go to your father. If you want to come back remember we have to buy a big car.' She had hidden some money away fearing the worst and now the worst was here. She took the bus to Chandigarh and told her father that he had beaten her the night before. Col. Pandher hugged his daughter but couldn't help crying at his misfortune. He had had such aspirations for her. She was the bright spark in the family. 'I felt she had something in her . . . she would shine no matter where she went. I wanted her to study further and complete her PhD. We tried to put this behind us.'

In the eight months or so since her marriage, Tikka had been through a lot. She had to flee so many times from her husband's house she began regretting the decision to marry. She tried to pick up the pieces, but she was a broken woman. She rejoined her office and tried to maintain a dignified front. There was no self-pity, no bursting into tears. It was as if she had been put to a tough test and moved on, a little wiser, a little quieter, a little more cynical. Her office colleagues welcomed her warmly. It was good to know that at least they had missed her greatly. She was one of the best trainers at the institute and her students loved her. But they could see she wasn't the same person. Something in her had vanished as if sapped from the very source. She seemed withdrawn. She managed to pass the day somehow, breaking it into hours, prolonging her tasks. But in the evenings she felt an awful void, a vacuum that only grew bigger. She didn't know where to go, how to fill that long twilight zone. She felt she had failed in the most important test – her marriage.

Zoya Randhawa told me how Tikka still could not bring herself to totally condemn her husband and his family. She wasn't brought up that way. 'Not everyone is like him. He just turned out to be a problem,' she would say while counselling her students not to paint everyone with the same brush. Not all marriages turn out badly. She found the dowry dispute puzzling at best. How can you go on asking someone for things? Weren't they embarrassed begging, she would wonder.

Then the threatening phone calls began. Bhupinder started calling Tikka in Chandigarh to berate her on some pretext or another. She didn't tell her father too many details for fear of burdening him. She had told her father once after his repeated visits to Ludhiana, 'Papa, I don't want you to fold your hands in front of such people. It hurts me a lot.' Whenever Bhupinder called, she would tell her father not to worry. But she herself was clearly worried. Col. Pandher wanted some kind of rapprochement for he couldn't foresee Tikka being on her own all her life. He sent feelers and some came from the other side. Bhupinder's parents came down to Chandigarh to talk to Col. Pandher to see if something could be worked out. But their demands were the same – another air conditioner and a bigger car. Col. Pandher said flatly that he couldn't afford to give another car.

He asked his daughter in private whether there was any hope of reconciliation and she said no. She did not want to go back to a man who had no respect for her. He then decided that separation and a divorce were unavoidable. He told Karamjit and Parminder that everything should be worked out amicably and that it was God's will. They seemed inclined not to make a fuss. He told them that they should return Tikka's dowry, including the jewellery and they agreed. They asked him to send them a list, saying they had no intention of keeping 'even a pin' from his house.

Tikka had resumed her life in Chandigarh but Bhupinder's frequent phone calls often shattered the shell she carefully created around her. She grappled the depression and confusion. He would scold her, even taunt her on the phone. She tried to keep busy with her work at ITFT, the institute being her refuge and her students her source of happiness. She took over the running of the house once again since her mother was still in the US for treatment. She tried to rebuild her sense of worth but it wasn't easy. Her father hinted sometimes that she should try to patch up. 'I thought separation might have created a place in his heart for Tikka. No parent wants his child to be alone,' he recounted later. He would discuss everything with his wife and son Ishpreet in New Jersey to try to figure the best way forward. He needed all the help to tackle the mountain of trouble his daughter was facing. 'My son said that in today's world divorce was okay. Our aim should be Tikka's happiness. Even my daughter-in-law said we should keep Tikka happy and she couldn't be happy there. I would keep quiet and listen,' he remembered.

Tikka went to Ludhiana in November 2000 to see if there was any way the two could begin again. She went on the pretext of collecting letters that had come from her university in the UK. Even though the envelope was lying right there, Bhupinder didn't let her take it. He said, 'You can get the letter when you get all your other things back.' He showed no sign that he was happy to see her. It was as if he had never missed her or even known she was gone. She came back despondent. When her father asked if she could live with him, she replied: 'No, Papa, never. I can't stay with him even for a day.' She began preparing the list of dowry items since her father hardly remembered or knew the details of the wedding transactions. Her mother had handled everything but she wasn't there to help. It was an onerous task but Tikka did it. Col. Pandher sent a polite letter, the dowry list and divorce papers prepared by a lawyer and friend, Anil Pal Singh Shergill.

The packet was sent to Bhupinder's parents in Moga on 17 January 2001 by courier to avoid any delay or confusion. The marriage hadn't lasted even a year. Karamjit called a couple of days later to complain about the list, claiming it was exaggerated. 'He said the jewellery was in Ludhiana and that only his son knew because he used to keep it.' He promised to consult Bhupinder who had been posted to New Delhi in the meantime and call back. But instead of hearing from the father, Tikka heard from the son. Bhupinder called and threatened her. 'What jewellery, which jewellery?' he shouted on the phone. She didn't know how to react but she was clearly frightened. He was denying there was any jewellery in his possession.

Tikka brooded a lot about her things – they were her precious possessions lovingly collected over the years. Besides what use were her mementos, her schoolgirl photographs, her letters, her clothes to them? She had taken her whole life to her new house and that was a mistake. That house never became her home. She couldn't understand their logic, no matter how much she tried to rationalize their behaviour. They were greedy, or else why would Bhupinder confiscate her jewellery on the very first day?

'She started going down. She seemed preoccupied and quiet. Her bua would tell her not to worry. Divorce is not a problem these days. You should make your life and marry again, she would tell her,' Col. Pandher recalled. But Tikka was not really listening. In her mind, Bhupinder's threats rang louder. 'I will fix you and your family if you try to get too smart,' he had yelled. It was after the dowry list was sent that his behaviour really changed. Bhupinder got 'ferocious' on the phone, using foul language and violent threats. He may not have wanted to return the jewellery worth several lakhs. He may have already sold it, no one knew. Karamjit was to claim later in an interview that he never got the list although he acknowledged receiving Col. Pandher's letter and the divorce papers.

'Tikka beta, take some milk and get ready,' Col. Pandher tried to wake up her daughter. She turned and went back to sleep. It was as if she did not want to face the world. The world meant his horrible phone calls and having to put up a brave front for people. She was just tired. She couldn't handle being the strong one any more. She wanted to be taken care of, coddled and protected. She had been standing upright for too long – through her mother's debilitating illness, her father's struggle against her in-laws, her own hellish ordeal in Ludhiana and against a callous and brutal husband. She wanted to double over and say 'no more'. Enough hardship for a lifetime. She was tired of being the good one. She didn't want to do her computer classes or her GRE course. She just didn't. It didn't make sense. She felt uninspired, even defeated. She somehow managed to carry on with her job at the institute but that's about it. She went to the office finally, she had to or she would sink further into depression.

Col. Pandher remembers clearly when the phone rang that night. It was the evening of 28 January 2001 and they had had dinner. Tikka answered it and she was on the phone for more than forty minutes. When he asked whether it was Bhupinder, she nodded. Her face was white with worry and she didn't look herself. 'When I persisted, she just said he was an "idiot". Don't worry I will sort it out.' She went to sleep that night, but her father could see she was frightened about something. She wouldn't tell him anything more.

'The next morning when I got up she was already gone. She had told the servant that she had to return some books at her office. She didn't even have breakfast,' the father recalled, each detail painfully fresh in his mind. 'We would always try to have breakfast together before going off for work. That was our routine.' But that day she hadn't bothered about the niceties and had just left. 'I got worried because of what had happened the night before. Something didn't seem right and I called her office. I told them to call me as soon as she reached. They called after twenty minutes or so to say she still hadn't reached the office.' He called his sister who lived nearby and asked her to come immediately.

Dark thoughts crept through his mind. Maybe she had gone to Ludhiana. Maybe Bhupinder had asked her to do something when he had called the night before. Maybe she was meeting him at that very moment. After all he used to come to Chandigarh often. Col. Pandher got into his car and drove to the bus stand looking for Tikka's Zen but there was no sign. He then drove to the gurdwara she used to visit sometimes and even to her office. But she was nowhere. Then his mobile rang and his sister told him Tikka had returned home. Just as suddenly as she disappeared.

Tikka was sitting in the drawing room when he got back. She looked pale and drawn. Her back was slumped a little; her hands rested on her thighs. She didn't respond when he called her, his voice left hanging in the air. He sat down next to her and held her hand. He tried to comfort her, but she was lost somewhere where voices didn't sound, they just evaporated. She tried to mumble something but the words were garbled. Then suddenly her whole body convulsed and she rushed to the bathroom. Col. Pandher could hear her tiny sobs, the pain wrenching her body, but she wouldn't open the door. With great difficulty she let her aunt in. Col. Pandher knew then that something awful had happened.

He rushed Tikka to Inscol Hospital as fast as he could, but the poison was seeping even faster. It was a race of Hades. They waited outside the operation theatre while the doctors struggled to bring her back but her insides already were burnt raw. When the doctor asked if she had taken Celphos, she raised her index finger to indicate she had taken one tablet. It was a strong pesticide commonly available in Chandigarh's grain market. She died at 1.40 p.m. on 29 January, a month short of her first wedding anniversary.

In order to reconstruct Tikka Preet's story, I went to Chandigarh to meet her father and some of her friends to learn more about her and why she was compelled to take her life. Col. Pandher was still in a state of shock and disbelief as he gathered his thoughts and resources to fight the case. It was July 2001, when I first met him, and we met a few times subsequently. He had already registered a case of dowry death, abetment to suicide and cruelty against Bhupinder under sections 304 (B), 306 and 498 (A) of the Indian Penal Code. The preliminaries were in progress. Soon after the case was filed, Bhupinder had disappeared while his lawyer tried to procure anticipatory bail. His bail was refused at all levels of the judiciary – from the sessions court to the Punjab and Haryana High Court to the Supreme Court of India – and he was declared a 'proclaimed offender'. He surrendered in early July and was lodged in the Model Jail in Chandigarh at the time.

Col. Pandher told me his painful story, difficult though it was to recount. He struck me as a gentle soul, gracious and helpful but with a will of steel. He wanted justice for his daughter. He had vowed to fight until the end. 'I am not going to leave him. I know my daughter won't come back but I will ruin him,' he told me, his eyes shining in anger. 'I will go on because justice is my mission now. We have two choices: either we can sit back or we can raise our voices. I can say, nothing will happen and carry on. But a happy slave is the worst enemy of freedom. If a man doesn't oppose injustice, he is part of the crime. It will be my "do paise ka" contribution.'

But sometimes he would talk of how his wife wanted him to move on and leave the case to the lawyers and the courts. He had turned sixty-three that year but age sat well on him. He was working a full day looking after his real estate business, his work as president of the All-India Human Rights Watch, his educational charity in his village in Punjab and a scholarship programme for orphan girls. I felt he gave me an accurate account of the events, neither embellishing nor diminishing the real story. He never tried to hide the fact that he had wanted the couple to reconcile until the end. After five days in Chandigarh and talking to Col. Pandher extensively, I felt I knew him well and his daughter too.

I also met Shergill, Tikka's lawyer friend, who was to appear as a prosecution witness in her case. He was angry with Tikka for committing suicide and running away from the world. 'If only she had told me in time that this was happening to her, I would have been able to help her.' He said it was a personal battle for him to fight Tikka's case and help her father on the long road ahead. He was preparing in earnest for the case, brushing up his criminal law, ordering new books and harnessing his energies. He was pitched against Rajinder Singh Cheema, a senior advocate and one of the best criminal lawyers in the area, whom Bhupinder had employed.

The more I heard about Tikka, the more I felt I knew her. She seemed like an unusual woman, someone who rode the roller coaster of life with dignity and self-assurance. She was independent minded but not strident, confident but not uppity, forthright but not aggressive. She had calmly stayed single until the age of twenty-nine in an environment where marriage, money and machismo are essential ingredients of life. She wasn't necessarily defying a tradition. She didn't oppose marriage per se but nor did she feel the compulsion most Indian women do under their parents' constant reminders. And lest anyone think there was something 'wrong' with her in terms of looks or health, just the contrary. Tikka was a good-looking woman, and very accomplished.

Her professors in the UK wrote to her regularly, asking her to come back and complete her PhD which she had left midway. She hadn't enjoyed living in Britain – it seemed too impersonal and cold. She felt an underlying racism she detested. She was in Reading, not exactly the hub of cosmopolitanism.

Her father told me a story of how she once brought a sick horse to the house from somewhere in Chandigarh to nurse it back to health. A dog or a cat is one thing, but a horse? Her parents were taken aback, worrying about who the owner might be. It turned out to be a police horse and a victim of neglect. Injured and stray dogs were common in the household, thanks to Tikka and her frequent visits to the local SPCA office. I also spoke to several neighbours who occasionally dropped into Col. Pandher's house to sit with him, give him courage to carry on. They remembered Tikka with great fondness, and it wasn't something borne out of necessity of having to condole a close friend in grief. They were genuine in their praise. An elderly gentleman who had known the family for decades said she would come regularly to his house to spend time with him and chat a little because all his children had moved away from Chandigarh.

'She had a strong nursing instinct and a very large heart. No one looked after sick people with as much selfless dedication as she did. If anyone was feeling low, she would try to cheer them up – sometimes at her own cost,' recalled Ishpreet. She took charge of her grandfather and even her mother's elderly buaji in their last days, caring for them. When one of their mother's school friends was diagnosed with ovarian cancer, Tikka arranged for her surgery, blood from the blood bank and took over the responsibility because her own husband was too shocked to deal with the crisis. Even two days before she took the drastic step, she was on the phone for hours to help one of Ishpreet's friends in New Jersey find his family in Ahmedabad which had just been struck by a devastating earthquake. To break her soaring spirit, to thwart her almost missionary zeal to serve others seems near impossible but it did happen. It happened slowly over an eleven-month period when she was Mrs Tikka Preet Gill.

I also went to Moga to meet Bhupinder's parents to listen to their side of the story. The contrast between the two families couldn't have been starker. If Tikka's family was a haven of love for the two children, Bhupinder's family was seeped in tension. Karamjit and Parminder Gill were extremely suspicious of my intentions and purpose. They had difficulty believing that I was just doing research for a book and not attempting to bury them deeper in the pile of trouble already facing them. They reluctantly agreed to meet me at their house but only after throwing me off the scent many times. They wanted to know exactly how I found their telephone number. When I said a reporter friend had given it to me, they wanted to know his name and address. I knew it was the psyche of the besieged but I felt a little concerned. Finally, we agreed to meet and I travelled to Moga by taxi. I was supposed to meet them around 5 p.m. and I must admit I was a bit nervous.

Over the past five days I had heard many stories about the Wild West nature of the Punjab countryside from local journalists and friends, especially about cases involving money, property and women. But I was relying on my old familiarity with one of my favourite states – I had been to Punjab several times as a journalist to cover the Sikh militancy in the 1980s. Although one was covering a grim story and there was a danger of random bomb blasts, one had felt safe. The hospitality and friendliness of the average

Punjabi was etched in my mind. For my trip to Moga, I found a driver who had taken me around on an assignment many years ago. I told myself that some chivalrous Sardarji would save me if I got into trouble and carried on.

I rang the bell at the Gill residence a few minutes after the appointed time. The solid iron gate painted red looked forbidding. But it opened after a few minutes and I was ushered into the living room. Karamjit and Parminder were civil but clearly bewildered by my presence. They asked me to sit down before giving me a quick but thorough look-over. The room had a divan, a two-seater sofa and two chairs – simple, basic furniture with no frills. The walls were mostly bare but for a rare frame hanging listlessly. The living room opened to the dining hall, which led to the bedrooms. One could catch occasional glimpses of a female figure moving quietly about, preparing the evening dinner. We sat down and I explained the purpose of my visit. They seemed uncomfortable about the whole thing and it took some time to convince them to talk. For them, any stranger those days was a potential spy from the other side.

We were soon talking about the tragedy of Tikka's suicide and the case against Bhupinder. First it was just Karamjit and Parminder but soon their eldest son joined us. They sat on three different sides of me, creating a chorus of voices, which I found overwhelming after some time. For the next three hours, I listened to them, trying to interpret the innuendoes and decipher the barbs. I let them do most of the talking because after about twenty minutes or so I realized that it was pointless to ask questions. They simply ignored them. They had a story to tell and they didn't brook any interruptions. I felt they were not talking *to* me but *at* me, sometimes all three at the same time. They were clearly worried about Bhupinder and how the whole thing had spun out of control. Parminder talked most of the time while Karamjit, sitting opposite me on the divan, mostly stared at me as if trying to read my mind. It was an uncomfortable feeling and it seemed as if I was on trial for a while.

Parminder, a forceful lady of considerable resonance, had small dark brown eyes. Her hair was tied in a simple bun and one could see a few grey stragglers peeking through. Medium height, medium built – she looked like any average lady in Punjab. She wore a brown salwar-kurta with a matching dupatta. But when she started speaking the illusion of normalcy was shattered. She was not an average mama going about her business of home and hearth but a woman with her back to the wall. For her the world was divided into friends and enemies, but mostly enemies. Fighting back was second nature to her, running to courts a habit. She had stood sternly beside Karamjit throughout his tormented life of lawsuits and family wars, egging him on, advising him, interpreting moves and plotting counter moves. She had never lacked for initiative. Even her school job had been a tool to exercise control over teachers and students.

Asha Dhillon, the principal of Summerfield School, told me that Parminder Gill was a woman of formidable resources and cunning. Unbeknownst to Mrs Dhillon, and taking advantage of her disabled leg, Parminder ran the school by fiat, threatening teachers, intimidating staff and spreading canards about those she disliked. She had won Mrs Dhillon's confidence by making herself useful but she abused the trust. 'I can tell you ten good things about her but I had to let her go because she was becoming more and more powerful. She took advantage of me after all the love and affection I gave her,' Mrs Dhillon recalled. 'She took full advantage of the fact that I couldn't climb stairs after my accident. I didn't realize what was happening in the school until recently. She had a psychological hold even on me.' Painful as it was to confess that she had been duped, Mrs Dhillon was brutally honest while recalling her long association with Parminder.

Mrs Dhillon asked Parminder to leave the school after it was revealed that she was leaking papers to children who took private tuition from her. No one knows how long it had been going on but Mrs Dhillon discovered the scam in early 2001 after some parents alerted her. The intricate web of deceit at the school was finally torn and Parminder was unceremoniously ousted. This happened around the same time that her son Bhupinder was charged in the case of Tikka's suicide. She sent messages back to Mrs Dhillon through intermediaries that she would 'ruin' the school after she settled her son's problems.

'She made a good friend but would make a very bad enemy,' Mrs Dhillon said after recalling many anecdotes of Parminder's cunning. How she kept the teachers in line by constantly dangling the sword of lay-offs over their heads. How the accounts never squared when she was handling them. How Mrs Dhillon would receive anonymous letters if ever she questioned Parminder on any of her decisions. How Parminder was spotted going through the cupboards in Mrs Dhillon's room.

The most unnerving story was about how Parminder once suggested to Mrs Dhillon to hold on to the 'love letters' they had discovered in the school to use as a potential weapon against the children who had written them. Discovery of love notes in a co-ed school is about as normal as finding wood in a carpenter's shed but for Parminder, the adolescent jottings represented a tactical advantage – something she sought in every aspect of life.

I got a taste of her single-mindedness in my three-hour meeting. She talked almost without a break telling me how Col. Pandher had ruined her son's career with his 'false allegations'. She would raise her hands up in the air in a gesture of despair and then suddenly drop them. Her voice would swell in a crescendo taking her audience with it and then fall with a thud. In that short journey, she would travel the range of emotions – anger, resentment, sadness and frustration. She began her story with a testimonial of sorts. 'My other daughter-in-law has been with us for nine years with no problem.'

But when I asked if I could talk to her, all three refused instantly. Persistence didn't work with the Gills and after a point I gave up, thinking they may shut me out completely if I showed too much interest in the other daughter-in-law. She would have had valuable insights into what happened. She didn't enter the room even once during the time I was there but I could see a thin young woman moving about the dining room. I assumed it was the elder daughter-in-law.

Bhupinder's parents gave a stout defence of their son, saying the whole case was fabricated to torment them. 'But no one is ready to listen to us. He (Col. Pandher) is the head of Human Rights so whatever he says is the God's own truth,' Parminder said, sarcasm dripping from her voice. Their contention was that Tikka hardly stayed with Bhupinder and rarely came to Moga so the question of her harassment didn't arise. She barely spent any time for anyone to mistreat her. It is Col. Pandher who was at the root of the problem. Under his tutelage, Tikka began to rebel against Bhupinder. 'The father was creating the trouble,' Parminder said. 'Seventy per cent of the time she lived with her father. No one is probing that aspect because he is an ex-army officer.'

Tikka, according to them, just didn't like living in Ludhiana and wanted to return to Chandigarh to her job. 'Why she was attracted to Chandigarh, we don't know,' Parminder said with her arms going up in the air, leaving the idea hanging mysteriously in the air. She and her son implied repeatedly that it was Tikka's father who was responsible for the marriage going sour while denying any suggestion that they demanded more dowry.

'Arre ji, why should we ask for anything? We earn first class and live first class,' she said, her voice getting louder than before. When I asked about the three lakh rupees in cash, it was as if I had uttered a blasphemy and polluted the air. There was first an outburst of disbelief and then Parminder came on: 'What three lakhs are you talking about? To whom did he (Col. Pandher) give the three lakhs? We never heard anything. We only asked that our baraat should be entertained. Nothing else. We come from a good background. We don't need to ask for anything.'

The absolute denial left me speechless. They were dismissing even a hint of a problem between the couple, any acrimony over dowry demands. According to them, it was all a creation of Col. Pandher's fertile imagination. But it was a logical strategy for them to adopt. Their son was charged with multiple counts of harassment and abetment to suicide. The last thing they would do is to confess there was any truth to the charges, experienced litigants that they were. Instead, they would muddy the waters, create suspicions, cast new aspersions and try to defuse the case.

I listened carefully, trying to look for clues. The excessive drama in Parminder's retelling of the story made me uncomfortable. Her attempt to go on the offensive was strategic but she went a bit far when she implied that Tikka's father was behind her suicide. 'Divorce papers reached us on

19 January and she was dead on 29 January. Only her father knows what happened in the interim. He didn't even inform us.' Then at her most outlandish best, she suggested that Tikka might have been murdered. Of course, she offered no support for her claim. It was meant to raise a doubt in one's mind and I let it pass. I didn't tell her what Mrs Dhillon had recounted to me earlier about Parminder's family showing little or no remorse at Tikka's death.

Mrs Dhillon, alarmed at the news of Tikka's suicide, had rushed to Parminder's house in Moga to be with the family and offer condolences. She found Bhupinder pacing up and down looking worried. 'I gave him hell for not being there for Tikka and hanging on to his mother's apron strings. He was flustered,' she had told me. No one seemed to be grieving that Tikka had died, instead the family was getting into battle gear. They were suddenly vulnerable since Parminder, Karamjit and Bhupinder were all named in the FIR filed by Col. Pandher in Chandigarh. Karamjit had fought dozens of civil cases acting as his own lawyer and even won some but now he was accused in a criminal case. His son was at the centre of the allegations. He didn't know how to deal with this reversal of fortunes.

'We went underground,' Parminder told me matter of factly. Their nightmare had truly begun. They fled their home in Moga and took refuge in different homes around Punjab while trying to procure anticipatory bail. It must have been a harrowing time but they didn't want to discuss it. Instead, they wanted to tell me about how the police had ransacked Bhupinder's flat in Ludhiana during 'recovery' – a procedure of collecting dowry items from the matrimonial home. With her usual flourish and sense of drama, Parminder launched into a tirade against the police and how they only work for the girl's side.

'They took the sofas, they took the curtains, they took the mattresses, they took the air conditioners. They took away everything. If he (Col. Pandher) had said this suit is his (pointing to the clothes she was wearing), they would have taken it off me. You should go and see the condition of our Ludhiana house. It is empty as if Bhupinder didn't have even curtains before marriage. He had been running the house before. It is not like they gave us everything,' she continued. 'I will show them that the boy's side is also something to contend with. But if I cry, they say it is crocodile tears. We can't even cry. Everyone is on the girl's side. All these dowry laws are like unlicensed weapons in their hands.' She took a deep breath. She then told me that Tikka's letters from Ludhiana complaining about harassment were fabricated. But it was on the basis of the two letters produced by Col. Pandher that the sessions judge denied Bhupinder bail.

It was their word against Col. Pandher's but circumstantial evidence pointed towards dowry harassment and physical abuse. Besides, Tikka had talked about the dismal state of her marriage to several friends – another pointer that something was really wrong. But for his mother, there was no truth other than her own. Then Parminder suggested something truly bizarre as a way out. Her arms in the air and voice rising, she threw a challenge to Col. Pandher to go to the Golden Temple with her and 'confess' the real truth. 'Let him come there, face the Almighty and then say if we are responsible for Tikka's death. I am telling the truth and I know God will punish the rest in his own good time.' She repeated the challenge several times, working herself into a frenzy. It was as if she was already at the Golden Temple bathed in divine light and vindicated while her 'tormentor' was struck down.

I was a little taken aback at this sudden recourse to God. It was hard to swallow – a family that had spent a better part of their life in earthly courtrooms battling for pieces of land now sought divine intervention. I listened quietly and did not question them. Instead, I requested a meeting with Bhupinder who was lodged in jail. They agreed and promised to call me the next day in Chandigarh since they were going to meet him. I thanked them for their help. It was getting late and it was time to take their leave. I had to drive back from Moga to Chandigarh. When I got ready to say goodbye, they insisted that I go with them to Ludhiana to see the condition of Bhupinder's flat and how the police had ransacked it. I politely declined, saying I would do it some other day, time permitting. They walked me to the car – not because they wanted to ensure my safety but *theirs*. I was to discover later that they came out to the main road where the car was parked to take down the license plate number and see the face of the driver. It was a piece of information to be filed away to be used later against me.

I drove back with my head buzzing with Parminder's voice. It was not easy being harangued continuously for three hours. She was overbearing and even seemed a little manic. Perhaps any mother with a son in jail and her back to the wall might do the same. I didn't want to judge her motives but her demeanour struck me. She was in constant attack mode, no matter what the context. I felt relieved to be driving back to Chandigarh; it was nearly 11 p.m. I was exhausted but I couldn't help thinking how different the two families were and how ill-fated the marriage.

I waited the next day for their phone call so I could go and visit Bhupinder with them in jail. But no one called until 4 p.m. – the evening visiting hours in jail. I decided to take a chance and try my luck anyway. I asked an old friend to accompany me and drive me to the jail, which was on the outskirts of Chandigarh. A red-brick structure, it had an open feeling. Almost welcoming, I dare say. It is a model jail and Chandigarh authorities are rightfully proud of it. We walked in and saw hordes of family members waiting to see their relatives in jail. Packs of mangoes, buckets of milk, boxes of sweets – there was an army of flies attacking the bags of food they had brought to supplement the jail diet. Policemen checked each bag thoroughly, taking down the names of inmates for whom they were meant. Fathers and mothers fussed to ensure the right bags went to the right person. I spotted bricks of butter being delivered. It was Punjab after all. Even jailbirds ate well here.

I was frisked by a woman constable and let into the visitors' room. A cacophony of voices greeted me. It was a medium-sized room with a cage in the centre into which the prisoners were released. All around the cage sat relatives, friends, lawyers and well wishers, exchanging notes and defence strategies. There was hardly any light and one had to peer at the faces to recognize them. I spotted the familiar face of Karamjit and went over to explain my presence. They were in deep discussion with Bhupinder who sat behind the iron partition. Parminder was holding his hand through the lattice. I stood around waiting for them to finish, not wishing to disturb the family in their brief time together. They were obviously discussing details they didn't want any outsiders to hear. When I thought there was a break for an opening, I introduced myself and asked Bhupinder if he would mind talking to me. He seemed reluctant. I felt I was going to lose my chance so I asked some questions anyway. He got angry and told me I was asking 'leading questions'. He said I had to submit everything in writing to his father if I wanted his side of the story. I decided to leave before the situation spiralled out of control.

What was to follow was a lesson in real life. Next morning, Karamjit and his elder son turned up unannounced at a friend's house where I was staying. I was shocked to see them at the door since I had never given them the address. But they had tracked us down from the phone number and just decided to 'check' me out. Later, they landed up at the house of a fellow journalist to find out if I really was who I said I was. But they never showed up for the appointment they made with me to meet at a restaurant that day. I started to sense trouble since they were known to be habitual litigants. It was a matter of time before I would be named in some complaint or another.

Sure enough, a few days after I left Chandigarh, Col. Pandher was visited by the police because of a complaint filed by Karamjit who had accused him of 'hiring fake journalists' to harass his family. The letter claimed that my friends and I were working for Col. Pandher and had gone to Moga on his instructions to make trouble. Riddled with untruths and factual errors, it tried to impute motives where none existed. The complaint was frivolous to say the least but it was the logical step in the world according to Karamjit – attack before the other can and chances are you will benefit from being the first out there. However, the case against his son Bhupinder is a lot more serious and Karamjit and Parminder have a difficult road to travel. Small tactical moves may not be sufficient to win this one.

Curiously, the judge at the trial court ordered that charges against Bhupinder be framed under section 304 (B) for dowry death rather than under section 306 for abetment to suicide. The move surprised Col. Pandher and Shergill because Tikka had committed suicide after continuous harassment and torture. They were witnesses to her desperate act and they had never alleged that she was killed. Tikka's family didn't want to comment on this latest inexplicable twist in the case but it was clear that Bhupinder's lawyers were up to something. Since murder was never alleged, it cannot be proved. Does it mean Bhupinder will go free? No one can say at this stage for the court case may carry on for years.

If convicted under 304 (B), Bhupinder could get anywhere between seven years and a life sentence while the maximum punishment under 306 is ten years and a fine. Bhupinder has also been charged under 498 (A) for cruelty which carries the maximum of a three-year jail term and a fine. Since Tikka's death, Col. Pandher has suffered another tragic setback. His wife succumbed to cancer in the US after a prolonged battle. His only satisfaction – he was able to visit her one last time in the US while pursuing the case in Chandigarh.

Tikka gave her life in the mistaken belief that her parents might find peace if she removed herself from the equation. But there will be no peace for Col. Pandher for years to come as the trial gets underway. He will have to marshal his resources, gather his wits as he recounts the story of his daughter's brief marriage to the judges. One can only speculate about the phone call the night before Tikka committed suicide and what might have transpired between the couple. But what is clear is that she saw a future darkened by shadows of her past and no easy escape. Death seemed easier.

American Nightmare

Archana's Story

The exhaust fumes from jostling vehicles almost obscured the sprawling court complex as Archana strode along the busy streets of Bangalore. I could barely keep up with her or our conversation but that didn't stop me from admiring the young woman a few steps ahead of me. She walked purposefully, confidently into the world of black coats and white shirts, carrying a big bundle of case papers. Papers related to others' problems, others' headaches that she must help cure. It was her first week at the job and she was going through a predictable mix of anxiety and excitement. She was a small-town girl in the big city to make a new life.

Her short hair in a neat ponytail, her dupatta draped sensibly around her neck, Archana walked from one court building to another, trying to keep track of three cases that would come up within an hour of each other. She requested a judge to grant a new date for a property case and rushed over to catch the next hearing but missed it. I was dismayed for her but she was unfazed. You can't be in two courtrooms at the same time, she said matter-of-factly and carried on. We munched on peanuts as we walked up and down flights of stairs, collecting papers, checking the case listings and doing the routine, rookie work she had been assigned as part of her initiation ceremony. She must learn the ropes before she would be sent for a 'real' hearing. She was a junior for an established lawyer who happened to be her cousin, a blessing for a young woman who had ricocheted from a protected life in Bangarapet – a small town in

Karnataka's Kolar district – to the unknown in New York to a painful courtroom drama back home and on to a new life in Bangalore, all in the span of six years.

But they were long years, never-ending, always agonizing and stretching eternally. They swallowed whatever dreams she had as a sprightly college girl. They left her baffled and mystified and sometimes defeated. It was as if her public trial would never end, her story never get back to the script. Everything seemed out of control, on auto pilot even as events ran away with her life. She desperately sought normalcy but it kept slipping away. Even today she felt she was in the spotlight, when fellow lawyers casually let slip that she was the 'Ambati girl'. How she hated it when they whispered that name even though she had left her married life far, far behind. It was as if her whole being was defined by that one event in her life – her marriage to Jayakrishna Ambati.

Archana was sitting in Judge H.S. Ramakrishna's adequately functional courtroom waiting for her case to come up. The room was filled with lawyers like her – men and women – weighed down by files. Many men sported a tilak on the forehead, a common sight in Bangalore where morning puja was a daily ritual. Would a defence counsel with a tilak make a better impression on the judge? Mercifully, the seats on the otherwise austere steel furniture were cushioned and comfortable. Stern notices of Silence Please and No Smoking abounded, lest the tension prompt anyone to start chattering and light up. Archana went up to the judge when her case was called and talked animatedly in Kannada. She came back smiling, her mission accomplished, and we rushed to another part of the city for her next appointment.

Archana's day began in the office of her cousin K.R. Ashok Kumar, her guardian and mentor in the new city. We first met in 2001 on a rainy October morning in his office after several exchanges over the telephone. She wasn't keen to talk about her past and relive the misery. When I initially contacted her in Bangarapet from Kolkata earlier that year, she gave me a flat no for an answer, rejecting all my pleas. She simply wasn't interested and no argument about her being a role model for others made a difference. I had to seek her father Nanda's help who put in a good word for me over his wife's serious objections. In the end, Archana agreed to meet me only after I promised not to prod her for details of her marriage. She was bound by her divorce agreement, which said that neither side would talk to the media about the case anymore. As a newly minted lawyer, she respected the agreement and abided by it. I assured her that since the case had been reported widely in the press, I didn't need to trouble her for details. I would depend on newspaper accounts and the public prosecutor who had handled her case.

With Archana, I wanted to discuss the present and the future, not the history. I wanted to know how she had rebuilt her life, day by day, hour by long hour, and jumped back into the arena armed with a new confidence. I wanted to know how she had escaped being a martyr. How come she didn't remind me of a character from any of the popular serials that purport to show lives of typical Indian women? Why didn't she carry centuries of sadness in her eyes? How come she didn't lament her fate or plead helplessness? I had so many questions about her 'today' because she didn't seem yoked by her yesterdays. The questions were overflowing specially because she came from a traditional background. She didn't grow up in a metropolis, nor was she exposed to feminist theory in college. She had led a humdrum life in Bangarapet in a provincial environment, going to school and on to college for a diploma in electronics. She had no special ambitions save to make herself useful to her family. She was unprepared for what life dealt her but she didn't go to pieces. So from where did Archana get her fighting spirit?

Her story had given me hope and I wanted to include it precisely for that reason. Her story had an air of optimism because she had fought back. She had overcome. And she was ready for life's next battle – to build a legal career and establish herself as an honest, good lawyer.

Archana's office was near the congested Chickpet Crossing. When I mentioned the area to Swamy, my faithful driver, helper and interpreter in Bangalore, he did a double take. Apparently, there was no place to park in the narrow lanes and bylanes and we were in the sturdy Tata Sumo – not a shrinking violet by any chance. But we had to get there and I was confident of Swamy's abilities and navigational skills. We found the area and after a couple of false starts, we found K.S. Market and D.K. Lane – a web of tiny spaces stacked with shops on either side. English and Hindi were useless on this excursion since most people spoke only Kannada. I quickly made Swamy the front man as we made our way into No. 14, the building that housed the office. I climbed up the darkened stairs and found the first-floor office with no difficulty. Archana was there, smiling and welcoming.

I sat in the small but bright 10 ft x 7 ft office while her cousin Ashok Kumar delegated cases to juniors, including Archana. He rattled off details from memory like a seasoned lawyer that he was as Archana struggled to grasp them. Her hesitation prompted him to finally reduce her case load by one, saying he would take care of it himself. The tiny office was dominated by gods – they were perched over filing cabinets, they peered down from the walls, and smiled from calendars. Not a stretch of space was left unblessed. There was a makeshift shrine atop the lone ventilator and an assistant balanced himself on a stool to do a quick early-morning puja before the start of business. Another searched for a missing file dodging Kumar's impatient instructions. The office was cramped and uninspiring but it had everything from computers to pagers to a fax machine and no one was complaining. A tiny balcony just big enough for two people opened out from Kumar's table, giving the boss somewhat of a view – of other crowded buildings and television antennas.

We set out in an autorickshaw since Swamy had been sent away to find a parking space inside the court complex for us to rendezvous later. I asked Archana if she was nervous appearing before a judge since she was just starting out. 'It's O.K. I don't have much to do, just get another date. I will read the file while we are waiting,' she said as we raced along, breathing exhaust fumes from the sea of vehicles around us. She was so calm, it seemed unreal. After her appointments we decided to stop and have lunch at one of the many vegetarian restaurants that dot Bangalore. She was excited about lunching out since the food at her hostel was 'so horrible', it made her yearn for home. Her hostel was actually a private residence, which the entrepreneurial lady of the house had begun renting to working women and students. It was Gandhian in spirit – stark, Spartan, simple. Four aluminium folding beds filled the small bedroom, leaving barely enough room to walk. There was one study table for all the girls and no place to really stretch out. Most of the women were living there because their parents had approved of the regime in place. The house-cum-hostel was safe and it ran under the stern eyes of a Tamil housewife. She maintained strict discipline, allowed few phone calls, discouraged loitering and turned off the electricity in the five rooms by day to prevent wastage. For the parents, it was just like home but for the girls – that's another matter.

Archana usually missed breakfast – it was not very appetizing and there was a rush to reach office on time. She didn't carry her 'tiffin box' either because she couldn't stand the brown water given in the name of sambhar. 'The hostel rasam reminds me of my mother-in-law's rasam. It is hardly spicy and so watery,' she laughed and her eyes twinkled. I could see there was enough distance between her and her experiences. She could look back without going to pieces. Her sense of humour was coming back and she was slowly gaining in strength. She was animated over lunch, clearly enjoying the outing. In our excitement, we overordered. There was dal, mixed vegetables, Chinese chilli paneer, rava idlis, tandoori rotis and fresh juice and after a valiant effort we had to surrender. She was happy at the prospect of eating leftovers for dinner.

I asked Archana how she saw her future as she grew more comfortable chatting with me about her personal life. She talked openly and without looking over her shoulder. She told me that her parents were looking for a suitable boy for her to get married again. She seemed reconciled to the idea but she was not waiting with bated breath for a Prince Charming to come along. When I asked if she was open to the idea of a love marriage since she must be meeting new people all the time in her profession, she asked with a straight face: 'Please tell me how that happens. I don't know.' The words came out softly from her but they stung. It was as if she had never even allowed the thought to enter her mind. It was not a concept she had grown up with, not even in her imagination.

She told me she looked forward to working as a lawyer but stepping into the real world was not without hurdles. People around her were largely supportive but some male colleagues couldn't help gossiping about her, sometimes to her face. Once she was trying to talk to a senior woman lawyer to congratulate her after a particularly good performance in court when a male colleague from Bangarapet broke in and said, 'You know, this is the Ambati girl.' Archana was mortified but fortunately the senior she was trying to get to know ignored the unwarranted remark. 'I don't want to be introduced like that. I tell them, "Please don't treat me that way." Some people salute me and say, "Hats off to you" and give me compliments. But I want neither. I just want to be like everyone else. I don't want to be identified with the case forever. I don't want to live in its shadow,' she says, her eyes flashing and glistening. Even though most people were good to her and even admiring of her courage, there were a few for whom she would always be an odd woman. Someone who didn't fit the mould, who couldn't make things work, who attracted attention, who went public – someone whom they feared because her story turned out to be different.

What kept Archana going was her desire to make a difference in the lives of women just like her who get caught in the web of marriage and demands. Studying law seemed the most logical option after she and her father decided to file a case against the Ambatis for dowry harassment. From then on, she lived and breathed law for the next five years while her case progressed through the system. She helped her father through the ordeal, getting a sense of the legal system in the process. She joined LLB in Kolar, the nearest town offering a degree, making a twelve-kilometre round trip by bus everyday for classes. She passed her LLB in the summer of 2001 and was enrolled at the Bar on 10 August the same year. When I met her she had just begun going to the courts to take care of small civil cases.

But clearly her heart was not in civil law, settling property issues or getting tenants evicted. Who wants to fight for fat cats on a property-grabbing spree? She already had a realistic sense of the legal system. The two cases she had followed as part of her practicals during her LLB course had given her a good sense of how justice is dispensed in India. Both cases involved poor people who came to the court for hearings for months, waited all day, lost their wages in the bargain, struggled to feed infants they brought with them while the lawyers and administrators of justice behaved in a cavalier manner. If the case was to come up in the morning session, it was summarily postponed to the afternoon for no better reason than a lawyer's convenience or a judge's predisposition. No one thought of informing the poor man and his wife sitting outside in the heat. 'At every step they had to pay bribes. They had to pay even for a copy of the judgment which by law is theirs for free,' she recalled. 'I have seen officers openly asking for bribes. It is in the veins of India. If you want to get depressed, go to the courts.'

Not encouraging words from someone about to set out on a new career but then better that Archana had no illusions about the system. She wanted to help women in distress but she knew her contribution might be limited by reality. She wanted to deal with women's problems because she knew them from inside. 'I am debating about criminal law but I don't want to defend criminals, that's for sure. I want to help women. You know, the first thing the defence lawyers do if a woman is involved is to establish that she had a relationship with the man she is complaining against and then they go about maligning her reputation by linking her with this and that. Character assassination itself should be a crime,' she said, obviously drawing from her own unpleasant courtroom experience. 'I want to take up criminal law but to become a public prosecutor one needs experience. Now I am just doing civil matters but let's see what happens.' Her governing emotion was clearly to help women who are double victims – once of the crime committed against them and then of the judicial system.

Archana was flooded with phone calls from parents and women once her story was published in the newspapers. They would ask her for advice, for a way out since she had managed to leave her former husband's home in New York and return to India safely. They were facing similar problems – daughters married to NRIs and being harassed for dowry. Stories of mental and physical torture were common and to add to the agony the women were trapped in a foreign country. They were brutalized in the isolation of the manicured suburbia of the US. They were abused in the working-class neighbourhoods of Britain. A parent called Archana to talk about his daughter who was 'locked up' in a London home, unable to leave. 'I was surprised how many cases there were and that the people involved were all educated. I told them education means nothing because all that glitters is not gold.'

After all, Archana herself was married into one of the most educated families in the US, a family that produced the youngest doctor in America and made history. The Ambatis were feted at the White House, felicitated by Bill Clinton, and given numerous awards by the Indian-American community. Their home state of Andhra Pradesh had rushed to honour them and shower them with recognition. They were the toast of southern India. The family's achievements were legendary. People brought their children to see the Ambatis so they could be in their illustrious company and be inspired. The Ambati boys had set an impossibly high standard – Balamurali, the younger brother, had got his medical degree at seventeen years of age. Yet, for all their achievements, the family in the end behaved worse than one that has no benefit of education. They may have got degrees, but in some essential way they were uneducated. And they had the unbearable arrogance of sudden fame.

When I went to meet Archana in her hostel a few days later, she said something that will remain with me forever. I asked her what gave her her inner strength and she said simply, 'I don't consider myself unlucky and I have no regrets. Yes, something went wrong but not everything. Otherwise, would I have found Janardhan or Suneel Kumar?' She was referring to the public prosecutor who fought her case and the police officer whose quick work and sustained efforts helped in the arrest of the Ambati family. Her own family was supportive and wove a web of comfort around her. Everyone in Bangarapet rallied behind the family too because of her father's active involvement in community life. The people acted as if the prestige of the whole town was at stake. Archana became *their* daughter and her plight was theirs.

In that, her story is truly unique and unusual. And moving.

I went to Bangarapet in October 2001 to meet Archana's family and some of the neighbours to learn more about what had happened six years before when by a quirk of fate she was married into an NRI family from New York. I knew that her father, who went by the name of Nanda, might not be able to talk to me for the same reason as Archana – the divorce agreement that forbade both sides from speaking to the media. But I decided to give it a try, if for nothing else than to see Bangarapet and visit her home. Swamy and I got into the faithful Tata Sumo and started bright and early from

Bangalore so that we would have a full day of work. Bangalore had been my base for the stories I was pursuing in south India. It was a rainy morning with an overcast sky hanging above as a constant warning. Getting out of Bangalore took a while but once we were on the highway, the greenery was breathtaking. Clusters of big rocks swept by, breaking the green carpet into uneven pieces. All the road signs were in Kannada but there were enough clues in English so one didn't feel totally lost. I thought over the questions I would ask but I grew apprehensive as we got closer to Bangarapet, wondering if I would find Nanda and if he would agree to talk to me.

Bangarapet's main street was bustling with activity. Trucks laden with all manner of things – from vegetables to building materials – were loading and unloading their wares. We asked several people the way to Nanda Textiles, a small cloth shop that Archana's father owned, and finally we found it. I stepped into the shop tentatively and greeted the man behind an old-style munshi desk on the floor. He looked up, smiled when I introduced myself and immediately produced a folding chair for me. I had been in touch with him and he had agreed to my visit. We exchanged pleasantries and chatted about the drive over to Bangarapet. Mrs Nanda, who may have been in her fifties, was looking at the account books. Once she understood the purpose of my visit, she was visibly disturbed. She apparently hadn't known that I would be coming. The husband and wife exchanged some quick, heated words in Telegu as I tried to look inconspicuous.

She grew more and more animated and I think angry with her husband. She looked at me with her large, beautiful eyes and said in English, 'The chapter is closed. Chapter closed.' She was telling me loudly to clear out and that Archana's marriage and divorce were both over. She repeated it several times in case I missed her message. For a minute, I was perplexed and didn't know how to proceed. But the gallant Nanda came to my rescue and explained that his wife didn't 'understand' and that she would come around in a while. Somehow, I didn't share his optimism. His wife was very clear and vehement.

Nanda didn't want to be rude to a visitor and tried hard to pretend that everything was fine. He took me into the house, which was above the shop. It was a small middle-class establishment and for a minute I was surprised that an NRI family looking for a big dowry would have settled on Nanda's family. We went up a narrow staircase to a dark living room dominated by long sofas along the walls. The upholstery and the style gave it a very '70s feeling. I sat down nervously, fully aware that I was there against the wishes of the lady of the house. One end of the long room was dominated by shelves filled with awards and plaques of all sizes and from different years. Nanda had been a mining engineer by training and had worked in nearly every Indian state. Now retired, he looked after his shop but apart from his professional pursuits, he was involved in a myriad other activities in town. His rather substantial business card carried an impressive list, identifying him as a 'journalist', a district commandant of the local Home Guards unit, president of the Cloth Merchants Association of Bangarapet, president of the Lions Club of Bangarapet, president of the local Scouts and Guides, joint secretary of Kolar District Volleyball Association, member of the District Blindness Control Society and a member of the Station Consultative Committee of the Railways, among others. Perhaps, Nanda's card had impressed the Ambatis.

Nanda was Bangarapet's first citizen, as it were. He dabbled a little in public life and seemed to know everyone in town. A bit of a busybody, he spoke rapidly with a heavy south Indian accent. Sometimes he was difficult to understand, and I had to conjure up all my listening skills to guess at the probable meaning. His narrow face seemed to have a perpetual smile, a kind of bemused expression. He told me about how the Ambatis had humiliated him right from the word go, recalling the constant insults at the hands of the family of four. He didn't want to talk too much for fear of incurring his wife's wrath and falling afoul of the legal agreement. But he agreed to tell me the bare sequence of events that led to his encounter with the Ambatis. Mrs Nanda interrupted him a couple of times and they exchanged heated words while I desperately wished I were invisible. I knew I was causing tension in the household but every time I tried to leave, he said everything would be fine. To show her ire and complete displeasure, Mrs Nanda refused to offer me even a cup of tea or coffee. Nanda had to finally ask his younger daughter Surekha to make some coffee as we talked.

Given that the family had been through hell, Nanda was remarkably objective and calm. But then he had managed to rescue his daughter from the hands of the Ambatis and secure fifteen lakh rupees as a lifetime alimony and compensation for the dowry he had given. He had won in a manner of speaking but his business was nearly ruined over the years as he made the rounds of the courts. The scars still showed from the harrowing daily bus rides to Kolar and then to Bangalore for hearings. It was mentally and financially exhausting. He still couldn't understand how some people could behave the way the Ambatis did. The Ambatis were openly shopping around in India for the highest bidder and he was a minor player but they got together.

Nanda showed me around Bangarapet and then took me to Kolar Gold Fields, or KGF as it is known, where the groom and his family had stayed. KGF is no longer the hub it used to be when the gold mines were still functioning. The exhausted mines, which put Kolar on the map, are now shut down, giving the town a forlorn look. But KGF still retains a colonial aura with old bungalows built by early British mining companies dotting the landscape. He proudly showed me the guesthouse he had procured for the groom and his family through his connections – the best in town – but which was thoroughly condemned as inadequate. 'Can you imagine Indira Gandhi stayed here when she visited and she was the prime minister at that time. What more could we give?' he asked, his voice rising in alarm. He took me to Sylvan Villa, an attractive hotel where the wedding ceremony was held. He had offered the best that his small town could muster but it didn't impress the New Yorkers.

I bid Nanda goodbye, thanking him for taking time out but feeling awkward for the domestic discord I had inadvertently caused. He had never hinted how vehemently opposed his wife was to discussing the Ambati chapter during our many phone conversations. Keeping in mind the gag order of the divorce agreement, he had been careful of what he said. I didn't want to press him and cause further problems in their already difficult life. I learnt the details later from court documents, police reports and newspaper accounts. I just wanted to meet him and see how a small town merchant's daughter had landed up in New York.

Nanda had been looking for a groom for his middle daughter Archana when he spotted a matrimonial ad in *The Hindu* in April 1994 by the Ambatis. He responded but didn't get a reply. Enterprising and a man of myriad connections, he wasn't the kind to give up easily. He called a few friends and learned that the two Ambati brothers were being felicitated in Tirupati. He bought train tickets for the family and set out on his pilgrimage, hoping to meet the famous Ambatis. They were visiting from New York and the news of Balamurali Krishna Ambati becoming the youngest doctor at seventeen had just hit the headlines. Since the family was originally from Andhra Pradesh, the news was specially enthralling for the Arya Vaishya community there to which they belonged. Balamurali's older brother Jayakrishna – the man who was to eventually marry Archana – was accompanying him alongwith the parents. Jayakrishna, also a doctor, was keenly exploring the marriage market on the side. The community had gone all out to embrace the Ambatis. They were awe-inspiring and the people couldn't have enough of them. They were held as shining examples of what was possible. Not only had they made a name in America, they had done so with aplomb. Everyone was walking with their chest just a little bit out, justifiably proud on Balamurali's behalf.

It was at one such felicitation that Nanda met the Ambatis through some common acquaintances. Like everyone else, he was awed by the family's achievements and dreamed about getting the elder boy for his daughter. He was willing to try his luck and why not? If his daughter married into the family, it would raise his prestige all around and possibly add one more legend to his considerable business card. It would be a matrimonial coup if ever there was one. The two families met and the girl and boy saw each other but didn't really talk or spend time together. Muralimohan Rao Ambati, the father, and his wife Gomathi were polite but didn't show any immediate interest in the Nandas.

There was no correspondence for almost a year, dimming Nanda's hopes of a famous groom for his daughter. He wrote a letter, saying he liked Jayakrishna and was willing to take Archana to America so she could see the place and get married. He waited for an answer for weeks and then months but there was no reply to his open overture. Nanda was by now resigned that his dreams for Archana would remain just that. But then one day his phone rang and it was Muralimohan calling. It was May 1995, a year after their first encounter. He wanted to meet Nanda and discuss the proposal. Nanda was a little surprised but also thrilled by the call. He immediately invited Muralimohan for a visit, nervously hoping the man would accept.

Muralimohan accepted and arrived the next day by train from Chennai to meet the family. He spent the whole day with the Nandas and saw the house and the shop – neither of which is imposing or ostentatious. The two sides talked for a while and Muralimohan seemed satisfied. He decided right there that Archana and Jayakrishna, his elder son, would get married. He called his wife in New York from Nanda's phone and informed her. A purohit was summoned and the date and time for the marriage was fixed for fifteen days later. A small ceremony was held and Archana's parents gave some money for the groom to formalize the arrangement and 'secure' him. The spot decision was surprising but Muralimohan was clearly in a hurry.

He left for Chennai soon, promising to return later. The Nandas were gratified. Who could have asked for more? They considered themselves lucky and their daughter fortunate to be marrying such an illustrious man. Nanda's eldest daughter also had been married to an NRI based in Abu Dhabi and they were happy. 'Since that marriage was in response to an advertisement, I fell for a similar one by the Ambatis,' he was quoted as saying in a report in *The Telegraph*. He clearly was enamoured of NRI grooms. One of Archana's photographs was sent to New York with a US-based relative to be handed over to the prospective groom.

But when Nanda's nephew went over to the Ambatis' house to deliver the envelope, they raised some demands. They asked for airfares for four or five people for the wedding. The nephew immediately called Nanda in Bangarapet and told him. Nanda refused, saying he couldn't afford it. But the nephew offered to help, saying he would pay the airfares in dollars in New York and Nanda could pay him back later in India. The marriage must not be stalled for this reason.

Between the four weeks the families agreed on the match and the actual wedding on 2 June 1995, several demands were made. According to press reports and police statements, the Ambatis allegedly asked for a bungalow in Chennai, a share in Nanda's own property and several lakhs in cash. Nanda agreed to give four lakh rupees in cash, jewellery and one-third share of the property, which would have gone to Archana. Despite their absurd demands, he didn't think of breaking off or telling them to take the first plane back to New York. Like thousands of fathers before him and after, his eyes were on the prize – the boy from New York. He was such a good catch, he lived abroad, and the family was everything a father would dream of for his daughter. Nanda ignored the warning signs, probably thinking of his good luck and enhanced prestige in the community. After all, everyone must be jealous that his daughter was marrying an Ambati. It didn't occur to him to question why the Ambatis had zeroed in on him. The matrimonial ad had come out more than a year ago and they surely must have been flooded with proposals, given their fame at home and abroad. Why had they not been able to find a bride for Jayakrishna so far? Was there a reason? Something was terribly wrong but Nanda wasn't thinking.

He was to learn later after journalists swooped in on the story that the Ambatis' quest for a bride had taken them through multiple rounds of negotiations with different families. Like hard-nosed bureaucrats bargaining at a trade round in Geneva, the Ambatis were interviewing candidates and checking them off a list. That is what had taken a year. And a broken engagement with a girl in Guntur. According to a report in *Frontline*, Jayakrishna was engaged to a girl and the marriage had been fixed for 1 June in Tirupati. The girl's family broke off the engagement because the Ambatis demanded 'an unreasonable amount as dowry'. The figure is said to have been above one crore rupees. A relative of the girl told *Frontline* that 'the only thing that matters to the Ambatis is money. They have been able to create a halo around themselves. It is a good thing their son's marriage didn't come through with our girl. The girl has been saved.'

One was saved but another became a victim. Perhaps the Ambatis insisted on solemnizing the marriage early because they had just been rejected by one family and they didn't want the word to get out. They even chose the same date – 1 June for the engagement to Archana as if denying that things had gone wrong with another girl. Even if anyone came to know, they would have a pat answer. Jayakrishna was still getting married and on the same day. Not many would guess to a different girl altogether. Everything was done in a hurry – the negotiations, the agreement and the preparations. The engagement was on 1 June 1995 and the marriage a day later.

Archana was married to Jayakrishna even after Nanda had seen enough of the Ambatis to know they were not the most amiable people around. Their achievements may have been laudable but they carried them heavily. Fame hung around them like lead – it hit you in the head the moment you got close. They bragged unabashedly about their importance. People who dealt with the family felt the father was unbearably arrogant – almost a cardboard caricature. He dropped Bill Clinton's name and flashed his photograph from the White House as a badge of entry all around India. It was so crass as to be funny but some people were impressed, even intimidated. He calculated the academic achievements of his sons only in terms of monetary compensation. In him, good old Indian greed came laced with the American penchant to equate everything with money.

Archana told *Frontline* in December 1995 that the Ambatis originally demanded 'sixty lakhs worth of gold jewellery, two lakhs worth of silver articles and airfares for the family from New York to Madras and from Madras to Bangarapet and back.' They made the demands in front of several people from Bangarapet. Nanda expressed his inability to pay so much money and after some bargaining, Ambati senior agreed to 'accept' three lakh rupees in the form of jewellery, fifty thousand rupees in cash, and fifty thousand rupees worth of silver, apart from airfares to the US and back. Of course, all marriage expenses were Nanda's burden.

'On the day the negotiations took place, my (future) father-in-law demanded the dowry amount but was satisfied when my father paid a token advance of Rs 10,501. Before the engagement on 1 June, the dowry was paid in full in the presence of elders. But still my in-laws were not happy, saying that there are people who are willing to pay two crore rupees as dowry. Because of the tension caused by their demands, my parents became ill. For the first time in my life, I saw my father weeping,' Archana told *Frontline*. Nanda wept but he did not change his mind. The reasons were the same – family izzat, tradition, being in denial about the truth, and misplaced hope that things would eventually work out. Like most Indian fathers, he seemed to believe in this peculiar magic.

Nanda had only a few days to make the wedding preparations. When the big day arrived, he went to the railway station to receive the Ambatis and with fanfare escorted them to the rest house. They walked since the station was close by but it offended the Ambatis no end. From the moment they arrived in Bangarapet, they began grumbling about one thing or another. They complained about the arrangements, claimed there were cockroaches in their bedrooms, that the coffee tasted like dishwater, that there were stones in their ghee-rice, that they got only cotton dhotis instead of silk ones and on and on. And that they were Americans and used to better treatment. Muralimohan, the father, terrorized everyone who came in contact with him – from the hotel manager to the sweeper. He abused the temple priest when he asked for a donation as is customary. Words like 'scoundrel' and 'bastard' seemed to slip off his tongue easily. For all the preposterous demands they made, they did not think of bringing a single gift for the new bride. No jewellery, no saris. Not even a flower.

The wedding photographs show the Ambatis standing sternly like guards besides the newlyweds. And tellingly, no one is smiling. The whole ceremony seemed joyless. Archana went through the motions quietly. Any protest from her would have only increased her father's public humiliation. A post-wedding trip to Ooty arranged for the groom's family by Nanda also turned out to be a fiasco because the car broke down, giving Muralimohan another reason to be abusive. He hadn't gone to America and broken his back, worked hard, saved his money, eaten frugally, protected his two boys from sin in that promiscuous society, beat them into shape for *this*! For a ride on bad Indian roads full of potholes where cars break down. Where people don't understand merit? Where cleanliness is not next to godliness and where flies intrude your personal space constantly? He hadn't come back for this.

Somehow the Nandas got through the ordeal of the wedding, only to discover that the Ambatis planned to take Archana to the US on a fiancée visa, not a spousal one. They didn't understand the full implications of this nor did they probe. It was odd that a newly married bride should travel as a fiancée after having gone through a full-blown marriage ceremony. The Ambatis were pretending in front of the US authorities that the couple were not yet married when they clearly were. The implications of the move are unclear but perhaps they wanted to avoid the long wait that an immigrant visa for a spouse entails. A fiancée or K-1 visa is given only in exceptional circumstances to exceptional people – the Ambatis qualified as 'distinguished' Americans – and the couple are expected to get married within three months of arrival in the US. But Archana's family and friends were surprised. After the wedding the Ambatis had seemed like they didn't want to treat Archana as a member of the family. A magazine had wanted to write about Balamurali being the world's youngest doctor but when the photographer wanted to take a picture of the family, the Ambatis pointedly asked Archana to stay out of the frame. At a community function organized by a family member to felicitate Balamurali, Archana was shunted aside and not even introduced to the gathering. She was to discover later that she was not married in the eyes of the US law since her status remained that of a fiancée.

The Ambatis' tantrums continued right up to the time the plane took off from Madras airport. They were leaving a week after the wedding ceremonies. A week that exhausted everyone who dealt with them. Nanda was asked to provide sweets for their relatives and friends in New York and when he delivered them, he was berated for not packing them properly. 'Don't you know we are going to fly at fourteen thousand feet? This will burst,' Muralimohan shouted, sending Nanda scurrying to buy a new suitcase for the sweets. Eventually he didn't take the suitcase. He created a scene at the airport on the day of their departure, demanding to walk right up to the plane. He flashed his photos with Clinton and the then prime minister, P.V. Narasimha Rao, who had met the family as a courtesy. The security official just laughed at the photographs, leaving the Ambatis fuming and perplexed. They couldn't understand why all doors didn't automatically open when they decreed.

Nanda had been watching and suffering the humiliation at the hands of this arrogant family. But he was still proud that his daughter had married into a famous and illustrious family. He pinned his hopes for Archana on the fact that the newlyweds would live in Rochester where Jayakrishna was to pursue his career, away from the domineering parents. It was a matter of time, he thought. And so did Archana who felt she could 'adjust' in the family. Did she have a choice? She had seen her father humiliated for her sake, she didn't want to make him feel worse. She decided she would follow the glass-is-half-full approach to life, not a pessimistic view. She entered her new home with an open mind. The Ambatis lived in a modest house in Bayside about twenty miles from the hustle and bustle of Manhattan. The neighbourhood was a typical middle-class suburb with small neat lawns encircling brick and wood homes. Residents knew the Ambatis, thanks to the army of television crews that had descended on them when Balamurali was in the news.

Archana tried to ignore her crotchety in-laws, trying to think of her husband instead. Her father's plight constantly weighed on her mind. She thought she would make a go of it but she was rudely shocked. She discovered that because her father couldn't give as large a dowry as the Ambatis wanted, she would forever remain a half-bride, a half-member of the family and a perpetual nuisance in their eyes. There was no welcome ceremony, no coconut broken in her honour. It was a bleak arrival for Archana in America, a country she had associated with excitement and friendliness. Her dreams of happiness under the Manhattan skyline quickly evaporated as she began to realize her real station in the Ambati household. She was there to serve as household help, not really be a member of the family. She wasn't even given a cupboard to keep her clothes, a corner to call her own. She was made to live out of her suitcases. Not allowed out of the house on her own except to water the lawn, she couldn't even move around inside the house freely. During the day she worked either in the kitchen or was made to sit in one part of the living room. If she was lucky enough to be taken to a gathering of Indian Americans and NRIs, she was not allowed to talk to anyone. She was introduced as a visitor from India, not as a daughter-in-law. In her short married life in New York, she never saw the basement of the house. When the family went out somewhere, Archana would be sent in one car with the mother while her husband travelled separately with his father. The couple were allowed little privacy.

Archana soon saw that her husband kept mum in front of his father, never conversing, never consulting, leave alone contradicting the senior man. Neither he nor his younger brother ever argued with the father, whose cheerless personality pervaded the whole household. Their opinions were not welcome. The house ran like a military camp and any deviation was considered dishonourable. There was no laughter, no after-dinner family chats. Archana tried to get close to the Ambatis but any attempt at conversation or joviality was met with a frown or, worse, insults. If she talked about her college days or her parents or her friends – she was declared a show-off who was trying to steal the limelight away from the Ambati boys. Muralimohan, an administrator and accountant by profession, even portioned food out on dinner plates and dictated how and in what sequence the meal was to be eaten. He cooked often, not perhaps for the joy of cooking but to ensure frugality. To describe him as a control freak would be an understatement. The house was cheerless and bleak. Such was the push for frugality that they wouldn't turn the airconditioning on even in the summer when the barometer in New York touches forty degrees centigrade. Fans too were in short supply, making the hot months hotter still. The austerity measures – unwarranted since all four were earning members – were worthy of a prolonged war situation. The mattresses in the house remained covered in their original plastic, lest human contact spoil them.

The Ambatis were frustrated that they hadn't been able to find a rich bride for their 'valuable' son. Their fame had spread across the oceans but it hadn't translated into instant riches. Why did they have to settle for Nanda? They couldn't accept the fact that they had failed in their mission. Muralimohan constantly harped on the 'insult' of having to receive a small dowry. He was deeply angry and somewhat bewildered by his lack of success in the marriage market. He took out his anger on Archana, the daughter-in-law whose very presence in the house reminded him of his failure. He abused her, harangued her, insulted her at every opportunity.

He constantly mocked her about her IQ, comparing her to his sons. He said her father had 'cheated' him. Archana listened and cried and always swallowed her anger. She was alone and in a new country, new culture with no friends around. There were no familiar South Asian faces nearby and if she were lucky enough to be taken to a social gathering, Gomathi, her mother-in-law, always hovered nearby. Once a sympathetic woman, gauging that Archana was unhappy, pushed a piece of paper with a telephone number into her hands but Gomathi saw them. Archana rushed to the bathroom and flushed it down.

Archana told *Frontline* when she returned to India: 'In the US I was abused physically and mentally by all the four. I was asked to write thousand word impositions stating that my mother was a prostitute, my father a scoundrel and so on.' To atone for what she was forced to do, she secretly wrote in blood behind her family photo that she loved her parents and hid it in her suitcase. The Ambatis went to the extent of trying to implicate her in theft. 'Jewels were put into my suitcase, photographs were taken and I was threatened that unless I signed some documents (before a notary), I would be accused of theft and handed over to the police.'

Referring to the physical abuse, Archana asked the *Frontline* correspondent: 'Did you shake hands with my mother-in-law? If you did, you will know what her slap feels like. They used to lock me in the house and I was only allowed to come out to water the lawns.'

There was no end to the Ambatis' insults and abuse. They never missed an opportunity to remind her that she came from a station below theirs. They asked her to look up the dictionary and find the meaning of the word 'textiles' and said her family didn't know the meaning otherwise why would her father name his tiny shop Nanda Textiles? It implied he owned a cloth mill, Muralimohan yelled. They had been 'fooled' by Nanda, a small trader. When she asked if she could study further in the US, her husband and brother-in-law refused to sponsor her. They said she must get the funds from her father. Even though each of the Ambatis had a car, they demanded that she get fifteen thousand dollars from her father to buy a car for herself.

When her uncle and cousins in America phoned her, the Ambatis would snoop and listen on the other line. They would berate her after each phone call and interrogate her about every word. She finally told her relatives not to call. When her cousin and his wife came to visit since they hadn't been able to attend the wedding, they were insulted by her in-laws. The wife was clad in jeans, a sign of wild abandon to the Ambatis and after the guests left, Archana was told that only prostitutes wore jeans. It had just been three weeks since she came as the new bride, but life was an endless list of complaints and insults. When Jayakrishna was leaving for Rochester, she pleaded with him to take her with him but he refused. He was neither able nor willing to go against his parents' wishes who wanted Archana to stay in their house. She began losing hope when she was barred from accompanying her husband. The mental torture and the dark, empty existence inside the Ambatis' home began to get unbearable. If she said anything, they behaved even worse. She couldn't imagine herself surviving years and years of this life. It would slowly turn her like them – unsmiling, austere and insular.

She was afraid and wanted to leave but she didn't know how. She couldn't call anyone because she was not allowed to use the phone. It had just been a month since she came to New York but it seemed like an age. The days were long and lonely, the evenings a trial in front of the in-laws. Her husband was no source of comfort. She would cry alone in the bathroom, trying to muffle the sound. She began to feel desperate and helpless. Not knowing which way to run, Archana began contemplating suicide. She decided to write a note to her parents but it was discovered by the Ambatis. They were alarmed. They immediately decided to send her back and she didn't resist. She was given a one-way ticket and put on a plane on 16 July 1995, after a bleak forty-five-day marital experience. She was given no money and her jewellery was kept back, according to the prosecution, but the Ambatis denied keeping any of her things.

Dispirited and depressed, Archana landed at Madras airport two days later and called her father. He rushed to pick her up, stunned by the news. When she came back to Bangarapet, she looked haggard and shattered from her nightmare, a mere shadow of her former self. There was no spirit left in her. She went into a shell and stayed inside the house for almost two months, never stepping out. She felt humiliated and ashamed and didn't have the strength to face people.

When her family heard her story, they were incensed. But the overriding thought in her parents' minds was still that Archana should somehow get back with Jayakrishna. They had never thought of or had a divorce in the family. They decided to find out if there was any chance for reconciliation. They sent feelers to the Ambatis through common acquaintances and relatives. But what they got was a written list of complaints, which was to serve as a piece of crucial evidence later in a delectable irony of fate. Muralimohan probably couldn't help making a list, coming from a culture where To Do lists are *de rigueur*. He came up with twenty-two specific complaints. To begin with, he didn't care for the walk from the railway station to the rest house. Nor did he like being served his vada on a banana leaf. He felt discriminated against because he and the groom were given cotton dhotis while Nanda wanted to wear a silk one. 'But we stopped him,' he wrote triumphantly. 'In the half a dozen functions felicitating Bala (Murali), Archana was given a front row seat but I never saw a smile on her face nor did she clap even once when the entire hall was full of applause,' he noted, his mind homing in on fine details. If it weren't so sad, it would be comical.

There were other letters demanding and complaining about the inadequate dowry. Gomathi wrote to Archana's mother blasting her for not sending this or providing that. Nanda tried pleading with the Ambatis in New York over the phone, incurring a huge bill in the bargain. But his efforts fell on deaf ears. He didn't know what to do next but then he heard from someone that the Ambatis were once again in India looking for a bride for Jayakrishna. They hadn't bothered about the minor detail of a divorce but then for them she was just a fiancée. Unable to take their cavalier behaviour any more, Nanda decided to go to the police. It was a big decision but he felt there was no other way out.

A complaint was registered in Bangarapet on 15 November 1995 under sections 498 (A) which covers cruelty and harassment for dowry, 120 (A) and (B) for criminal conspiracy, 323 for simple assault, 342 for wrongful confinement and 506 for threatening a person's life. The Ambatis were also booked under sections 3 and 4 of the Dowry Prohibition Act for demanding and taking dowry. There was no hesitation or delay tactics by the police in lodging the complaint. The compelling nature of the letters and Nanda's own standing in the small community perhaps played a role in the smooth course of action. Police officials showed unusual alacrity and sensitivity in Archana's case.

T. Suneel Kumar, district commissioner, swung into action once he received information that the Ambatis were in Vizag for a function, being feted once again for the achievements of Balamurali. The Rajalaksmi Foundation of Andhra Pradesh was planning to present the annual award to Balamurali. Kumar immediately sent two constables led by Sub-inspector Konappa Reddy to Vizag to arrest them. Kumar's prompt response – rare in a dowry case – was crucial to the much-needed success. He asked Nanda to accompany his policemen to identify the accused. He also called Vizag's police commissioner, R.P. Meena, to seek his help since the arrest would be made in Andhra Pradesh, not Karnataka. Meena was known in the state for his successful raids against the Naxalites. He liked action and promised to deliver.

When I met Kumar six years later, he was modest and philosophical about his role. He said it was a winning combination of good luck and fortuitous circumstances that the Ambatis were nabbed. He remembered the details of the case and recounted those eventful days when Archana's story had gripped the headlines.

The police party had left Bangarapet on 18 November and reached Vizag in time for the function a day later when Baramurali was to be honoured. Everything was moving like clockwork. Meena had assigned some local policemen and women to help Kumar's visiting posse. They went to the hall where the award was to be given, thinking they would be lucky to make one arrest. But when they saw all four Ambatis there soaking in the glory, they couldn't believe their luck. It was a bonus they hadn't expected. They found out that the Ambatis were staying at a local politician's house. The police decided to swoop in on them well after midnight when the family was sure to be at home and asleep, making the arrest easier. But they were in for a bit of a setback. When the police knocked at the door, Muralimohan came out and began abusing them. He threatened he would 'take their uniforms off' if they dared arrest him. Didn't they know who he was? That he knew Bill Clinton? That he knew Narasimha Rao? And so on. He named lesser mortals down the line who could fix them in no time.

The inspector, already timid about arresting a guest at a politician's house, was intimidated by Ambati's loud harangue. The end result – he came back empty handed that night. The inspector went to Commissioner Meena the next morning to ask what they should do since the Ambatis were invoking the prime minister's name. Meena gave them a green signal, saying a culprit is a culprit and should be arrested. He decided to lead the charge himself. It mattered little to him if the Ambatis were related to anyone or flashed photos with bigwigs. Emboldened and thirsting for a showdown, the Vizag police decided to arrest them in full public view the next day at a five-star hotel where the two sons were scheduled to give a talk on 'medical ethics'. The press was already there to listen to the young prodigies. As soon as the seminar ended, the police surrounded the Ambatis. It was a scene that gladdened Nanda's heart.

Muralimohan started abusing Meena as the full impact of the police action sunk in. 'Don't mess with us. We have contacts,' he yelled helplessly. Meena kept his cool and continued to do his job. As he took them away, Muralimohan vented his anger on the journalists gathered there, calling them sensationalist. The famous four were packed off to Kolar by car that day itself. It was a twelve-hour journey on Indian roads, not something that the Ambatis savoured. They complained the police hadn't fed them or even offered them water but the canny constables produced receipts for everything. They had been treated politely. Once they reached Kolar – Nanda's sphere of influence – black placards greeted them. A hostile mob of people was ready not with garlands this time but angry protests. 'Dowry Devil Ambati, Down Down', 'Shame, Shame, Youngest Doctor of USA', they shouted.

Kumar couldn't believe that all four Ambatis had been snared into his net. He told me later that if he hadn't acted promptly and missed the chance to arrest them, there is no telling what may have happened. They would have simply returned to the US, far from the reach of a Bangarapet police officer. The local police would have contacted Interpol and requested help but given the number of offenders each country is looking for, the Ambatis would have been low priority. 'Luck played a big role. The Ambatis were probably thinking that Indian laws didn't apply to them. That's why they were roaming here with impunity. They also didn't expect that Nanda would go to the police. They were so arrogant that they damaged their own case,' said Kumar, sitting in his office in Bangalore. 'They even threatened me and said that I won't have a job left because I arrested them,' he said with a smile.

Once the Ambatis were deposited by the police in front of the magistrate in Kolar, the judicial process took over. Determined not to learn from experience, they tried to throw their weight around even in court. They said they were 'distinguished' US citizens who could not be tried in an Indian court. But Judge H.M. Bajanthri cut them short and simply said, 'The law does not make a distinction of distinguished persons.' He overruled the defence lawyer's claim that since the crime was committed in the US, the Kolar court had no jurisdiction over the matter. He went with the assistant public prosecutor's argument that the crimes against the complainant had commenced in India and therefore violated Indian laws. The Ambatis were remanded to judicial custody until 25 November but three of them were allowed on medical grounds to be admitted to the local hospital. On the appointed date, Judge Bajanthri released all four of them on bail on a personal bond of twenty-five thousand rupees and a cash deposit of the same amount. He asked them to deposit their passports as a guarantee of their continued presence in India. Muralimohan claimed the passports were at the US consulate. But when the judge said they might have to continue in custody, the passports were immediately available.

A vice-consul from the US consulate in Madras had arrived in Bangarapet to provide help to the besieged Americans but remained largely on the sidelines as an observer. She told reporters that the Ambatis had contacted their Congressman in New York presumably to seek his help in their release. But the Ambatis' bail applications were rejected twice by the high court. In a statement given to the press at the time, they denied all the charges, saying they were fabricated. They denied harassing Archana and instead accused her of wanting to blackmail them to extract money. Their accusations carried little weight as sentiment against them grew in Bangarapet.

There was a distinct sense of 'us against them' in the air. They were NRIs and therefore half-outsiders. How dare they torture *our* girl? The small-town cohesiveness was much in evidence and Bangarapet residents were rallying around the beleaguered Archana. Nanda was flooded with letters of support, many offering help as he battled for his daughter's dignity. The arrogance of the Ambatis by now had become the stuff of urban legend – anyone who had even been in the same room with them had a colourful story to tell. They had fallen from the high pedestal and become the laughing stock of the town. Newspapers carried daily stories of their encounters, their tantrums, their threats and obnoxious behaviour. Even their lawyers were tired of them. A.C. Yaduraya Gowda, a lawyer who had hosted them and fed them for nearly three months because they seemed so helpless in a hostile environment, said they were 'brilliant people but lacked humanity'. He told me that they had behaved badly in court and when he tried to get them admitted into a hospital to save them the agony of custody, they fought with the doctor. As the case got underway and they began picking up legalese, the Ambatis felt qualified to tell the lawyers how to do their job. 'That old man (Muralimohan) is also bright and he has a good job in New York. He works with a budget of millions of dollars. But he can't spend even hundred rupees here. They didn't bring any money with them when they were arrested. I helped them on humanitarian grounds. But they didn't even have the courtesy to thank me,' Gowda said in a telephone interview.

Legal preliminaries took nearly two months after the arrest as the Ambatis desperately tried to get their passports back and return home to New York. They pleaded that their jobs were in jeopardy and their careers could be ruined. In a message faxed to a friend in the US and reported in *The Asian Age*, the Ambatis said they were being held hostage in India for a ransom of $100,000. They claimed Archana's family would withdraw the case if they coughed up the money. The message urged Americans to tell their Congressmen and Senators what was happening to the Ambatis. Their human rights were being violated.

The lawyers working for the Ambatis had been trying to get the Karnataka High Court to relax the bail conditions set by the lower court which effectively prevented the accused from leaving India. The high court had rejected the application twice, sending them back to the lower court. Finally, on the third attempt, the Ambatis were able to get a high court order for releasing their passports following a bank guarantee of two lakh rupees each. It was January 1996 and the Ambatis had tasted a bit of the real India by then. But the order set an onerous condition – Muralimohan and his two sons could leave India but not Gomathi, the mother. She was required to stay back for the legal proceedings. The Ambati men, although free to return home, were required to appear before the Indian consul in New York once a month. The case continued to attract public attention and extensive press coverage, especially in the southern newspapers and magazines.

The government had appointed one of the best public prosecutors in Karnataka to build the case. K. Janardhan was quite a legend in his own right in the state. A dark, brooding man with a girth that gave him additional gravity, he was known for his honesty and integrity. 'Incorruptible' is how everyone, including women activists, described him. He was the rarest of rare. Defence lawyers worked harder and extracted higher fees from clients when they faced him in court. He had prosecuted many dowry cases and successfully so. In recognition of his courtroom skills, the government had assigned him to a special court dealing with cases of violence against women. Janardhan tended to get involved with the lives of the families he was helping. He seemed genuinely concerned about women when he talked about their problems. No, he didn't need a seminar on gender sensitization, I felt. He took a hands-on approach, often helping his clients beyond the call of duty. He would even feed them if needed.

I met Janardhan in October 2001, a full six years after he had prosecuted Archana's case, to find out what happened and how it happened. He remembered the case in great detail; he also gave me an insider's view of the system. He was now the deputy commissioner of police (prosecutions), a desk job he had taken because of failing health. Instead of pinning down shifty defence lawyers in court, he was now advising the state on prosecution strategy. He looked over case files and decided which verdicts should be appealed. He had time for visitors. We met twice and talked a great deal about dowry cases and why the conviction rate was so low. Janardhan had opinions and insights and many criticisms of the way the criminal justice system worked. He was honest and not afraid to speak the truth.

He didn't want any credit for hounding the Ambatis in court – he was merely doing his job. He said the first credit should go to Suneel Kumar, the senior police officer, without whose diligent investigation the chargesheet wouldn't have become a reality. And then to Nanda, the father who decided to fight. 'One should appreciate his fighting spirit. He had a lot of it,' Janardhan recalled. Archana had been very lucky unlike thousands of other Indian women whose stories and cases get lost in dusty police files every year. She had honest policemen, a good prosecutor and consistent public support – a heartening combination.

'Usually in these cases only the aggrieved party supports the prosecution. All others turn hostile. In this case everyone supported us. The people of Bangarapet were saying: "She is not Nanda's daughter, but our daughter." ' Nanda kept up the fight despite losses to his business. Ambati's overactive and inventive lawyers tried to slow him and break his spirit by filing a counter case against him for 'giving dowry'. They got an order from a judge of the Karnataka High Court, saying that giving and taking of dowry are both offences under the Dowry Prohibition Act and therefore Nanda should be prosecuted as well. The judge even directed the police to arrest Nanda.

Nanda was flabbergasted at the judgment. He was forced to appeal to the Supreme Court in Delhi, which unfortunately was on vacation at the time. But a woman lawyer who was active with NGOs went out of her way to help him when he landed in Delhi. She represented Nanda in front of a vacation bench and cited the relevant provisions of the Act which were as clear as day. The highest court straightaway dismissed the case without commenting on the high court order. One can't emphasize enough that all the stars were aligned right for Nanda and Archana – everything was working in their favour despite the political and financial clout of the Ambatis. It is rare that a victim of dowry harassment gets immediate attention from the police who, by a rarer stroke of luck, find the accused and take the decision to arrest them. For one case like Archana's there are thousands of others where the police won't arrest the husband even after a dying wife has directly accused him of burning her.

Janardhan, helped by good evidence and efficient police work, started building his case in earnest. He had been appointed as a special prosecutor by the Karnataka state government for the case which, in effect, meant that he had to appear in a magistrate's court when he normally did not appear in anything lower than a sessions court. The government was well aware of the media interest in the case, to say nothing of the Ambatis' international connections. It did not want to leave anything to chance and one of the best prosecutors was sent over to Kolar to fight. Janardhan was the man of the hour. He had to travel by the state roadways bus from Bangalore to Kolar and must have made over fifty trips. A car could have been arranged for him but he chose to do it the right way. 'Apart from that girl, I too was subjected to cruelty in this case,' he told me, the bus rides still vivid in his mind.

I asked him to recall some of the highlights of the trial period and he came up with vivid details. Janardhan said the proceedings were well into the first year and evidence was being recorded when dramatic encounters between the two sides were witnessed.

'The girl was being humiliated in court by the defence counsel. Whatever a lawyer can do to humiliate a girl in a criminal case, they did. I was just short of assaulting them at times. Fortunately for Nanda, I was there. They did not succeed in their mischief,' he said. From anyone else the statement may have sounded boastful but coming from Janardhan, it sounded flat and normal. There was a ring of honesty and passion in what he said. He was just being the big brother, protecting a woman who was being verbally abused in front of him. When the defence counsel got into details of Archana's married life, he stepped in and asked the judge to record her statement in camera. He tried to stonewall the cheap but common defence tactic of maligning a woman's character. When he talked about cases, strategy, deception, lies and misinformation inside courtrooms, he was matter of fact and blunt. If he referred to himself, it was not to brag but to separate himself from all the lies. He was simple to the point of being unimpressive in today's razzle dazzle world of image projection.

Janardhan told me the main planks of the prosecution were:

> Demands for cash, jewellery during negotiations.
>
> During the wedding, the Ambatis acted as a unit and all four humiliated the parents and the girl. They commented on the food, gifts, their house, clothes and

> arrangements. They found fault with everything and were unhappy with the dowry given.
>
> Fifty thousand rupees was given in cash in front of witnesses apart from gold and silver articles.
>
> On the night of the wedding, Gomathi started pressuring Archana to ask her father to hand over her share in the family property.

The defence argued that Archana was a troubled person and that she disliked the Ambatis from the beginning. She made no effort to accommodate them. In the five hundred or so photos taken during the wedding and during various functions to honour the youngest Ambati, she is not smiling even in one of them.

Janardhan argued back: 'Archana's smile was taken away. How could she smile when she saw her father being constantly humiliated by the Ambatis? They treated her father as a servant. When she went to America, they treated her as one too. To prevent her from going to the police, they took her photographs with suitcases filled with the family jewellery as a means to blackmail. They told her they would lodge a complaint that she had stolen all the jewels. How could she smile?'

At one point during the arguments, Gomathi said that Archana was not good-looking and charming enough. Janardhan shot back with some unkind but effective words. He pointed at Gomathi and told the court: 'This lady is standing before the court and arguing about the complainant's charm. Has she seen herself in the mirror?'

There was a hushed silence in the room. The defence protested loudly but the prosecutor continued calmly: 'I said what I did purposely. You couldn't digest the insult for a minute but you expect Archana to bear it for life. This is mental cruelty. My purpose is served. I am satisfied.' Gomathi started crying in the courtroom. She faced the brunt of Janardhan's charge since she was the only one present for the trial. Her husband and two sons were back in New York. It was perhaps unfair to make Gomathi the main villain when clearly her husband was the unquestioned head of the family. The high court somewhat typically had decided to keep Gomathi in India for the trial while allowing the three men to return home. Even Janardhan said he felt sorry for her after a point. 'Although I fought against her, I started pitying her. No one showed her any sympathy. She got the maximum punishment – she had to stay in a small hotel, come to court and become the villain of the case.'

The case proceeded along but the way it finally ended was a surprise.

It had been conducted in full glare of the media and Archana had become well known around the state. Although Nanda was overtaken by a spirit to get back at the Ambatis, something that no one could begrudge, the tension and stress of daily court proceedings took their toll on the family. His wife was hospitalized and even his youngest daughter suffered. Surekha couldn't concentrate on her studies when the whole family was caught in the vortex of a legal case. As a result, she didn't do as well in the medical entrance examination as she might have in better times.

As time went by, the stress started to tell on both sides even though the prosecution case was going strong and conviction was a near surety. It had been nearly two years since the trial started when the first hint of a 'compromise' came. Nanda was losing his business coming every day to court. He had spent a fortune pursuing the case and had even taken loans. He still had to think about his youngest daughter's college and marriage. Archana, on the other hand, was mentally exhausted. From the beginning she had resented being in the limelight and hated the constant publicity. Her life had been invaded by an army of strangers who called themselves reporters. Everyone around her was always asking her about the case and how it was going. She just wanted the whole din around her to end and normal life to begin. Both she and father were beginning to feel overwhelmed. By now they had understood how the legal process worked. Nanda knew that even if the trial court convicted the Ambatis, they might not go to jail. They would file for suspension of their sentence and appeal the verdict in the high court. At the appellate stage, they wouldn't even be required to stay in India. They could conduct their affairs through highly paid lawyers. At the trial stage at least Gomathi had to be present. The appeals process could take years. How would they go on fighting?

According to Janardhan, Nanda was struggling by then even to come to court. He had exhausted his savings. 'He was a totally shattered man. It made him vulnerable to offers from the other side.' At the same time, the Ambatis began to realize that they might be convicted and they didn't want that qualification in their carefully built resume. They began thinking of ways to settle out of court. Their lawyers and wellwishers suggested approaching Nanda with an offer of cash. The Ambatis agreed and made an initial offer of ten thousand rupees with a demand for a mutual consent divorce for Jayakrishna and Archana. It was a laughable amount and as expected Nanda rejected it outright. The tables had turned. Instead of the Ambatis calling the shots, they were at the receiving end. They had to up their 'bid' if they wanted to be taken seriously. Senior lawyers again told the Ambatis that their conviction was a near certainty because of the prosecution case. The evidence was exemplary and the arguments strong. The public sentiment had turned against them over time. The adulation was over, the felicitations had ended. They were going to be pinned down. If they wanted to escape conviction, they had to move fast and offer a reasonable amount.

The Ambatis were keen to preserve whatever reputation they had left in the community and the Nandas were equally eager to forget the painful past and move forward. As the negotiations about the final settlement got underway, lawyers close to the Ambatis began leaking stories about Nanda's greed and his demands for a large compensatory amount. Nanda had asked for a minimum of fifteen lakh rupees as a permanent one-time alimony for Archana. It would cover the wedding expenses, the dowry and the time and money spent in court proceedings. After a few rounds of negotiations, the two sides agreed and worked out the financial details – both being adept at the job.

With the monetary aspect settled, they went to the family court to file a mutual consent divorce petition. The divorce decree was obtained without much difficulty but it contained several conditions. It was agreed that neither side would pursue any criminal or civil cases against the other or talk to the media. The divorce decree made the criminal case for dowry harassment against the Ambatis irrelevant and brought Janardhan's efforts to a naught. He was at the end of the trial and a verdict was expected. It would have been a big feather in his cap. 'I had conducted the prosecution with all the vehemence but I was forced to file to withdraw from prosecution. It was a sad end to a very good fight,' he told me five years later with just a hint of regret.

The Ambatis deposited the cheque for fifteen lakh rupees with Janardhan – such was his conduct that even they trusted him – which was to be given to Nanda only after the criminal case was dropped. Ambatis' lawyers filed a petition in the Karnataka High Court asking the state to withdraw the dowry case. There was a precedent for their move. There had been sixteen previous decisions by various high courts, which said that when a mutual consent divorce is obtained with a reasonable permanent alimony, there is no use pursuing a criminal case for dowry-related cruelty under section 498 (A).

But the Karnataka High Court didn't agree. Laying bare the pragmatic compulsions of both sides, the judges raised a pointed objection. Why didn't the Ambatis file the petition earlier? Why at the fag end of the trial? 'Now that the trial is almost over and you feel you are going to be convicted, you have come to the high court. You have not approached the court with good intentions,' the judges opined. The saga was to continue. Surprised and shocked by the rejection, the Ambatis complained bitterly to Janardhan but the matter had gone beyond him. They decided to approach the state government and met the then law minister of Karnataka, M.C. Nanaiah, to plead their case. They asked him to recommend withdrawal of the case. It was an unusual move but the Ambatis were in a corner. The more time they spent in Indian courts, the more they lost in America in terms of time and money. Nanaiah gave them a patient hearing and interviewed both Archana and Jayakrishna personally. He recorded their statements and convinced himself that the couple really could not ever come together. In light of the permanent alimony already having been decided, he recommended that the criminal case be dropped. He also weighed the fact that both were young and would marry again so the sooner they were free of legal encumbrances, the better. Nanaiah then directed Janardhan to withdraw the case.

I asked Janardhan if this kind of intervention by the law minister was common. He said it was done only in rare circumstances. The state withdraws a criminal case only in situations of national importance – for public good or when communal harmony is at stake. This was an unusual case because of the high quotient of public and media interest. 'In my opinion the government took a proper decision. The law minister himself interviewed the parties and convinced himself,' said Janardhan without apparent rancour, being a good soldier that he was. Perhaps this kind of end to an honestly investigated and well argued dowry case was preferable to what he faced most of the time – his own witnesses turning hostile in court after making a compromise deal. He told me of countless cases where he had put his heart and soul fighting for a dowry victim only to watch the girl's father change his story in court and his case fall apart. He had seen mothers turn around and tell blatant lies about their dead daughters because they had made a deal with the boy's side to drop the case. This was more acceptable, although still disappointing in some ways.

During the three-year trial period, Janardhan had got to know the Nandas quite well. He knew their difficulties. In fact, it was he who had suggested to Archana that she should study law and help other victims like her. The two still meet and when I told him that she had just begun practising, he was visibly moved. It was heartening to know the system also had compassionate, competent officers.

I drove over to Archana's hostel at the other end of Bangalore to bid goodbye. She was cheerful and showed me around the place, including the 'bunker' or the basement room for renters, which had few windows. She had just finished washing her clothes. They lay drying on the beds as we chatted. We talked about her childhood and her friends, and how they had stood by her during her ordeal. Her eyes moistened at the mention of one of her girlfriends who had been a rock of support.

As I left Archana I couldn't help feeling a mix of optimism and tension inside. She had risen to the challenge life had thrown and given a good fight but whether she could sustain her courage depended on how well she was accepted by her milieu. She was still fragile and needed to be saved from future shocks for a while. Or the pain she hides inside might come pouring out.

Fight to the Finish

Maria Bai Ki Kahani

Maria Bai Ashrafi's small face was dominated by a pair of big, brown spectacles, which moved down her slight nose every now and then. They gave her a serious and worried look, almost obscuring the fire in her eyes. But the fire was there, and it leaped out at unexpected moments, singeing the subject of her conversation. She sat ramrod straight adjusting her no-nonsense green nylon sari once in a while. The green sat well on her dark skin. It was the same green you see in mosques, on flags.

Maria was a devout Muslim and quoted often from the Quran, to illustrate how God was with her in her struggle or to send thunderbolts on all mankind. She had little patience for men, in fact none when you came right down to it. She had lived without their help most of her life. They formed a necessary – although she would question it – but not an important part of her world. At sixty-one years or thereabouts, she had grown so weary of men, she didn't even waste her anger on them. She needed to deal with them as most victims must but she didn't think they were worthy adversaries. They seemed puny despite their big crimes and faded quickly when faced with her simple faith and courage. They put hurdles in her path, but she kept going. She had goals and those had to be achieved.

Her goals were many and varied – to punish the man who she says burnt her daughter to death, to procure from him the mehr that she had wisely set so high, to make the legal system work for her, to survive on meagre earnings, to fight her many ailments, to worship her pir and to keep on the austere path she had chosen for herself. Life had rarely let her rest. So when it all came tumbling down with her only child's horrific death, Maria Bai cried a lot. She wondered if her God was being fair in his dispensation. But such thoughts lasted only a while and she quickly pulled herself together and carried on.

Men had inflicted a big blow this time, killing her daughter mercilessly, her beautiful Fatima. It would have broken anyone's spirit, especially after a lifetime of struggle and deprivation. Maria Bai had worked so hard to lift Fatima out of the morass of a peripheral existence. She had overcome the walls of her sprawling slum to make her daughter a doctor. Regular meals were not routine, nor was rest from the many jobs Maria had taken to earn money. It was a gruelling cycle – work, more work, tuitions, cooking, taking Fatima to school and bringing her back, typing at night for extra money and finally praying for long hours. She was a teacher at a small school and in her extra time she taught the Quran. After retirement, she had sold stamp paper for more than a decade in the Bangalore court complex for a small commission. Her hard work was rewarded when her daughter got her medical degree and began earning a living. She had made her daughter independent.

Fatima had died a doctor of Unani medicine. Maria Bai didn't understand Allah's ways but she didn't ever question them. She simply worked with whatever she had. No complaints, no bitterness in being hounded by the very force she had worshipped all her life, waking up before sunrise to read the Quran for two hours. It is a peaceful time to remember God – fewer noises, fewer distractions from her crowded living conditions.

'I need the peace it gives me to read the Quran. At night I am alone with my thoughts and no one can bother me,' she told me when we met in Bangalore. Her faith was her strength and it gave her the inner peace to carry on. Her poverty had blended well with her spiritual quest – so used was she to missing meals that fasting during Ramzan was not a problem, she told me with a laugh. Her rozas were frequent. She was a follower of Syed Tyyab Ashraf Jeelani, a pir who had come to the Hyderabad area from Pakistan and settled down. 'I am his mureed (devotee) and he protects me from the flood.' I was riveted by now as we sat across from each other and she opened her life up, chapter by chapter. Her story was all about courage and fortitude – the two words often used to describe the generals and armies of history. She was a general and an army rolled into one with a piercing voice, sharp enough to cause alarm. She used it effectively to command attention.

We met in the small two-room office of Vimochana, a group of women activists in Bangalore that had been helping Maria Bai fight her case. I had been in touch with Donna Fernandes, Vimochana's director, to seek her help in locating dowry victims in south India. Donna, who has been actively fighting for dowry victims for more than two decades, was responsive and immediately suggested several cases in and around the city. She had been in the trenches with the victims and knew them well. It was Donna and her group of dedicated caseworkers who had forced political attention on the high incidence of dowry deaths in Bangalore, a city otherwise associated with most things salubrious. They had led a successful public campaign in the late 1990s, backed by systematic research, forcing the state politicians to take notice. Vimochana's sterling work in the field had resulted in the formation in April 1999 of a Joint House Committee on

Atrocities Against Women to investigate the high rate of unnatural deaths and make recommendations. It was one of the few groups in India that was forcefully raising its banner against dowry deaths and working in a sustained manner. Donna was a storehouse of experience and information, who still hadn't become a cynic or a pessimist. I was lucky to have spent time with her, learning about how a grass-roots organization battles this ever bigger problem in the new century.

Donna's colleagues introduced me to several victims, some of them Muslim, who had come to Vimochana for help. They were at different stages of the long fight – some were just in the process of deciding whether to make their pain public, others were determined to seek legal help and still others who had been at it for years. The Muslim women seemed especially vulnerable because of the ease with which their husbands could abandon them if dowry demands were not met. They used the method of 'triple talaq', pronouncing the word three times to divorce a woman. One of the victims told me that she was always afraid when her husband drank and fought with her because in the heat of the moment he could always say the word.

The modern-day scourge of dowry demands and associated violence had over the years spread to the Muslim community through a seamless process of osmosis. The practice of dowry was present in the Muslim community since the medieval period but it wasn't as widely followed as among the Hindus. References to dowry are found in literature from the times of Balban, Firoz Shah Tuglaq, Akbar, and even Noorjahan, when charitable trusts were established to help parents straining to meet marriage expenses for their daughters. But the custom didn't assume the level of institutionalization seen among the Hindus because Muslims emulated Hindu patterns only to an extent. In the 1970s when dowry deaths were recognized as a specific form of violence against women, there were hardly any reports of this being a problem among the Muslims. But thirty years down the line, there are NGOs specifically working with Muslim victims of dowry violence.

Today the poor and lower-middle-class Muslim families are as likely to be victims of dowry demands as their Hindu counterparts. The shift took place slowly, over time, as Muslim families with sons saw utility in the practice. The logic was similar – dowry was an easy way to extort money and gifts from the bride's family. Middle-class families with sons in government service or on a dollar-earning job in the Gulf began demanding bigger and bigger dowries on grounds that they had invested more in the sons. The market value of Gulf-returned men automatically went up. In Bihar, Maharashtra, Andhra Pradesh, Karnataka and Kerala, where there was a significant Muslim population, reports of dowry deaths began surfacing as demands rose but a corresponding ability to deliver did not. NGOs working in Muslim-dominated areas recorded the phenomenon with alarm but the spread largely remained hidden from the pages of mainstream press.

Donna suggested I meet Maria because her story in many ways exemplified the particular difficulties Muslim women faced. Once I met Maria, I knew she was the right person. She struck me as an adamant feminist at first as I listened to her simple but strong beliefs about justice and fairness. But then I wondered if calling her a feminist would detract from her true stature because of the burden the word carries today. Many use the term more as an insult than a label of identification. Maria was not a feminist by training or conscious belief but by nature. A natural feminist, if I can call her that. She believed that women were just as able, as competent and as deserving of life's munificence as men. 'A woman can do a lot. She is not a lesser being by any means,' she said. She had lived her life with that core belief and worked within a system essentially unfriendly to women like her. She was a poor Muslim, a widow and alone, without a ring of supporting relatives. They kept their distance because they didn't like her fierce independence of mind. They were weary of her and even a bit afraid. She demanded her rights and was willing to fight for them. When I asked how she had managed all these years to survive alone as a woman, she recited a couplet with aplomb:

'Aurat kya kuch nahi kar sakti agar iraada kar le
Mard to sochta reh jata hai, aurat kar guzarti hai.'
(There is nothing a woman can't do, if she so decides,
The men keep ruminating, while the women just do it.)

Then she added with a final flourish: 'Hum kar guzre (I did it).' She threw her head from one side to another for emphasis then quickly adjusted her large glasses. 'A woman can survive without a man but a man can't survive without a woman. They need to feed their urges. They will shame themselves in brothels, wherever.' The pity in her voice was unmistakable. I wondered about her confidence – she had oodles of it. From where did she get it? Not from her traditional family which had never encouraged independence of thinking or action. Not from her environment, which was the typical veiled environment of a poor Muslim community where women stayed in the background and men called the shots. When I asked her, she simply said: 'You get self-confidence from Allah. You get confidence from Baghdad's pirs. You get confidence from Medina.' Her faith was clearly her guiding light. She looked to the Quran for solving the riddles of life, interpreting it far more progressively than the reigning mullahs might. Keeping women uneducated or undereducated and suppressed was not her creed. She knew her book well since she had been a Quran teacher in her younger days.

'If I get into trouble, I just go to my pir's mazaar and pray. He often appears in my dreams and tells me not to worry. You will win, he tells me. Inshallah, hum jeetenge (God willing, we will win),' she told me. The royal 'hum' sounded natural from Maria's mouth, not awkward. 'He (her son-in-law) won't come out of jail. He will die there. But his punishment is only a part of my quest. I want to live and abide by Islam and die according to it. I have already chosen the place for my burial. I have kept my clothes aside. I have to go someday but I am not afraid. I don't want to hurt anyone. Allah says all souls belong to him – Hindus, Muslims, everyone. All are human beings but humanity is what so many lack.'

The battle-scarred yet combat-ready woman in front of me was impressive. A big powerhouse packed in a tiny frame. A great raconteur, she remembered details without having to be prodded. She had had considerable experience dealing with journalists – she counted some among her friends and inquired about them. 'I call them once in a while when I feel lonely,' she told me. She had testified in front of the House Committee on Atrocities Against Women set up by the Karnataka government in response to the Vimochana campaign for action. Standing before members of the state assembly, she loudly condemned the policemen who had investigated her daughter's case. She pointed at the police commissioner and said, 'You have cheated me.' The final report of the House Committee contained Maria's testimony along with the answers the committee had sought from the police in connection with her allegations. The police commissioner defended himself and his force, saying blandly that there was nothing wrong with the investigation. 'Laymen have so much pain, they will tend to exaggerate,' he said, leaving both Maria and Vimochana volunteers aghast.

Maria's fight is uphill all the way. She is the only prosecution witness. The only other friend and well wisher who met Fatima on her deathbed and listened to her version of events left Bangalore and settled in Saudi Arabia a couple of years ago. Maria has to convince the judge that Fatima did not die an accidental death but was killed by her husband. Her daughter told her how her husband had poured kerosene on her and lit the match. But the case is complicated because Fatima gave more than one 'dying declaration' – one of the most crucial pieces of evidence in a dowry-death case. In her first dying declaration, she said she was burnt in an accidental stove burst while in the second statement she accused her husband of setting her aflame. Maria claims that the police refused to record her 'real' statement even though Fatima was fully coherent and conscious and had told her everything clearly. A police inspector called Pratap Singh allegedly listened to Fatima but did not write anything down. 'Not one word was written. He told me later, "Let the girl get a bit better and then we will record her statement," ' Maria remembered. She must establish that the police played unfair by not seizing the evidence and by delaying every stage of the investigation.

Fatima was a pretty girl with large, dark eyes. On her wedding day, she had worn a red dupatta laden with silver gota and covered her head. She looked confident and secure in her world. She knew her husband-to-be and they had met each other several times during her mother's illness. Syed Khwaja Peer was a rakishly handsome fellow who hovered near her as she ran between her college and her home, tending to her mother. She was in her fourth year at the Unani Medical College in Bangalore and trying hard to cope with the demanding schedule. She would soon be a doctor, a dream she and her mother had shared forever. But Maria had fallen sick with meningitis and Fatima had to look after her, the house and her studies. They had only each other in this world. The mother had worked hard for Fatima and now she must be there in her time of need. She couldn't neglect her college – ammi won't be happy. But she simply couldn't cope and had to take leave from her college to nurse her mother. It was sometime around 1996 and Syed had recently moved next door to their house in Wilson Garden. Very soon he was visiting Maria Bai's house to meet Fatima. His parents befriended the family too.

Fatima was vulnerable – her mother was seriously ill and there was no one else to lean on for support. Syed and his family seemed like nice people. She did not resist his attention. Syed said he was a computer engineer and that had made even her mother sit up and take notice. When his parents suggested that the two get married, Fatima welcomed the idea. Syed was 'educated' just like her and with her medical practice meshing in nicely with his job, they would be comfortable. At least there won't be any need to keep out-of-season rozas, she thought to herself with a smile. She could even help her mother financially. Syed seemed like a good prospective husband – he was employed (at a multinational company, he had told her) and he had potential. She was excited about moving to her 'own' house even though she loved her mother dearly. As Maria Bai recovered from meningitis, Syed increased the pressure to get married. His parents pestered Maria daily and Syed didn't even want to wait till she had completed her degree. But fortunately for Fatima, Maria Bai put her foot down. She certainly wasn't going to allow her daughter to get carried away by some young man's fleeting passion and destroy her career. Young Syed would simply have to wait, the mother decreed. But he kept up the pressure, as did his parents who visited often.

Syed and Fatima were married on 23 October 1997, soon after she completed her last exam. He had been in such a hurry to claim her as it were. Thanks to Maria's foresight, most of the big items needed for the marriage were already there because she had been buying them slowly over the years. Whenever she collected a few thousand rupees, she got something for Fatima's big day. There were mattresses, bedsheets, clothes, jewellery and even a few new pots and pans. She was not giving a big dowry because, for her, Fatima didn't need one. Her daughter was educated and would earn all her life. Still she spent more than 1.5 lakh rupees on the wedding what with food and other arrangements. Her pir's wife came to bless Fatima. It was a happy time for Maria – the hustle and bustle, the good food, people all around.

The newlyweds moved in with Maria because she had more room and Maria didn't mind. This way Fatima would be close to her – what more could she want? In case she fell sick or hurt herself, at least her doctor daughter would be around to take care of her. After all she was getting on in years.

But the new member of Maria's family did not make a smooth transition. Any change is difficult but Syed showed every trapping of a traditional son-in-law. He expected Fatima to wait on him and satisfy his every whim. He would shout across the room, demanding this or that. The two women in the house were irritated at first and slowly grew alarmed. His attention-seeking behaviour was difficult for Fatima who was struggling with the demands of her profession on the one hand and household responsibilities on the other. Within a few months of marriage Syed stopped working altogether. He would disappear in the morning and come back home drunk. He began asking for money from his aged mother-in-law. He had told them that he had a job at a Pepsi bottling plant but today Maria doubts even that along with all his other claims. She was ashamed of her son-in-law but couldn't say much. He would create a scene every other day and storm out of the house. Poor Fatima had to run after him. Once she found him in a park, sitting on a bench.

'I used to tell him that one must live with dignity and die with dignity but he paid no attention. He would only shout. He misbehaved all the time,' Maria told me. After about six months of grating on each other's nerves, Maria told Fatima that it might be best if they moved out and looked for a new place. 'I didn't want all these games. I told her to take him away and I left for a month. I locked up my room and told them that I expected them to move out by the time I came back.'

'But when I came back, he threatened me and asked me to leave my own house. I said none of this nonsense would work with me. So he grabbed my neck. I thought this was the limit. I couldn't tolerate all this. I told Fatima to take him away and told her I didn't want to talk to him again,' Maria recalled. She didn't suggest divorce because she wanted Fatima to make that decision on her own. She remembers the exact date when Fatima and Syed left her house. It was 19 March 1998, a day she won't easily forget because of another date that is lodged in her brain. 'She was burnt on 5 December 1998. She was away from me for eight months. He did all this in eight months.'

Fatima and Syed moved to another place in what Maria referred to as a 'third-class area'. It was in a poor, dirty part of Bangalore, far worse than where Maria was living. But separation was the better part of valour in this case. It was no use living with constant bickering. He might behave better with his wife if Maria wasn't around. Mothers-in-law create their own tension in a spousal relationship. But he wasn't going to let go so easily. He kept pushing Fatima to ask her mother for more money and other household items. Then he came up with a totally outrageous demand.

He demanded that Maria pay for a clinic for Fatima and him. Maria was taken aback. She didn't have that kind of money lying around. But he insisted and even Fatima seemed to think the idea of a private clinic in itself wasn't bad – it was a logical progression for her. Fatima had finished her medical degree and instead of working in a hospital, she could start her own practice. The idea began appealing to Maria too. The more she thought about it, the more sensible it sounded. She somehow arranged for twenty-five thousand rupees for the clinic but attached a condition: the young couple would have to give her one thousand rupees every month from their earnings for her upkeep. A fair stipulation, she thought. Maria had raised Fatima single handedly, educated her, made her a doctor and even provided the money for her to open a clinic. She herself needed help now that her bones were slowly giving way. She wasn't able to work anymore.

The clinic was soon opened and started doing well. Patients began coming in droves since it isn't easy to get a woman doctor in a poor Muslim area. Fatima soon had a thriving practice but Syed wasn't happy. He resented the monthly payments to Maria. He didn't like his mother-in-law's strong and practical bent of mind. Besides, she was always advising Fatima on what to do. He was jealous of the mother-daughter bond, which seemed to exclude him. It was as if he weren't there. He felt the need to establish who the boss was. So what if they were living in Maria's house and he was unemployed and even unemployable. No one was clear about his alleged 'computer engineering' degree – did he really have one? But he didn't feel the need to explain himself. He was Fatima's husband and the only male around. If she was a successful doctor, it was because he was 'allowing' her to be one. Her mother's time was done.

Syed demanded that all the clinic's earnings be handed over to him. Fatima and Maria resisted the idea but he got abusive. He then decided to 'play' doctor at the clinic himself, saying Fatima should just teach him the basics on the spot. The rest would be easy because he would get a false certificate from Hyderabad where apparently any degree can be bought for a price. Fatima was appalled at the dangerous scheme. How could anyone dream of playing with people's lives? She had got her degree after five years of hard work. She didn't want to be part of this fraud, which would threaten people's lives. When she refused, Syed lost control. Maria remembers there was a big fight over it.

'I supported my daughter and told her he shouldn't come near the clinic. He would ruin her reputation too,' Maria told me. 'Medicine is not like selling onions and potatoes. He couldn't just become a doctor overnight. What if the police found out about the false certificate and took him away? But he wasn't concerned. He began fighting about everything. He said he didn't want to give the one thousand rupees to me every month. When Fatima came to visit me, he wouldn't let her spend any time with me.' At first, Fatima visited every week to see her mother and make sure she was alright, then it became once in two weeks and slowly it was once a month. The mother started to lose touch with her daughter and when Maria tried to send messages, she was rebuffed. Maria remembers that whenever she asked Fatima to come back to her to stay, her daughter would say, 'Amma, don't worry, I will take care of myself. I can't be a burden on you again after you have done so much for me. Little did she know what he would do to her . . . ,' Maria's voice trailed off.

It was on 5 December 1998, when Syed came to Maria's house and told her that Fatima was burnt in a stove burst. It was about midday when he broke the devastating news. He told her that she had been admitted to the Baptist Hospital, a private hospital in Bangalore. Maria begged him to take her to the hospital. It was around 2 p.m. when she finally reached the hospital and saw her daughter lying on a bed. She was charred with 90 per cent burns. Maria couldn't bear to look at her little Fatima, her daughter whom she loved so much and had so proudly brought up. Maria wanted to scream out loud but someone had robbed her voice. She could only feel anger and grief welling up inside her.

'Asalaam walekum, ammi. Mujhe Quran baksh do (Greetings, mother. Please bless me with the Quran),' Fatima said, her voice faint but clear. Maria sat down beside her. She felt so helpless that day. She couldn't do anything for her daughter. She couldn't even hold her in her arms. The doctors and nurses were rushing about but no one had the time to answer the million questions surging through Maria's mind. She felt a deep pounding inside her head. Maria began getting angry, so angry that she wanted to break something. She asked Fatima how it happened and her daughter told her the whole story.

Syed had gone out early in the morning, maybe around 8 a.m. It was a Saturday, and Fatima was busy cooking for the day. She didn't think anything of it when he left the house so early. They had been quarrelling for the past four or five days over the same old things – get more money from your mother, don't give her the monthly allowance, and on and on. Fatima was tired of the constant fighting but felt trapped in the situation. She didn't think it wise to return to her mother's home – what would people say? They would only blame her. That she couldn't make her marriage work. That she has no mercy for an old mother who had already done more than her fair share for her daughter. That because she was a doctor, she had airs and didn't want to look after her husband. Walking out and living on her own didn't seem practical. These thoughts were going through her mind when she heard the door open an hour later.

Syed staggered in drunk and banged the door shut behind him. Fatima went back to her cooking when she suddenly felt something cold on her shoulders. She turned around and saw Syed behind her. The next thing she knew she was in flames and struggling. He had taken the ultimate revenge. She tried to run but the door was locked. She rolled on the floor to extinguish the flames and she screamed in pain. Nothing seemed to help, the pain was excruciating, the shock of it all even worse. She begged him to take her to the hospital but he wouldn't – not until he had cleaned up the place. She knew her chances of survival were dimming with every passing minute. She begged him to call her mother at least but he wouldn't even do that. He told her that he would take her to the hospital and inform her mother on one condition – that she should not implicate him or his family in any statement to the police. She agreed, hoping to live long enough to tell her mother the truth. Syed finally called a taxi and took Fatima to the hospital.

As Maria listened to her daughter, she felt her head was going to burst. She didn't know whether to comfort her daughter or to hurt the man who had done this to her. She had braved a lot in life but this was a test she hadn't prepared for. Her Allah hadn't given her any clues about this one. She felt helpless and angry but she knew she couldn't afford to get immobilized, not now. She had to act.

She ran to the police station with some people and demanded action. It was about seven in the evening. Maria claims that valuable evidence of the murder was lost because of the callousness of the police at the K.G. Halli police station. They delayed going to the scene of crime for hours despite her pleas. Even registering her complaint took some time. Sub-inspector Appa Ji, whose name Maria clearly remembered, repeatedly told her that her daughter was a victim of an accident and there was no need to lodge a complaint. Only when she put pressure by taking some of the neighbourhood people to the police station did the police agree to visit the house where Fatima lived. Maria accompanied the police team – a sub-inspector, two constables and her son-in-law to the house to find the stove, which is said to have burst, intact with no apparent signs of damage. The house was clean. 'The police didn't seize the stove. I kept asking them to,' Maria recalled.

She named two police officers as prime culprits for the shoddy manner the half-hearted investigation was done. The police seemed to have decided beforehand that it was a case of accidental burning, not murder. At one point, an inspector told her that since it was a love marriage, it was unlikely that the husband would have burned her. Maria even saw one of the inspectors laughing and chatting with Syed and feting him with coffee and dosas inside the police station. It broke her heart to see her daughter's tormentor hobnobbing with the police with impunity. 'If the police had given him two kicks, he would have confessed. Instead they were looking after him like a guest. He had paid them off.' No one seemed to be bothered about Fatima's fate. Maria told me that she doesn't know if her daughter's statement had been recorded honestly because it was written in Kannada, a language she neither reads nor writes. 'I don't know what they recorded in my name so I refused to sign it.' She alleged that Syed and his family had bribed the policemen with the money from the clinic and that the murder was planned. The wedding album had been removed from the house, presumably to hide or destroy evidence of the marriage itself but the police did nothing to try to find it.

Even Maria, who had faced life with a quiet stoicism, felt defeated that night. She didn't know whether to run after the police to make them do their job or to take care of her dying Fatima. She had to arrange for money to get medicines. When she went to the bank to withdraw money, she desperately hoped her daughter would still be alive on her return. The nurses were of little help, hardened as they tend to become after years in a hospital watching burn victims. Maria did most of the nursing herself – from cleaning Fatima to reminding the nurses about the glucose drip. 'My daughter was in bandages from head to toe. But she could talk clearly. She used to say, "Allah, forgive me for whatever sins I have committed and give me a place in heaven. I am coming to you. They have done this to me, punish them." '

Maria told me that even though Fatima was conscious and coherent, the police failed to come to record a new statement, preferring to stay with the first one given immediately upon arrival in the hospital in which she had exonerated her husband. 'I called Inspector Pratap Singh several times but he kept making excuses.' Maria begged him because she knew Fatima didn't have much time. When he finally came it was a few days later but it was as if God was keeping Fatima alive. Pratap Singh told Maria to stand outside the room while he went inside to speak to Fatima who told him everything about how Syed had poured kerosene on her. Maria was standing outside and listening. 'I heard everything – about the fight, about the burning.' But the inspector didn't write anything down. When Maria demanded to know why he hadn't recorded the statement, he allegedly said he would come later when Fatima was a little better. Whatever he did record was in Kannada, a language that Maria couldn't read. In the end the police recorded three separate statements by Fatima. According to a report in *Frontline* of 27 August 1999, in the first dying declaration Fatima said she was burnt in an accidental stove burst. In the second and third statements, she accused her husband of setting her ablaze. The doctors signed the papers but didn't get involved.

Fatima died on 11 December 1998 after struggling for her life for six whole days. She had been married for just over a year, a year that was long on discord and short on happiness. Maria Bai Ashrafi was suddenly all alone in the world with not a soul she could call her own. It was evening when Fatima left her charred body, just after the azaan, the call to prayers. Maria had spent the whole day running about lodging complaints and trying to get copies of police reports. She was sitting by her daughter when Fatima asked her mother to read the Quran. Maria knew the time had come. Her breathing was erratic and she was losing consciousness. It was a miracle that she had lived so many days and in such pain. The doctors ordered a postmortem and wrote down the cause of death as 'shock' even though Fatima had 90 per cent burns, according to the distraught mother. And it was several hours before the body was handed over to the mother. Maria took her to the cemetery, bathed her and buried her. It was nearly midnight by the time the prayers were done and she came home. Syed didn't show up for the burial or any of the formalities.

It was a sad homecoming. Maria couldn't sleep that night. Her mind kept racing from one thing to another. She paced up and down her small room, sometimes sitting on the bed, sometimes looking out on the road. She felt drained and tired but there was no rest. For the first time she was afraid but she didn't want to admit it even to herself. The darkness of the night scared her. It was not like any other night. It had the power to black out anything, everything. She tried hard to save herself from being swamped but the dark waves kept lashing at her. She waited for the first sounds of dawn which always seemed to come too early when she was reading the holy book but that night the birds were silent. Their busy sounds of first hint of activity were always Maria's favourite. They were like a band leading her very own procession to face another day.

A total of three FIRs were filed in the case, all because of Maria Bai's doggedness and fearlessness. The first FIR was filed on 5 December 1998, the day Fatima got burned, under section 498 (A) dealing with cruelty against a woman for dowry. The second FIR was filed on 11 December, the day she died, under section 306 for abetment to suicide following Maria's second statement to the police. But the police still would not consider Fatima's case a murder no matter how much Maria tried. She got help from Vimochana, the activist group, whose volunteers showed up in strength to ensure the police would listen to her and follow the rules. She also wrote to the state home minister, Roshan Baig, asking for help. He called the police on her behalf and a senior level police officer began overseeing the case.

It was only on 6 January 1999 that a third and final FIR was lodged under section 302 for murder. Over the next few months, Maria ran to the police station many times to ensure that the police were doing their job but the progress was slow. They first wouldn't give her a copy of the FIRs and when they did, it was incomplete, she claimed. She had to call the senior police officer again to pull up the inspectors investigating the case. A chargesheet was filed six months after the crime and charges were framed under sections 498 (A) and 302. Syed was in jail for a few weeks but he was released on bail conditional to his appearance in court for the hearings. Finally, the case was committed to the sessions court.

'Everything has taken so long that that boy (Syed) has manipulated all the neighbours. He laughs at me openly when he sees me in court. He says he would never go to jail,' Maria told me during our long interview. Her life was now centred around the many court cases she must fight. Rarely did a day go by without a run to a lawyer's office or to the court. She carried a thick diary with reminders, important dates, names of people and messages to stay abreast of her many appointments with the law and lawyers. She consulted it often to check on her facts. Her meagre resources were stretched but Vimochana volunteers were a constant help and source of strength.

After Fatima died, Maria's landlord told her to leave the house because of the court case. As if she needed any more calamities to befall her, any more knots in her life. She ran around and got an injunction with the help of her friends. But the landlord made it known that she wasn't welcome and her continued stay would not be easy. He said she was 'trouble' and began harassing her. She got a cassette by post filled with abusive language and other threats. 'I took the cassette to the DCP and to the judge and made them listen. It is so horrible, you would cover your ears,' she told me.

Maria clearly knew how to fight back and that was a blessing. She was not intimidated by the thought of going to court or facing a judge. After all, she had spent a lifetime selling stamp paper in the Bangalore court complex, thanks to the kindness of a judge who had helped in getting her started. She was familiar with the system and to some extent even the law. She knew about injunctions, orders, hearings, evidence, judgments. She had survived for nearly two decades as a stamp paper vendor – a highly competitive and charged world. Of her 3 per cent commission, she had to hand over 1 per cent to the lawyer who brought clients to her for stamp paper. 'I had to give income tax on my sales but the lawyers got it for free,' she recalled with a smile. She also did some typing sitting in the corridors. When she started her vending business in 1977, the cost of typing was three rupees per page and by the time she stopped in 1995, it had gone up to five rupees per page. It wasn't a princely rate by any means but Maria had to eke out a living somehow and this was a respectable way to do it. She earned about two to three thousand rupees a month from selling stamp papers and typing.

Those days her work day began before dawn when she prayed to the Almighty to make her little Fatima excel in school. She then filled water in drums and got milk. As dawn would break, Maria would be in the kitchen packing lunch boxes for the two of them. Fatima would wake up and get dressed herself – she was quite self-sufficient even as a little girl. Her mother had ensured that for her own sanity. It was important for little girls to take care of their own chores and then help with additional ones. In this respect, Maria was no different from an average Indian mother. A daughter was expected to turn into a mini mother as soon as possible and learn cooking, sewing, cleaning. Once the mother-daughter team was ready, Maria would sit Fatima in the front of her bicycle, and load her typewriter on one side of the back wheel, and the school bag and tiffin boxes on the other. Maria couldn't ride the bicycle because the weight was too much for her frail and petite frame to pull. So she walked the cycle until the school, dropped Fatima and then rode to the court.

Once in the court, she did some typing and selling. She got to know some lawyers and judges who became her mentors. They would help her out financially whenever she was in dire straits. One such was Zaheer Ahmed, a law clerk, who helped Maria and Fatima through some bad patches. He treated Maria as a sister and kept in touch. It was Ahmed who went to the police with Maria when Fatima was in the hospital to plead with them to arrest Syed. He also heard a full account of what happened from Fatima before she died. He could be a crucial witness but he recently moved to Saudi Arabia to join his son. He was the only person Maria trusted and treated as family. He was there when Fatima died and she would never forget that. 'I lost my daughter. I was distraught but none of my real relatives were there to even condole with me. Why shouldn't I hate them?' They had been of no help in her dark days, she said. 'Men say I am a woman and I must talk like a woman. I tell them, I don't wear bangles because I gave them all to you.'

Fatima's murder case is not the only case Maria must fight. She is also fighting a civil case against Syed to get the mehr of 1.5 lakh rupees but that too is proving to be an uphill struggle. Even though she has the nikahnama, which clearly sets out the terms of marriage, Syed has failed to pay the money so far. 'The mehr has to come to me. There are no two ways about it,' she told me confidently. So far there have been about twenty hearings in the civil case but Syed has evaded them all. He somehow managed to evade the summons although Maria said he would have to be served sooner or later. The money would be helpful now that she has no real earning capacity. She told me that she had to sell her belongings to raise money to live. She often eats one meal a day, sometimes if that. 'If I get the mehr, I will go to Mecca and Medina. I have no other desire now.'

Maria's stoicism was strong, almost frightening in its enormity. She was a real-life heroine and listening to her recount her life story, one felt small, very small, in comparison. She had the conviction of truth and the strength of a dynamo. She believed with her whole heart. 'Allah will take care of me till I die. He hasn't made me beg or lose my dignity so far. I still have my izzat,' she said. 'I have lived on my will power. And I am still alone – it's my fate. It must be written on my forehead,' she said, drawing an imaginary line across.

But her loneliness is not tinged with sadness because Maria has lived alone with aplomb. She lost her father when she was very young – she couldn't remember exactly how young but she doesn't remember his face. She lived in purdah as did her mother and the women around them in Bangalore. India was newly independent and Maria has a few memories of 1947, the heady year when everything seemed hopeful and resurgent. Her mother married her off when she was only thirteen years old and her first husband turned out to be abusive. He would beat her up just to show his power over her. When he realized that she could sing, he took her to Bombay and tried to put her on a kotha. Her marriage lasted a little more than two months. Maria asked for a khula (when a woman asks for divorce) and came back to her mother. Her mother died in 1963 and her relatives tried to get her married off again. But Maria resisted and said she wanted to study. 'I will marry when I want,' she told them flatly.

She came out of the purdah and shed her burqa to start on her lonesome journey. 'I wanted to show my uncles and aunts that I could do it. So what if I was a girl? They told me to come and live with them but I refused. Ever since childhood, I have been like this – a hard nut to crack,' she said with relish. She would cook herself, eat by herself and sleep alone in her father's house. She enrolled herself in seventh standard in a government high school and passed her matric exam in home science. She then decided to go to Hyderabad to Osmania University to learn Urdu. She had to fudge her age in order to get in, she told me. Those were hard times – she had to look for ways to finance herself. She sold saris to earn money. She often had one meal in two days, surviving on a cup of tea and biscuits. 'I had no choice. For years I have lived on a cup of coffee decoction and one roti. I fasted but I never begged anyone for help. I worked and got paid. Food and water are not that important – your izzat is.' The frugal meals and a largely liquid diet of caffeine have left their own legacy on her delicate body. Her oesophagus has been affected – it has shrunk because it imbibed mainly liquids.

Sometime during those hard years she met a man who pursued her with zeal. 'He told me he would take care of me and I believed him.' Maria married him in 1969 but he died when she was pregnant with Fatima. But it wasn't a happy marriage and Maria was reluctant to talk about it. 'Why do you want to know all this, ma?' she would endearingly ask every now and then, adding the ma at the end as many do in south India. I told her I was fascinated by her story and how far behind she had left her burqa, the veil that she had shed without ceremony. But to her there was nothing unusual about anything. Her progression was as natural as growing old. After Fatima was born in 1970, Maria went to Hyderabad with her to try to make a new life and spent nearly seven years there. She did odd jobs selling household items and earning a commission. She somehow made ends meet while ensuring schooling for her daughter. But it was a hard life in a new city. Her cynicism grew in direct proportion to her experiences. 'People are good there. They stab you from the front, not from behind as in Bangalore,' she told me. Maria's pain and anger often spilt out unexpectedly through her studiedly calm exterior.

Some time in the mid 1960s, she had visited the courts for the first time when her uncle filed a case, claiming a share for his son in her father's property. She fought but the house had to be auctioned and proceeds divided. She got ten thousand rupees, which she put away in the bank for later.

Maria has been fighting court cases ever since and is obviously familiar with the law and her rights. She has fought successfully and received compensation from the court for an accident injury. All her efforts were directed towards one goal – to educate Fatima. She even considered going to Saudi Arabia and paid an agent in Mumbai fifteen thousand rupees to get on a ship. She abandoned the plan when she realized the nature of the work she would be required to do. To finance Fatima's medical college expenses, she sold one of her kidneys for fifty thousand rupees, she told me calmly. As I listened, I had no doubt that Maria would fight to the finish. And receive justice for her daughter.

Love Story Gone Wrong

Mary Shaila's Story

College was something Mary Shaila Pereira had always looked forward to – it had meant freedom and opportunity. Freedom from the small town she lived in and opportunity to pursue her ambition to be an engineer. She had always dreamed about moving to a big city and getting a job in the real world. It was boom time for techies and she wanted to be one. Everyone she knew was either studying computers or doing a management degree. The luckier ones had gone abroad. She too wanted to be part of the rush – it seemed so exciting. Very soon she would get her degree and be out applying for jobs.

Her mind was focused on making something of her life. Her parents had encouraged her to be independent. They had given their two children the best they could offer but they didn't want to stand in the way of future opportunities. They knew a better life awaited them beyond Chickballapur, which wasn't the centre of the universe or even a minor hub of activity even though it was near Bangalore and benefited somewhat from its shadow. Their children had a feel for what was possible beyond the boundaries and Mary Shaila was eager to explore and experience that world. She was a bright student and full of promise.

Her father, Francis Pereira, was a teacher in a primary school and her mother Rosy a government health inspector. Their standard of living was comfortably middle class, no frills but they had everything they needed – a small house, some savings and enough to take a vacation or two. The

Pereiras had always emphasized education, believing firmly in the wisdom of hard work and rewards. Mary Shaila did well at school, always working conscientiously to improve her marks. The teachers liked her cheerful and enthusiastic disposition. They could depend on her for extra tasks during crunch times – be it the annual day function or the sports day. They knew she would succeed in life because she had a rare combination of grit and dedication. She was keen to get on and take responsibility. When she decided to enrol for a bachelor's in electrical engineering in nearby Karkala, her teachers felt she was on the right path.

It was a big day for the Pereira family when Mary Shaila left home for higher studies. The little girl in pigtails had grown up and was venturing out on her own. Rosy and Francis had never let her stay out of sight for too long but that day they bid her a cheery goodbye. A part of them was being separated but the joy of seeing one's own all grown up was greater than the sadness of separation. They gave her the usual set of warnings about being careful in a new place, not to stay out late and not to trust total strangers. She was their first born, special as all first borns are to parents. Mary Shaila listened carefully to the advice and promised to follow the rules. She herself was a bit afraid but she didn't want to make any confession of fear lest her parents change their mind and keep her back. But inside her a giant ferris wheel of emotions was whirling. What if she felt lonely? What if she couldn't cope with the studies? What if she didn't make any friends? But underneath the fears was a distinct bubble of excitement and wonder. She had always waited for this moment and now it had come.

It was a rite of passage for Mary Shaila. She had pinned all her hopes on going to college, imagining it as a new world where she would count for something, someone. She was stepping into adulthood, unchaperoned. She would make her own decisions, decide when to study and when to chill out. A room of her own in a hostel with other girls and they would talk late into the night. There would be marathon sessions of fun to look forward to. The anticipation had been building for months. She had plans but fuzzy ones – of travelling to different parts of the country and just watching and absorbing. College would give her the opportunity to do that, she thought. Trips with friends on long train rides. New avenues. There was a world of promise waiting to be explored. And she was ready for it. It was 1995, the year she crossed a major threshold in life.

She hugged her mother really hard – Rosy had been Mary Shaila's mentor, confidant and advisor rolled into one. She was going to miss her mother, she knew. No one could pamper her more. She didn't have to worry about a thing with her mother around – her clothes were always washed and ironed, the food was always on the table and even her messages were taken down meticulously. As the day of departure had neared, Rosy had become even more lavish and loving. She cooked her daughter's favourite dishes in succession and fussed over her as never before. It was all an attempt to hide the anxiety beneath, the sadness that was about to overwhelm Rosy. She had got Mary Shaila's clothes ready, shoes mended and even bought a supply of basic medicines. After all, her daughter shouldn't have to run to the pharmacy in time of need.

Mary Shaila enrolled at NMAMIT College at Karkala in Udipi district for her bachelor's in electrical engineering. The first few days passed off like a dream. She sailed from class to class, learning the ropes and getting to know her new professors. She made new friends and got into the swing of things. Her first year at college passed quickly, in fact too quickly, she thought. The routine of classes, exams and visits home kept her busy and she hardly realized when the months melted away. And before she knew, she was in the fourth year.

Early in 1999, a young man by the name of Ivan D'Souza introduced himself to her. She remembers the day when Ivan, a slightly portly guy, came up to her and struck a conversation as young men tend to do. It was clear that he was interested in her. She was an attractive young woman with a wide, open smile. Her short, cropped hair gave her a bouncy, fun appearance. She gradually became friendly with Ivan who seemed to follow her wherever she went. She began enjoying the attention. The fact that he was a little older seemed exciting. He said he was a BCom graduate and owned the Golden Gate, a bar and restaurant in Karkala. Mary Shaila liked him and soon they began dating each other. They went out often for long, lingering cups of coffee and to the movies. Before she knew it, she was in love, or so she thought.

'I started visiting his house and his family. They took to me very well. His mother and father both seemed to like me,' a distraught Mary Shaila told me more than a year later when we met. She carried with her a heavy bundle of court papers, which she pulled out to prove her point every now and then. We met for the first time in October 2001 at the office of Vimochana, the Bangalore-based activist group that has been helping her fight her case of dowry harassment. She was about five feet three inches and was dressed in a pair of blue jeans and a short white patterned T-shirt. Looking at her, one wouldn't imagine she was a victim of dowry harassment. She seemed so young, so trendy in some ways and capable of looking after herself. You could imagine her sitting in a college cafeteria sipping tea and cracking jokes with her mates. But I had learnt that there was no 'typical' victim – I had met and heard about women and families who one could never associate with dowry harassment or torture. Education, status or wealth was no indication of social behaviour. An educated man was just as capable of raw greed as an illiterate country bumpkin. A rich family could be just as crude in its demands as a small-time trader.

Mary Shaila seemed vulnerable in her suffering, but defiant in her will to punish the man, who she said had defrauded her and ruined her life. She wanted Ivan to go to jail. Nothing less, nothing more. Her determination was clear and so far her parents had supported her in her fight. She had seen a lot in her twenty-four years, more than she had bargained for. The whole episode with Ivan had left her broken and embittered. But what was disturbing was her postscript. She told me repeatedly that after she finished the court case, she would simply 'end' her life. 'I don't want to live anymore,' she said, her eyes carrying the sadness of broken dreams. 'I just want to die. What is there for me now?' Words failed me as I listened to her – what could one say to such a declaration? When I tried feebly to contradict her, she simply laughed at me with her big, teary eyes. She said her mind was made up. All I could hope for is that she would begin to look at life again. I wondered if her parents knew what she was thinking.

It was a bright sunny day when Ivan took Mary Shaila home to introduce her to his family. The D'Souzas had a decent house with four bedrooms and a large compound. They had a large grove of coconut trees, apart from mango and cashewnut trees. There was an air of tranquillity, that languid feeling of a semi rural setting, which forces you to lie back on a charpai and soak in the heat. The warm air made everything seem more comfortable. Ivan's mother Anna Severine welcomed Mary Shaila into the home and showed her around. There was the usual round of tea and snacks and the family chatted about this and that. Ivan's brother Joy was around but his father sat quietly on his chair, not saying much. He seemed lost in his own world and she learned later that he was suffering from a mental disorder. She was not told the exact nature of his problem but it was clear he was not all there. He needed help to feed himself. Mary Shaila felt very much at home at their place. They all seemed friendly and eager to get to know her. She was fortunate, she thought.

She soon became a regular visitor to the D'Souza household, visiting them for Sunday lunches and often staying on for dinner. The family doted on her and adopted her as a future permanent member. She enjoyed her visits, getting to know Ivan's mother really well and other aunts and uncles. She soon began helping out in family chores, and they in turn sought her opinion on family matters. Two of the brothers were in the Middle East earning a good living. When they visited India, Mary Shaila was there for the get-togethers. She doesn't know when the transition happened from being a girlfriend to a prospective daughter-in-law but it did. Anna Severine started depending on her as one – asking her to take care of small errands, household chores and even a bit of cooking.

It had been just a few months – April 1999 to be precise – since she and Ivan had met but it seemed that she had always been part of the family. He suggested they get engaged. This meant she was the one for Ivan, a man she now loved dearly and couldn't imagine living without. Things were moving fast but Mary Shaila didn't mind. She called up her family and told them that Ivan and she were planning to exchange rings as a mark of commitment to each other. They told her to be careful and give the relationship some time. But she was on fast forward and didn't want to hear any words of caution.

Mary Shaila's family went to meet the D'Souzas in May the same year and everything went off well. The two sides got along well as the prospective bride's nervousness gave way to pure joy. Anna Severine showed Rosy photographs of her family and shared anecdotes. Rosy was pleased to see her daughter smiling in the photos, glowing, in fact, standing next to Ivan. It was indeed a pleasant day for all – Rosy's fears about her daughter's future were set at rest and Anna Severine was able to judge and assess the family. What Rosy didn't know was the tenor of things to come. She came away satisfied with the choice of her daughter, thinking Mary Shaila had been lucky to find such an accepting and accommodating family on her own. She was proud of her daughter's mature judgment.

A few days later Ivan asked her to move into his house and save the rent on the hostel. She hesitated a bit, wary of losing her independence, but a part of her was genuinely flattered. She was excited at the prospect of living in his house but thought it would be best to ask her parents first. After a bit of argument and convincing, they agreed. After all, the two were going to get married soon.

Mary Shaila started living in Ivan's house and was soon taking care of most of the needs of the D'Souza family, including looking after the invalid father. She would clean him and change him and see to his meals. It was seva in the true sense of the word. Anna Severine was happy to have such a devoted young woman for a future daughter-in-law. She decided to include Mary Shaila's name on the family ration card and even asked her to apply for a passport giving their address in the application. It was the D'Souza's way of showing how much they cared for Mary Shaila who would soon be a permanent member of the household. She started relinquishing more and more of her responsibilities to Mary Shaila, who kept accepting them without complaining. Soon she was washing everyone's clothes and even looking after the kitchen. The lone servant in the house did odd jobs but mainly took care of the outdoor compound. When relatives visited, the workload increased manifold. A part of her felt overwhelmed – she found it difficult to manage the household and her studies. Ivan was sympathetic but whenever she tried to talk about the problems, he didn't offer a solution. He would simply tell her to cope. 'This is your house and you just have to do it,' he would tell her. But he would deftly evade her queries about marriage.

'Everyone misused me. I used to even shave Ivan's father and give an oil massage to Ivan. In that house I have done the kind of work that I never did in my own. Even when I had typhoid, they didn't let me rest. I had to draw water from the well. I got boils on my palms and Ivan wouldn't even bring me medicine,' the young woman recounted. When I asked her why she didn't walk out of the house, she said: 'I loved him and I thought the situation would improve after marriage.' They had talked about marriage in the past but as time went by there were fewer references to it. What worried Mary Shaila was Ivan's reluctance to talk about the wedding date. When she raised the topic, he either avoided it completely or evaded it by making false promises.

It had been more than a year since she had moved into his house. She felt it was time to get married. They had already been living as husband and wife. Sometimes he said he would marry her after he visited his brother in Dubai. At other times, he just laughed it off. It was some excuse or another and she began to get worried. Her studies suffered but he didn't seem to care. He would ask why was she so worried since she was already the daughter-in-law of the house. All his relatives regarded her as such. They always asked about her and sent her greeting cards. That was all true but there was something not quite right with the situation. When she pushed too hard, Ivan would get abusive. He had a drinking problem and tended to get melodramatic. He would put his hand on the Bible and swear on all that's holy that he would marry her soon. Sometimes he made up by bringing her flowers.

'I believed him because I loved him. But I was a glorified maid, a qualified servant in his house. I served him and his family but they just abused me,' Mary Shaila told me. The situation was beginning to get unbearable and she asked Ivan if they could move to a room nearby so she would have some freedom from the household responsibilities. But that didn't help either. Ivan began getting abusive and moody. He didn't need an excuse anymore to be harsh to her. His drinking got worse and so did his behaviour. He began hitting her and once even threatened to 'sell her'.

They had gone by bus to Bangalore when the incident took place. They were returning to Karkala when he started scolding her over something petty. He then got off at some bus stop and she was forced to follow. He began abusing her in public and a crowd gathered. 'I am going to sell you here,' he bellowed. Mary Shaila was scared for her life that night. He was yelling at the top of his voice and pinching her. Somehow they got back safely but she knew that a line had been crossed. The fights became more frequent and the beatings too. When she was taken to the doctor for treatment, Ivan would say she fell down.

'I felt he would change after we got married. I thought I would change him with my love. I had hoped that when we lived separately, things would be better and he would be more responsible,' Mary Shaila recounted with an air of helplessness and a look that said – 'Please don't ask me why.' I simply listened. All she could do was to hope. She was young and believed that she could transform her man. She had lived with him for nearly two years and neglected her studies. She was attending college but not regularly. The blunder had been made. To walk out now would mean she would be left with nothing. She had also learnt over time that Ivan's bar and restaurant business was not all above board. He had links with undesirable elements of the area. She felt a little afraid of getting on the wrong side of the D'Souzas. But she also didn't want to continue with the status quo. This could go on forever and she wouldn't be any the wiser. She forced Ivan to commit to a proper engagement and to meet her family once again.

It was December 2000 when Mary Shaila's parents once again visited the D'Souza household to discuss the future of their daughter. Ivan and his mother agreed that a date for the wedding should be fixed. It was decided that the betrothal ceremony would take place on 29 December in Chickballapur, where the Pereiras lived. The D'Souzas came to Mary Shaila's house along with her and rings were exchanged in front of friends and family. The document of engagement was prepared to be handed over to the church authorities. The marriage date was fixed for a month later – for 29 January 2001 and the ceremony was to be held at the Immaculate Heart Church in Ivan's hometown. It was during these talks that the subject of dowry first came up. Anna Severine said that the 'amount' should be fixed during the ceremony itself and should be given right away.

In her complaint to the Chickballapur police station, Rosy said that she agreed to give twenty thousand rupees as dowry and handed it over that day to Ivan. She also promised that she would give a chain and ring at the time of marriage. Ivan took the money but said that the families must discuss the 'total' amount that had been demanded. Rosy and Francis were puzzled by all this talk but didn't want to raise an alarm. Everyone was around, their relatives and friends were milling about the house and any heated words would immediately be broadcast to the rest of the community. It was best to wait and talk in private. The D'Souzas left soon after and Mary Shaila went back with them. It was an unusual arrangement for a girl to be living with her in-laws before marriage but Mary Shaila was engaged and about to be married.

The next day, Rosy got busy with the wedding preparations and sent the invitation cards for printing. But a few days later, on 4 January 2001 to be precise, her daughter called her to say that the D'Souzas were asking for a meeting to 'settle' the dowry amount. Rosy rushed to their house the very next day along with her mother. It was then that Ivan's family openly asked for five lakh rupees as dowry.

Rosy could only stutter in response. She didn't have any words – her mind seemed to freeze. Things were crumbling in front of her very eyes and all she could do was watch helplessly. It was an impossible demand and she knew she couldn't meet it, however hard she tried. It was not a sum within her family's reach. It was absurd. She called her husband on the phone and told him about the outrageous demand. He too was speechless. They had saved some money for the marriage of their two children but they hadn't planned on giving a big dowry. They thought educated people didn't need or ask for it. Their daughter was going to be a qualified engineer after all.

Rosy stayed on for nearly five days in Karkala trying to persuade Ivan and his mother to drop the demand but instead of backing down, they became belligerent. Anna Severine said that five lakh rupees was a reasonable dowry and the twenty thousand rupees already given at the time of engagement was a mere token amount. It was exclusive of the dowry. No matter how much Rosy pleaded, the D'Souzas would not relent. They seemed to have metamorphosed into different people, not the ones Rosy had first met. Their manner had changed. They were talking as if they were doing Rosy a favour by agreeing to the marriage when it was clear that the girl and boy had chosen each other. What really hurt both mother and daughter was the attitude of Ivan, the man they thought was essentially decent. He had been living with Mary Shaila for so long, but now he threatened to walk off if the dowry was not paid up front. The marriage would not take place as agreed. Rosy was desperate as was her daughter who had already suffered enough abuse and mistreatment at the hands of this family. She had neglected her studies and chosen to be a 'glorified maid' in their house and now she was being literally abandoned at the altar. The wedding invitations had been printed and ready.

The mother and daughter talked over things and Rosy told Mary Shaila that it was better to end it all now rather than face the problem later. They seemed adamant on their demand and since Ivan hadn't shown any resilience, it was wiser to walk out and forget the whole thing as a long, bad dream.

Then something happened that jolted both Mary Shaila and Rosy into action. Rosy had left Shaila for a few hours to collect her belongings from the rented room so the two could go back home. While Rosy was away, Ivan and his mother tried to kill Mary Shaila by pouring kerosene on her. 'Fortunately, her mother came back suddenly to the house in an auto and at the same time Shaila ran out of the house crying for help,' according to the police report prepared for the state public prosecutor. A relative of the D'Souza family was witness to the assault on Shaila and told Rosy about it.

Mary Shaila escaped the attempt on her life and went to the local church frequented by the D'Souzas and told the priest everything. Father Onil D'Souza assured them that he would call Ivan and his family and advise them. He asked both families to come to the church for a meeting on 8 January 2001 and that he would try to convince Ivan to drop his outrageous demands. Mary Shaila and Rosy went to the church on the appointed day but Ivan didn't show up. His brother and mother came to the church and repeated their demands. They said they did not need anyone's advice and they won't allow the marriage to take place unless their demands were met. The priest was helpless and told Rosy to 'go according to the law'.

After consulting her husband Francis over the phone, Rosy told her daughter to file a police complaint against Ivan and his mother. Mary Shaila readily agreed. She was afraid for her life and thoroughly disgusted and disillusioned with the man she was ready to call her husband. She contacted a lawyer and lodged a complaint on 9 January 2001 at Karkala, accusing Ivan, Anna Severine and her son Joy of attempting to kill her, demanding dowry and cheating them of twenty thousand rupees. Instead of going to church to sort out last-minute details of the wedding celebration, the family was running to police stations. But despite the explicit nature of the complaint, the Karkala police failed to take immediate action and didn't order an investigation. No interrogation or attempt to determine the veracity of the complaint was made.

Mary Shaila says that Ivan had 'links' with the police and no one dared cross his path, especially on what they considered 'a family matter'. In desperation, she called the superintendent of police of Udipi who was sympathetic and gave her a patient hearing. He said he would intervene and ask the DSP of Karkala to pursue the case. But nothing happened. Mary Shaila then went to the sub-inspector and requested him to initiate the investigation but was told that there was 'no offence'. Having tried their level best to move the police and failed, Mary Shaila and Rosy returned to Chickballapur. They went to meet the DSP of their town, Mohan Hegde, and narrated their story. He contacted the Karkala police over the phone and inquired about the case but was told that 'no case can be made out'. He decided to register another complaint in Chickballapur in February under sections 3 and 4 of the Dowry Prohibition Act and under section 420 of the IPC for cheating to try to prod his counterparts into action.

Instead of celebrating her wedding in the New Year, Mary Shaila embarked on a lonely battle to seek justice. Humiliated and disillusioned, she began doing the rounds of police stations, lawyers' offices and NGOs. Her final year of electrical engineering remained incomplete – so afraid was she to go back to Karkala for classes. 'They will get me killed and call it an accident if I go there. The police there won't help me. Ivan's family has links with all sorts of people. I can't complete my engineering and I can't transfer my degree to another college,' she told me during our meeting. The Karkala police had showed no sympathy for the victim and she was forced to file a complaint against the sub-inspector and others in the office of the Lokayukta for

Karnataka. She said in her complaint that a crime police inspector from Karkala by the name of Peter visited her parents' house and forced them to sign on blank papers. He claimed he had been sent by his superiors to investigate. Suspecting something amiss, Mary Shaila's parents informed the local DSP who asked this policeman to come and meet him. But 'Peter' disappeared into thin air. The family was terrified since the man purporting to be a policeman may not have been one at all but he took their signatures.

They sent a flurry of letters to senior state officials, from the governor, to the state home minister, the minister for women and child development, the state secretary and the state director general of police expressing their fears and requesting action. They got a reply from almost everyone, promising help but nothing concrete happened on the ground.

When I met Mary Shaila, she was in the midst of pursuing her case against Ivan and his family. She had missed her final year exam because of all the trouble and had to ask the college for a 'completion certificate'. Frustrated by police inaction and their inability to arrest Ivan, she contacted the National Commission for Women for help, thinking they could make things move. They gave her a patient hearing but were unable to influence the police to do their job. Sometime in early 2001, she heard about Donna Fernandes of Vimochana and decided to go to her. Donna took up cudgels on her behalf and made several phone calls to the police and other officials. It was because of the persistence of Vimochana that a friend of Ivan's, who had been threatening Mary Shaila openly on the streets and outside the court, was arrested. Donna has helped her at every stage, intervening with the district authorities and the police to ensure th correct procedures are followed. But it is an uphill battle all the way.

Ever since Mary Shaila decided to take Ivan to court, she has been subjected to every indignity imaginable. She gets obscene phone calls from boys whom she suspects are Ivan's friends and cronies. Every time the phone rings, she feels a chill going down her spine. 'We will kill you. We will ruin your family if you continue with the case,' the voices shout at the other end. They have threatened to throw acid on her and even kidnap her. Male voices introduce themselves to her mother, 'Hi, I am Mary's new lover.' To live with this kind of terror is not easy and in the Indian context, it is all the more devastating.

Ivan has been using the lethal weapon men wield over women with ease – that of ruining her reputation. Spread a few rumours, tell a few lies and start a whisper campaign and the job is done. No blood spilt either. It is almost effortless and the result is crushing for the girl. Not only is she temporarily incapacitated, she carries the scars forever. But Mary Shaila fought back and every anonymous threat made her resolve stronger and her desire to get justice deeper – no matter what the price. She had already paid a high price for falling in love with the wrong man. Nothing worse could happen now. Her education, her career and prospects for marriage were all destroyed by one man who used her and then discarded her like an old shirt. To counter the obscene phone calls, she filed a defamation case against Ivan in May 2002, seeking damages worth fifteen lakh rupees.

She said the police have done little to help contain the conflagration around her. Ivan hadn't been arrested despite three visits to Karkala by the Chickballapur police with the specific aim to nab him. A contingent of five armed policemen went each time with Mary Shaila whose job was to identify the culprits but came back empty handed. She paid for the travel and food but they made no real effort to catch him. They simply went to his house and he jumped out from the back. Once his mother hid him in a room and bolted the door from outside. Mary Shaila overheard the mother talking in Konkani and realized what was happening. She alerted the policemen but they didn't bother to search the house. Another time they looked around in parks and came back. 'They could have gone in the middle of the night but they didn't want to. When I insisted, one of the policemen said: "Even we have family." Another asked for money to catch him. They are all afraid of Ivan because he has links with various people.' The Pereiras have already spent two lakh rupees on these trips and other expenses. They have got documents photocopied, often done the personal work of policemen on the job. Even though they have provided all the information and done a lot of the spadework for the police, the information is not included in the charge sheet.

There are certificates and announcements and wedding invitations – for anyone to see that the two were about to get married. There is even a certificate for a 'marriage preparation course' that Ivan and Mary Shaila attended at the Family Life Service Centre under the Diocese of Mangalore. She has letters from the church. The priest of the St Francis Xavier's Church in Chickballapur had called two 'banns' – formal announcements in the parish about the upcoming marriage – and corresponded with Ivan's church about the marriage. There is proof that the wedding was imminent but for some reason it didn't take place. The reason was dowry.

As I was leaving, Mary Shaila said something that would always stay with me. She told me she knew her life would end violently and soon. 'I know I am not going to live very long because they will get me sooner or later. I am fighting them. He has already sent his goons after me. They have spread rumours about me because I have filed a case. One of Ivan's friends threatened to rape me.' I just stared at her, fumbling and fidgeting, unable to say much. No words seemed appropriate. It was like watching the death of hope, the end of joy. It carried all the sadness of a young woman betrayed and a vision shadowed. It was her truth and her reality and I could do little to mitigate the intensity with which she felt them. She covered her head with her arms and buried herself in her knees. She was trying to hide to get past the momentary crisis of retelling her tale. It was a love story gone awfully wrong. Tired and dejected, she had few expectations from the future. She felt no one would give her a job because they would brand her as a troublemaker. 'I will just wait until the judgment and then I won't live,' she said and broke down.

In the End . . .

In the end, there is some hope and some despair. Victory seems distant and the terrain rugged. In the fight against dowry, there are no heroes, only soldiers. There is a sense of pessimism among those who are engaged in battle but they will continue the assault.

Dowry deaths became more common during the 1990s, ironically a decade that created a sense of progress for women. There were many more women on television, there were women sarpanchs, and there was a rise of fashion models as the new divas. Women became pilots, manned all-women police stations and even started rural broadsheets to inform each other of strides made in their villages. Many more fought elections. Medha Patkar of the Narmada Bachao Andolan created history by triggering a rebellion in villages in three states against big dams. Her selfless devotion to the cause inspired hundreds of young men and women from the cities to join her protest. Women in Chennai showed grit and smarts when they decided to break tradition in 1994 to become masons and electricians, moving beyond being construction workers. Political parties in their manifestoes were forced to acknowledge half the people who hold the sky. The autonomous women's movement moved forward, sometimes definitely, sometimes gingerly.

Gains were made but the problems facing women did not lessen proportionally. Every major crime against women recorded a rise – rape, molestation, domestic abuse, trafficking, kidnapping, sexual harassment. The number of cases pending in the courts grew, locking with it the fate of

...ions of women who sought redress. With it had come an uneasy sense of acceptance – *it happens* – not among women activists but in the society at large. It settled like smog over the nation's consciousness, absorbing the outrage. New crimes were rationalized by the old idea of fate. There were a few demonstrations, but not nearly enough to focus the country's attention long and hard. Dedicated activists continued to fight lonely battles against dowry deaths in pockets across India – Sakhi in Kerala, Swayam and Nari Nirjatan Pratirodh Manch in Kolkata, Shaktishalini and Saakshi in Delhi, Aawaaz-e-Niswan in Mumbai, Vimochana in Bangalore, to name just a few. But their numbers were small compared to the gargantuan proportions of the problem.

Those on the battlefront deserve plaudits for they have chosen to continue despite the lure of settling into more comfortable jobs. Talking to activists engaged in daily counselling and crisis intervention was in itself sobering. They offered an even darker version of reality than one saw in the media. They were surprised that I was surprised at the mind-numbing stories they told of police negligence and corruption in the legal system. Everyone in an abstract sense is aware of corruption being an integral part of the Indian reality but to hear concrete examples of it involving life and death situations was chilling. It is still difficult to imagine that a person can bargain over a dead body but hundreds of policemen do it daily.

For a few thousand rupees, a policeman may actually 'adjust' the section of the IPC under which he books a man who burnt his wife and perpetuate a lie that will resonate throughout the trial. He may 'fail' to interview key witnesses or seize incriminating evidence. A doctor conducting postmortems at a government hospital where thousands of burn victims end up may casually write 'death due to shock' despite signs of physical injuries and bruises because he wants to reduce the burden of medico-legal cases in the hospital. He may 'fail' to notice or mention details that might help in the prosecution later. A public prosecutor paid by the government may still extract Rs 250 from a poor slum family in Kolkata every time he deigns to appear in court on their behalf. Even the 'extra' incentive may not persuade him to take the case seriously and do his homework. Even when his homework is done for him by the victim's family, he may not use the information because he may have been paid from both sides. His incompetence is written on his face, yet he won't be removed from his job. He is there on political patronage and his job is to make sure party cadres are well taken care of, not to ensure justice for dowry victims.

Donna Fernandes, an old-style activist leader who heads the Bangalore-based group Vimochana and has been working with dowry victims for over two decades, says that unless a deeper social movement emerges, not much will change for women. 'A woman is still seen as someone lesser and to compensate for her "lesserness", her parents give dowry. Laws alone can't help to combat this because we have a terrific capacity to twist laws. There should be a movement to restore human values. We have to look deep within ourselves.'

In the end, it is all about how little we value women in our culture. Some things have changed but for the few. Pervasive violence is only the extreme manifestation of women's low status in society but 'devaluation' of women may show up in a myriad ways even for the privileged. For high women achievers, doors are slammed shut by corporate India simply because they are women. Companies like Videocon can have four thousand women employees in factories and a number of women engineers but their corporate floor is still out of the women's reach as a 'matter of policy'. The chairman says he runs 'an orthodox family'. Bajaj Auto has few women in the middle and senior management and the policy changed only around 1996. Women occupy only 3 per cent of the senior positions in the private sector and most companies have an average of 5 to 6 per cent women employees. In the manufacturing sector, not much has changed since 1974 when the Tatas advertised for jobs, saying: 'Ladies need not apply.'

All the manifestations of Durga and Kali, which in my three-year tenure in Kolkata had loomed menacingly large, seemed like a big joke. A sad contradiction was at work – between the yearly and elaborate Puja pandaals celebrating the power of Durga riding a lion and killing demons and the Left-ruled and therefore admittedly more progressive state of West Bengal doing little to save women from dowry deaths. Card-carrying party members prayed at the feet of the goddesses but failed to act when real-life Durgas and Kalis died in government hospitals of burns and poisoning. The preoccupation at the national level with the might of the Hindu nation was even more insulting. The women were dying daily, mostly quietly, away from the debates on coalition politics, match fixing, stock market crashes, border clashes and celebrity worship. This is not to say that other issues were unimportant but women's issues did not seize the politicians in the 1990s in the way they did a decade before.

The government had created the National Commission for Women in 1991 and moved on to other business. But the NCW lacked the teeth it needed to be heard and felt. It sought a review of anti-dowry laws and asked for several legal loopholes to be plugged but its recommendations languished in various ministries for years. Finally, it launched a nationwide exercise in the late 1990s to review the provisions of the Dowry Prohibition Act with twenty-one state-level workshops. The exercise delved into the larger question of women's economic status and whether the problems of dowry should be linked to the demand for equal inheritance rights for women. The NCW also raised the issue of compulsory registration of marriages along with a list of gifts and dowry items which could act as a deterrent against harassment. Finally, it said that the Dowry Prohibition Act wrongly treated both the giver and the receiver of dowry as offenders. Although the courts are lenient to the 'giver', an amendment is awaited. For the past decade.

But the NCW failed to generate the kind of momentum it takes to make the government move. The various state commissions for women that it oversaw for coordination of activities were working on their own. The NCW and its state counterparts showed sporadic bursts of enthusiasm, but there was no sustained campaign to focus legislative attention. For the most part they were like a tired bureaucracy filled with members who were comfortable with the ruling elite, having been appointed by them in the first place. They rarely rattled the cage. Of course, there were many notable exceptions where commission members made a mark despite the limitations imposed on them by the structures. But most were not interested in upsetting the apple cart and demanding better implementation of laws or keeping the enforcement machinery on its toes. They made recommendations but didn't always follow them with well-organized campaigns to create pressure for action. They didn't coordinate or cooperate on a regular basis with the hundreds of NGOs who could have helped build the momentum for change.

But then who can blame them – activism itself seemed to have become déclassé over the past ten years. The women's movement in modern India had started with aplomb during the struggle for independence when women actively participated not only in the Congress-led traditional boycotts of foreign goods and non-cooperation movement but also in the revolutionary strand spearheaded by the Bengal nationalists. The movement consolidated in the 1970s and '80s with significant gains but diversified in the 1990s with multiple goals and trying to reach larger parts of the hidden society.

Was the women's movement evolving into something different? Maitrayee Chatterjee, an old-time feminist and leader of a Calcutta-based organization, says today's activists lack a coherent strategy. As a result, the movement today is different in its feel and grasp. Also, the times have changed, forcing changes in strategies and outlook. But it is also true that the movement has lost its political ideology. 'We are no longer challenging authority. We could have countered the BJP openly on so many issues but we didn't. We let them walk away with our issues. Then all the ills of mainstream politics came into the women's movement – hierarchy, identity and culture politics and what not. I feel the women's movement is not the place to show the superiority of one's culture as some of our women thinkers seem to do. The basic issues of women's rights are the same everywhere.'

There was a bit of chaos of the marketplace even in women's issues – new, more attractive areas of study and research gained over the older, more 'downmarket' problems of dowry deaths and other violence. Gender sensitization seminars were in and street protests were out. In a strange bifurcation of commitment, even as the number of NGOs rose dramatically, more and more went into research-oriented projects, gender training, policy formulation and consulting and fewer into pure activism.

Was it because no movement can sustain the heated momentum for too long and must have the inevitable downward phase? One might argue that activism began being looked at as somewhat proletarian compared to networking, training, documentation, attending seminars and starting women's studies departments. All these were not inherently less important but the original aim of women's studies and activism being two legs on which the movement could walk was lost along the way. The new generation of women leaders appeared less eager to stick their necks out while the older generation moved on to jobs more suited to their age and energy. After all how long could the women's movement look to a Subhadhra Butalia, a Veena Mazumdar, a Kamla Bhasin or a Vibhuti Patel for leadership?

Another major reason for dimming of loud voices was the entry of foreign donor agencies, which funded hundreds of NGOs across the country. In turn, they had a dominant voice in setting the agenda. While the NGOs played a crucial role in taking up causes, popularizing them and reaching a larger number of people, they did not have complete independence of action. If donor money was coming for the Year of the Child, project proposals were hurriedly written for the child until the next year when it might be time to focus on the physically challenged. The child projects would then get pushed behind or be followed half-heartedly while the NGOs rushed to get funds for new projects.

'If domestic violence is what the donor agency wants, that's what it will get, not necessarily what is most important in a certain area. Many NGOs are trapped in this,' one of Kolkata's prominent women activists, Rajashri Dasgupta, told me. My interaction with NGOs in Delhi also highlighted the funding trap. This has led to a shrinking perspective o women's issues because the NGOs have begun to see wom problems in isolation. 'Women's issues are not just dov rape but also education, food security, health and not having a nuclear bomb looming over their heads. The linkages between issues are missing,' Dasgupta felt.

Those linkages were very much present in the 1970s because the women's movement grew out of a soil fertile with movements and agitation. There was the Shahada movement of Bhil landless labourers against landlords and the anti-price rise movement in Maharashtra; the movement for better wages led by Ela Bhatt which resulted in the Self-Employed Women's Association and the anti-corruption movement in Gujarat; and the various Left movements around the country, which mobilized thousands of poor and tribal women. On the international front there were student protests, anti-nuclear and anti-Vietnam movements which inspired many educated middle-class men and women in India.

'When we came out to protest we understood the politics of issues even though we may not have been able to articulate as well. We reacted with gut instinct. Today, getting a job with an NGO is seen as a good career move. It is like any other job. Many young social work graduates bring a freshness and enthusiasm to the table at one level but at another level, they lack perspective. They tend to reinvent the wheel, repeating studies already done instead of taking them further. This is not because they are less intelligent but because they lack the political perspective,' Dasgupta observed after long years in activism that began on the radical edge of Naxalism. 'There is a certain naiveté about issues. We are not drawing clear conclusions. Some of us no longer know who our friends are and who the enemy.'

While this NGO-ization took away some issues from the autonomous women's movement, the NGOs lacked the grit to question state policies. Many groups put the spotlight on domestic violence but failed to relate it to the dominant ideology of the state which denies women real rights over property. And they made little noise against state violence. The state was not made to confront the skeletons in its own closet – police brutality, custodial rape and police corruption. They took up dowry deaths but didn't link them with the larger issue of patriarchy and how it perpetuates women's subordination in society. They failed to question the family power relations and the repercussions on wom Foreign donors that fund many large NGOs are queasy questioning the host government too loudly lest t barred from working here. The autonomous women's g which depended on membership and volunteers for fu could not compete in this new marketplace for vario reasons. They were on the wrong side of the resource flows. A large part of their agenda was kidnapped by political parties, which quickly saw women as a large voting bloc and began incorporating women-friendly promises in their manifestoes. When in power, they announced new pro-women policies but without adequate infrastructure. Women's groups felt cheated but they made few attempts to recapture territory.

Some of their issues were co-opted openly by political parties – the most glaring, blatant and ultimately damaging to Indian women was the surrender of the demand for a uniform civil code. When the BJP took it up as one of its major planks, the women's groups were caught unawares, upset and confused. They let the BJP walk away with it even though they had strongly lobbied for it in the early 1980s. They knew 'personal laws' of all kinds were a great source of sorrow for women. After the BJP came out in support of a uniform civil code, the women's groups couldn't bring themselves to lend their voices because of the heavy baggage of being associated with the BJP. They debated among themselves and called for gender-just laws, looking for alternate terminology to say essentially the same thing. The Left parties simply abandoned the cause instead of fighting it out with the BJP, their sworn enemy in the political arena. They didn't have the deftness to mount a campaign to win the hearts of minorities in favour of the issue. And this happened post–Shah Bano when the State had showed clearly that the rights of Indian women were subordinate to obscurantist demands and bluster from fundamentalists. The State saw every issue in terms of electoral gain – even destitution of Muslim women.

In what is now seen as a time when Hindu communalism as well as Muslim fundamentalism rose, the Shah Bano case became a bitter lesson for the women's movement. In a landmark judgment in 1985, the Supreme Court said a divorced Muslim woman was entitled to maintenance by her husband under section 125 of the Criminal Procedure Code which entitles divorced, destitute and deserted women to support from their husbands. It was a progressive judgment but religious leaders saw it as an attack on Muslims and started an orchestrated campaign for its repeal. After battling indecision for a while, the government of late prime minister Rajiv Gandhi succumbed and a year later introduced a new bill, which undermined the judgment. The new bill specifically excluded Muslim women from the purview of section 125 and left them at the mercy of financially strapped Waqf boards. It was one of the most regressive, anti-women moves in post-independent India. The State was accommodating voices of Muslim fundamentalism, without a care for the rights of women. It allowed a few conservative men to speak for the entire community and assert control over Muslim women, mixing religion with the question of fundamental rights.

If this weren't bad enough, the women's movement suffered another setback when it was confronted with a pro-sati movement mounted by the Rajputs, Shiv Sena and traditionalist forces in society after a case of sati was reported in Deorala, Rajasthan, in September 1987. Women activists speaking out against sati were dubbed as Western, modern and pernicious influences on Hindu society – a charge that would resonate for years. Debates raged within the women's movement about strategy – whether to work with the government, whether to go with politics of identity/ethnicity and whether to look for small gains or mount larger battles. The movement unfortunately was painted as an urban, modernizing force, one that was opposed to the 'traditions' of rural society and thereby essentially unfriendly because it campaigned against sati and supported Muslim women's right to maintenance. The opposition by the communal-fundamental combine grew with time.

Women's groups attached to various political parties had ideological problems sharing a platform. How could the women's wing of the Congress party make common cause with the CPM's All India Democratic Women's Association even if the cause was as immediate as the murder of thousands of women every year? Ideological 'purity' was more important. The less said about most of the BJP's women activists, the better. They believed in the traditional, ever-suffering, never-complaining, always-on-the-grind, all-embracing, son-adoring, Mother India. Any hope of redemption from them was misplaced. Women politicians inside Parliament and outside didn't adopt many women-related causes in the 1990s, spending time in the same kind of backroom survival games that their male counterparts played.

Over time, the women's movement seemed to cede more and more space to the political parties, religious leaders and even communal forces. The 'traditionalist' forces have been strengthened enormously over the past decade under the umbrella of the Hindutva philosophy, which sees women essentially in a sacrificing mother role living in Vedic bliss. These forces are essentially opposed to fundamental social changes and project themselves as the keepers of 'real' India and Indians. They propagate myths about women in the popular imagination – the most pernicious being that today the men are under siege and need protection from the pro-women laws. The 'new woman' is in charge and the nation must press on with other business. The new woman is aware, educated and employed but she also 'fits' the traditional straitjacket. An impression has gained that enough strides have been made otherwise the 'feminists' would be at the door. Superficial references to women's issues in party manifestoes and election rallies have created a sense that attention is being paid to problems by officials. All this is nothing but an attempt to soften the focus and create red herrings.

In the charged communal atmosphere of the new decade, where Hindu and Muslim fanatics fight on the battleground of women's bodies, it is hard to expect politicians paying attention to serious problems. Muslim women, doubly burdened by the conservatism of Islamic law and the social stay-in-the-veil mentality, are the worst sufferers when the madness of communalism rules. They are told to stay low and not raise demands about their 'rights' when the entire community is under attack. The fissures within must be kept hidden in times of trouble. Whatever little progress they made in the past through painstaking representations in front of the Muslim Personal Law Board to demand an end to triple talaq or enforceable rights for maintenance is quickly negated. After the mind-numbing violence against Muslim women in Gujarat in February–March 2002, even activists are afraid to continue their fight for better rights under the Personal Law. They might be seen as 'traitors' to the larger cause.

If the backlash against feminist ideology came from the establishment, it also came in some part from the media. After an initial interest in women's issues in the popular media, which coincided with the rise of the women's movement in the 1970s and '80s, there was a disdainful drop in the 1990s when the popular press was engaged in chasing a phantasmagoric India. That India was energized in equal part by machismo, market and a new-found 'masti' of the soft drink culture and it rarely acknowledged ugly, social problems. Women's issues were treated as just another item of consumption on the news pages. The serious 'women's' pages began disappearing from large national dailies and in their place sprung glossy, colourful supplements filled with fitness news and diet fads. Urban India was changing and many argue that the changes in the women's movement were a response to the different times.

So different were the times that the media would celebrate a boom in women-centred serials, even though the main characters were more like cartoons driven by rituals and petty domestic squabbles rather than women with real problems. Most of them were spun around the 'ideal bahu' theme. Their women characters were obsessed with marriage, always scheming to get one either made or broken. They existed in the overall ambience of Hindu traditions and symbols at their paper thin worst. These serials can't be dismissed simply as fodder for the lowest common denominator. They developed and prospered in an atmosphere resonating with the Hindutva philosophy being propagated at the national level. The strong women of the earlier serials were gone. There were hardly any characters reflecting the 1990s reality when more and more urban (since these serials are centred around cities) women were performing delicate balancing acts between careers and homes, modernity and tradition.

A spate of Hindi films, many of them blockbusters, added their weight to the national propagation of 'traditional' values. Although popular movies have always emphasized traditional mores, the new crop shimmered with an abundance of foreign locales giving them a superficial modernistic feel. The heroines donned the clothes of vamps of the old days and made the genre itself redundant but in the end, they were in the Sati Savitri mode. They were shown as happy appendages of men, fasting and feasting at their beck and call, dancing around in skimpy designer outfits waiting for the karvachauth moon. Despite outward appearances, conformity to convention and tradition were the dominant themes, creating a sort of cultural schizophrenia.

Alongside mushroomed beauty pageants and 'talent search' programmes on television which had children – sometimes girls as young as five and nine years – dressed as clones of movie stars in cheap, tinsel clothing, gyrating to film songs with their parents clapping among the studio audience. There was a glinting sense that we were all moving towards modernity, helped by kitsch and karma. The market would take care of the rest.

But many women fought back this glossing-over of the problems because they *are* and will be the most important agents of change in India, a country whose grid of socioeconomic problems is the most complex in the world. Committed women and men worked on in many districts, without a national thread tying them into a powerful knot. But then the women's movement, as it grew, did not attempt to become a single, large body of office-bearers with top-down thinking. Some saw it as a weakness while others considered it a major strength because of the vastness, diversity and complexity of India's problems. The same issue may have to be tackled differently in different states. The strategies of the anti-alcohol movement mounted by women leaders were very different in Manipur, Garhwal and Andhra Pradesh. The movement's richness came from this bottom-up approach.

The past decade where evolution and change and doubt and debate marked the women's movement has brought us to where we are today – at a crossroads in terms of the future. There is a diversity of views, differences of approach and a proliferation of causes – reflective of India's myriad problems and size. Various women's groups are doing commendable work in their areas and many of them are networking amazingly fast, thanks to e-mail. But they cannot share their experiences on a regular basis with each other to repeat their successes because of a lack of resources. As for the persistent problem of dowry deaths, women leaders engaged in active intervention on behalf of the victims rarely have time to breathe and little time to methodically record what they have learnt. They are too busy dealing with the day-to-day problems of victims. Rarely do they have ready figures even on the total numbers of victims they may have helped, leave alone statistics on different types of crimes against women or their own success rate – the very figures that could help build pressure on the government for change or better law enforcement.

Successful strategies discovered by one group could be made available to another if the research-oriented NGOs collaborated regularly with those actively involved on the ground and helped in documentation and dissemination. The bureaucracy of the National Commission for Women along with the various state commissions does some of this but it could do enormously more given its reach. It can be more proactive and engage more regularly with the state commissions. A group in Punjab may have valuable insights to impart to a group in Andhra Pradesh but new ideas often get lost because they are not widely disseminated.

The lack of an overall strategy and fragmentation of goals have been detrimental for the women's movement. Today, the movement doesn't have many nationally recognizable faces or names. What is sorely needed is a national coalition of representative groups that can be mobilized when needed to bring attention to important issues, especially dowry deaths. A model for it exists in Kolkata where the Maitree Network has shown how various groups working on vastly different issues can come together to fight a common cause when needed. The network successfully took up the case of a Bangladeshi woman who was raped at Howrah station and mounted pressure on the state government to own responsibility. The woman was given ten lakh rupees in compensation as a result of a PIL suit. She was supported, sheltered and mentored throughout her ordeal by the Maitree Network. The coalition meets once in two months, has a rotating leadership and maintains strict records of its deliberations and strategies.

A similar national coalition of groups working on dowry deaths could help refocus attention on this growing problem [illegible] devise strategies and combat it on a war footing. Just as [illegible] omen's movement had rallied around the issue once and fought against it, it can and should again come together. The times may be different but the problem still is the same.

After two years of listening and recording oral histories of women victims of dowry, it was difficult to be optimistic. I had met survivors, seen them clinging to life maimed by burns and learnt about countless others from NGOs working in the field. Most hadn't made it to the newspapers, so 'common' was their fate.

But many women have fought back despite the Sisyphean labour of waging a court battle. Most of the stories I selected for this collection show in some manner the triumph of their spirit. I decided deliberately to include only those cases which had a ring of optimism, however faint and nebulous. Either the victim herself or her family – in many cases her mother – had picked up the baton and decided to bring the man to justice for the torture and humiliation inflicted on her. In most cases they had got little help from either the police or the judicial system but they had persevered over the years and more. If these were positive stories in what they said about the human fighting spirit, there were countless others which ended before they had even begun – in the police station. Looking at innumerable cases of half-hearted investigations and lazy prosecution, one knew they wouldn't stand the scrutiny of defence lawyers. Conviction would be a dream.

Women's groups over the years have come up with many suggestions to improve the situation and most of them agree that making new rules or more laws is not the answer. What is needed is better implementation of existing laws with a few changes here and there to tighten the system. Special and new laws may give a false sense of action being taken but in [illegible]e of dowry deaths, stringent laws don't seem to have worked as a deterrent given the rising graph of crime. Implementation is the key, not an edifice of new laws.

Sujata Mehra, a Delhi-based lawyer who has advised NGOs and written a manual on laws for women for a legal literacy campaign, says special laws have made the system more inefficient. 'Special laws have a tendency to be strictly interpreted. It is better to ensure that the system works rather than enact special laws because nothing will work if the system doesn't work. The knowledge that you are going to get caught and punished is a more effective deterrent than any set of special laws, however radical. A special law made for a particular crime sometimes creates loopholes because the more you try to fit the crime into a tight definition, the more difficult it becomes to prove it and the more likely it is that the perpetrator will get away. A better option for combating social evils is for the existing system to work better within a time frame.'

She suggested mandating special 'day-to-day evidence' for dowry death cases where court dates are given on consecutive days to speed up the process. The best way is to make the system work faster with the existing safeguards. It is not necessarily helpful to make piecemeal changes in the Criminal Procedure Code for special laws because any deviation from normal procedure invariably causes the courts to be much more cautious. Besides, the dowry laws already have an in-built bias, however inadvertent, against women because their murder is considered somewhat less of a crime. 'Even in cases where it is a clear case of murder for dowry, there is no death sentence. You have the discretion to give anywhere between a seven-year to a life sentence while murder is punishable by a death sentence or life imprisonment. You are sending a signal that society doesn't want to give the same punishment for killing a woman. So what have the special dowry laws achieved except to show in one more insidious way that women are not valued equally as the men?'

Donna Fernandes, who has done pioneering work in creating awareness around the rising dowry deaths in Bangalore, threw up her hands in despair when I asked her about her experiences with the legal system. 'You can have laws, you can punish, but most of the time, with the kind of evidence that is needed, it is not possible to convict. I would be happy even if the courts gave minimum sentences as long as they punished the guilty. I don't want life imprisonment. I don't want someone to be hanged. I would be much happier having the minimum as the maximum sentence but punish they must. I can see how the law is practised, no one can be a 100 per cent sure of convicting a person.'

Constantly hammering against the legal system has made Donna despair and she has begun advising families to reach out-of-court settlements. If the police can take six months to a year to arrest a man, what is the point of pursuing a case where collecting evidence is so difficult to begin with? She recalled a case of a woman called Laxmi who allegedly was killed and then hanged by her husband. He had raised the volume of the television to block the screams of his wife. Watching what was happening to the mother, their little baby started crying, alerting Laxmi's old parents who lived upstairs. They came down to check and saw their daughter hanging from the ceiling. The parents filed a case and Donna's organization followed it for two years. When the trial reached the stage of evidence, the husband offered the parents two lakh rupees as a settlement amount to help raise the child and to drop the case. Vimochana advised the parents not to compromise, assuring that they would get justice. In the end, the husband was acquitted. The parents said something to Donna, which still rings in her ears. They told her: 'We believed in you more than in God but we neither got justice nor the money.'

In the end, for Donna, no excuses could or should be made for the way things are. 'I don't want to hear how the police are so burdened and how the system is jammed. Then fix your system. Add more police. Just because your system is bad, women don't have to die for it. Do something but don't deprive me of justice. Otherwise you are saying women are not worthy of justice.'

Groups working in the field have suggested ways to improve the current backlog in the legal system. Court delays can be reduced by fixing a time frame for conducting trial and disposing of cases through special courts designated to deal with unnatural deaths of women. Retired judges can be a helpful resource, an idea that the law ministry has considered in the past. To improve police investigations of dowry deaths, special training should be given to officers so they can deal more sensitively with families and witnesses. Tact and sophistication are key to eliciting information from neighbours and in-laws but very often the first person on the scene of crime is a constable or a sub-inspector, not a senior officer as mandated by law. Police must ensure that a senior officer investigates unnatural deaths because it affects the quality of evidence and the FIR. He should be accompanied by a fingerprint and forensic expert to help collect evidence. There is a tendency on part of the police to classify dowry murders as suicides and accidents because it reduces their workload.

Time is of essence in investigating dowry deaths and cases of torture. Since it is difficult, if not impossible, to get an eyewitness, because the crime is usually committed inside the four walls of a home and with collusion of the in-laws, it is crucial that collection of other evidence be done fast to make the case stick in court. The culprits must not be allowed time to doctor the evidence or destroy it. If the body has been moved, it should be treated as a violation of the law.

A national handbook could be prepared for the police containing the laws and all the relevant guidelines issued over the years covering deaths of women under suspicious circumstances. It should be available in all languages so that policemen and women can thoroughly understand the implications of the rules.

But these are just the practical problems faced by victims and their families. To combat the scourge of dowry, policy makers have to look deeper and further. The dowry problem has to be tackled with a multi-pronged strategy. On the inside the innumerable instruments of subordination and subjugation of women within the family must be fought and on the outside the many disadvantages in inheritance laws, employment opportunities and attitudes of the state. Dowry seeps deep into the social fabric and connects fundamentally with the low status of women. If women are to have equal rights, they must have more options besides marriage in life.

They must be able to come out of Manu's embrace.

References and Bibliography

Introduction

1 *National Crime Records Bureau for the Years 1990–1999*, Ministry of Home Affairs, Government of India, Government of India Press, New Delhi.

2 *The Laws of Manu*, translated by Wendy Doniger and Brian K. Smith, Penguin Books, New Delhi, 1991.

3 K.R. Malkani, *India First*, Ocean Books, 2002.

4 Dipankar Gupta, Professor of Sociology, Jawaharlal Nehru University, New Delhi, personal interview, April 2002.

5 Samita Sen, Reader, History Department, Calcutta University, personal interview, April 2002.

6 M.N. Srinivas, *Some Reflections on Dowry*, Centre for Women Development Studies, 1984.

7 Malavika Karlekar, *Domestic Violence*, EPW, Vol. 33, No. 27, July 4–10, 1998.

8 Patricia Uberoi, Institute of Economic Growth, personal interview, May 2002.

9 Ranjana Kumari, *Brides Are Not for Burning*, Radiant Publishers, New Delhi, 1989.

10 Ranjana Kumari, *Brides Are Not for Burning*, Radiant Publishers, New Delhi, 1989.

11 Hasina Khan, member and secretary, *Aawaz-e-Niswan*, Bombay, personal interview, September 2001.

12 Ranjana Sheel, *The Political Economy of Dowry: Institutionalization and Expansion in North India*, Manohar Publishers, New Delhi, 1999.

13 Syeda Saiyidain Hameed, *Voice of the Voiceless: Status of Muslim Women in India*, National Commission for Women, New Delhi, March 2000.

14 *The Telegraph*, 13 August 2001.

15 Malavika Karlekar, *Domestic Violence*, EPW, Vol. 33, No. 27, July 4–10, 1998.

16 *National Family Health Survey (NFHS-2) 1998–99*, International Institute for Population Sciences, Mumbai.
17 Ranjana Sheel, *The Political Economy of Dowry: Institutionalization and Expansion in North India*, Manohar Publishers, New Delhi, 1999.
18 Romila Thapar, *Ancient Indian Social History: Some Interpretations*, Orient Longman, New Delhi, 1978.
19 *The Laws of Manu*, translated by Wendy Doniger and Brian K. Smith, Penguin Books, New Delhi, 1991.
20 *Deccan Herald*, 30 August 2000.
21 *Indian Express*, 5 May 2000.
22 *The Pioneer*, 16 June 2000.
23 Dhanuk family, interviews arranged by Swayam, Kolkata, 2000.
24 Donna Fernandes, member Vimochana, Bangalore, personal interview, October 2001.
25 Suman Nalwa, personal interview by e-mail, 14 February 2001.
26 Radha Kumar, *The History of Doing*, Kali for Women, New Delhi, 1993.
27 Madhu Kishwar, *Off the Beaten Track: Rethinking Gender Justice for Indian Women*, Oxford University Press, New Delhi, 1999.

Bibliography

Altekar, A.S., *The Position of Women in Hindu Civilization: From Prehistoric Times to the Present Day*, Motilal Banarasidass, Delhi, 1983.

Butalia, Urvashi & Sarkar, Tanika, Eds., *Women and the Hindu Right: A Collection of Essays*, Kali for Women, New Delhi, 1995.

Davies, Miranda, Ed., *Women and Violence: Realities and Responses Worldwide*, Zed Books, London, 1994.

Devasia, Leelamma & Devasia, V.V., Eds., *Women in India: Equality, Social Justice and Development*, Indian Social Institute, 1990.

Jethmalani, Rani, Ed., *Kali's Yug: Empowerment, Law and Dowry Deaths*, Har-Anand Publications, 1995.

Kishwar, Madhu, *Off the Beaten Track*, Oxford University Press, New Delhi, 1999.

Kosambi, Meera, Ed., *Women's Oppression in the Public Gaze*, Research Centre for Women's Studies, CWS Gender Series, Book 2, 1995.

Kumar, Radha, *The History of Doing*, Kali for Women, New Delhi, 1993.

Nair, Janaki, *Women and Law in Colonial India: A Social History,* Kali for Women, New Delhi, 1996.

Ranjana Kumari, *Brides Are Not for Burning*, Radiant Publishers, New Delhi, 1989.

Sarkar, Lotika & Sivaramayya B., *Women and Law: Contemporary Problems*, Vikas Publishing House, Delhi, 1994.

Sen, Mala, *Death by Fire: Sati, Dowry Death and Female Infanticide in India*, Penguin Books India, New Delhi, 2001.

Sheel, Ranjana, *The Political Economy of Dowry: Institutionalization and Expansion in North India*, Manohar Publishers, New Delhi, 1999.

Sinha, Niroj, Ed., *Women and Violence*, Vikas Publishing House, New Delhi, 1989.

Sood, Sushma, Ed., *Violence Against Women*, Arihant Publications, Jaipur, 1990.

Thapar, Romila, *Status of Women and Dowry: Traditions Versus Misconceptions*, Manushi, No. 42–43, New Delhi, 1987.

Umar, Mohd., *Bride Burning in India: A Socio-Legal Study*, APH Publishing, New Delhi, 1998.

Verghese, Jamila, *Her Gold and Her Body*, Vikas Publishing House, New Delhi, 1980.

Reports

Towards Equality: Report of the Committee on the Status of Women in India, Government of India, Ministry of Education, 1974.

Unnatural Deaths of Women in Marriage: A Campaign Diary, Vimochana, CIEDS Collective, Bangalore, 1999.

Voice of the Voiceless: Status of Muslim Women in India, Syeda Saiyidain Hameed, National Commission for Women, New Delhi, 2000.

Annual Reports, National Commission for Women, New Delhi, 1996–98.

Violence Update, Centre for Social Research, New Delhi.

Articles

'I Should Not Have Been the Traditional Indian Father,' *Illustrated Weekly of India,* 10–16 July 1993.

'Till Death Do Us Part,' *Far Eastern Economic Review*, 28 Oct. 1993.
'Her Story,' *The Indian Express*, 9 April 1995.
'Former Orissa DGP Absconding,' *The Telegraph*, 17 July 1995.
'Killed by Greed and Oppression,' *Time*, 11 Sept. 1995.
'Illegal Demands,' *Outlook*, 31 July 1996.
'Dowry Laws Nail Innocents,' *The Week*, 6 April 1997.
'Ordeal by Fire,' *The Week*, 17 Aug. 1997.
'Victims of Sudden Affluence,' *India Today*, 15 Dec. 1997.
'Exploding the Myth of an Evil Practice,' *The Telegraph*, 18 Feb. 1998.
'Dowry Scalds Beauty Queen,' *The Telegraph*, 8 Jan. 2000.
'Hindu Bride Wins Back Dowry After Divorce,' *The Daily Telegraph*, 4 April 2000.
'Having Lost Her Daughter to It, She Now Fights Dowry Monster,' *The Indian Express*, 13 May 2000.
'Bridal Suit,' *The Telegraph*, 14 May 2000.
'The Happiest Day Was When Cops Came,' *The Indian Express*, 15 May 2000.
'Room to Kill,' *The Telegraph*, 24 May 2000.
'Dowry Again,' *From the Lawyers Collective*, June 2000.
'Victims of Greed,' *The Pioneer*, 29 June 2000.
'Blow by Blow Account,' *The Telegraph*, 18 Nov. 2000.